SNOWBOUND

BY RICHARD S. WHEELER
FROM TOM DOHERTY ASSOCIATES

SKYE'S WEST
Sun River
Bannack
The Far Tribes
Yellowstone
Bitterroot
Sundance
Wind River
Santa Fe
Rendezvous
Dark Passage
Going Home
Downriver
The Deliverance
The Fire Arrow
The Canyon of Bones
Virgin River
North Star

Aftershocks
Badlands
The Buffalo Commons
Cashbox
Eclipse
The Fields of Eden
Fool's Coach
Goldfield
Masterson
Montana Hitch
An Obituary for Major Reno
Second Lives
Sierra
Snowbound
Sun Mountain: A Comstock Novel
Where the River Runs

SAM FLINT
Flint's Gift
Flint's Truth
Flint's Honor

SNOWBOUND

RICHARD S. WHEELER

A TOM DOHERTY ASSOCIATES BOOK

NEW YORK

This is a work of fiction. All of the characters, organizations, and events portrayed in this novel are either products of the author's imagination or are used fictitiously.

SNOWBOUND

A Forge Book
Published by Tom Doherty Associates, LLC
175 Fifth Avenue
New York, NY 10010

www.tor-forge.com

Forge® is a registered trademark of Tom Doherty Associates, LLC.

ISBN 978-0-7653-1662-2

First Edition: March 2010

Printed in the United States of America

0 9 8 7 6 5 4 3 2 1

To Tom Doherty,
who asked me to write about the Pathfinder

SNOWBOUND

Senator Thomas Hart Benton

I shall never forget the months I spent as a spectator in the Washington Arsenal watching the fiendish glare that Brigadier General Stephen Watts Kearny directed at my daughter's husband, John Charles Frémont. I had never seen anything like it. General Kearny had fixed his unblinking scowl upon my son-in-law with the full intent of intimidating the young man.

The court-martial of Colonel Frémont began on November 2, 1847, and ran eighty-nine days. General Kearny had brought the charges, including mutiny, disobedience, and conduct prejudicial to good order. These sprang from the period when Frémont and his battalion of irregulars, along with Commodore Robert Stockton, had largely conquered California with little help from the regular army. Commodore Stockton, the senior United States officer in the region, had appointed Colonel Frémont the governor of the newly conquered province, a position he ardently defended against the meddling of Brigadier General Kearny, until the malice-soaked Kearny stripped him of the office, accused him of insubordination, and then hauled him east as a prisoner.

Kearny must have seethed, for the young and celebrated conqueror of California was neither a veteran line officer nor a West

Pointer but a junior officer, an explorer and mapmaker with the Army's Corps of Topographical Engineers, who happened to be near the Pacific coast when war broke out. Not only that, but Frémont and Stockton had won California with minimal bloodshed, and Frémont had made a generous peace with the conquered Californios.

It didn't end with that, either, for the young man was also a national hero, well known to his countrymen as the Pathfinder. In previous explorations he, along with a company of gifted scientists and cartographers, had mapped large portions of the little-known West, and the accounts of these journeys had been published by the government and made available to pioneering Americans bent on settling the West. Thus the Pathfinder had been a great instrument of westward expansion, an enterprise dear to my heart, and one to which I had devoted my entire career in the Senate.

But all this success, which seemed to wrap my son-in-law in a golden aura, was too much for the old guard in the army, and in General Kearny it found the means to ruin the most celebrated young officer in the republic. I knew, even as the two sides prepared for the trial, that Colonel Frémont would have to endure a special burden, the rage of envious senior officers who vented their rank hostility and contempt toward my son-in-law at every opportunity, sometimes stating their case in the sensational daily press.

I took steps in my own fashion to salvage my son-in-law's career, one day interviewing President Polk about the matter. I noted his tepid response, and I marked him as a pusillanimous opponent of the Bentons, though we had made common cause for many years. I took to the Senate floor, where I still commanded a faction of my Democratic party, and did not hesitate to let the whole body know of the malign effort to disgrace Colonel Frémont, and by extension, bring ruin upon my family.

How I ached for my daughter Jessie, who was forced to listen day after day to the most disgraceful and base accusations against her beloved husband, even while she bore his unborn child. It was plain to the whole world that the charges against my son-in-law were utterly without merit, concocted by a vindictive old general who had arrived in California too late and with too little force and had suffered the mortal indignity of defeat by the Californios. Was it any wonder that a bilious stew began to boil in the bosom of the old soldier or that it was soon to spew over the true conqueror of California?

I took my own measures as I watched the trial progress through the weeks and months. When General Kearny took the witness stand, I stared back, as relentlessly and unblinkingly as he had glared at my son-in-law, and my steadfast gaze had its effect. The general exploded in rage, and the tribunal directed its attention toward me, even as I sat with glacial calm among the spectators. But the conduct that was perfectly acceptable to the tribunal in Kearny's case was not acceptable to them in my case, and I suffered the rebuke of its presiding officer, Brevet Brigadier General G. M. Brooke. That gave me the measure of the thirteen members of that tribunal. I knew where the Bentons stood with them, and some things I do not forget or forgive.

I like to think that the whole lot of them were recollecting an earlier utterance of mine that still follows me around, much to my advantage: "I never quarrel, sir, but I do fight, sir, and when I fight, sir, a funeral follows, sir."

They found Frémont guilty on all charges and directed that he be thrown out of the army. The miserable Polk affirmed the charges but remitted the sentence, permitting my son-in-law to remain in the service. But that additional rebuke was too much for the young man; he resigned in deepest sadness, and thus the Pathfinder, the young republic's most honored young man, found himself tarnished and alone. Those were hard days for my daughter Jessie and her husband, and I ached for them.

It mattered not that the American people, along with the press, were solidly behind Frémont for it was plain to the whole country that sheer spite among senior army officers had brought the Pathfinder to his ruin. It mattered not that this vindictive verdict caused grave illness in Jessie and threatened the life of her unborn child. It mattered not to the Polk administration that it had wrought an injustice and that the American people were aware of it and outraged by it.

But I have my own ways and means, and I thought of an enterprise that not only would regain Frémont's reputation for him as the nation's foremost explorer but also would open a way for Saint Louis to funnel the entire commerce of the West and the Pacific into the States and to hasten the day when the republic would stretch from sea to sea. I proposed to several Saint Louis business colleagues that they fund a private survey along the 38th parallel, with the intent of running a railroad to San Francisco along the midcontinent route. I received somewhat hesitant backing because the gentlemen feared that Frémont might once again fail to use sound judgment, but in the end, we raised enough to finance Frémont's fourth expedition. It would be up to the Pathfinder to restore his name and reputation. But in this case he would not be defying a superior officer; he would answer only to himself. This time there was no one looking over his shoulder.

CHAPTER ONE

John Charles Frémont

General Kearny killed the baby. I would never say it publicly, but I knew right down to my bones that it was true. Jessie would come to it also; she thought that Benton was sickly because of the court-martial.

Ten weeks was all the life allotted my firstborn, named after Jessie's family. The ordeal in Washington City was more than Jessie could endure, and it afflicted the child she was carrying, and now the bell tolls.

Stephen Watts Kearny and his cronies brought the charge, mutiny and disobedience in California; put me and my family through the ordeal; and triumphed. He who was a friend of the Bentons, supped at their table, could not contain a raging envy of me, and now the bell tolls.

Benton was a sickly infant, delivered by a worn woman, though Jessie was but twenty-four. Even Kit Carson, almost a stranger to children, said as much. He had visited Jessie in Washington only a few weeks ago, having completed his courier duty for the army, and thought that Benton would not live long.

I watched the pewter river slide past in the dawn. We were aboard the *Martha*, plying its slow way to Westport from Saint

Louis. Most of my men were there, awaiting me, receiving and guarding the expedition's materiel and mules. I didn't much care to go on this expedition. It would not be the same. A great weariness has afflicted me ever since the verdict—no, ever since General Kearny marched me to the States as the rear of his column, in disgrace.

I had read in the press that I have changed: "Colonel Frémont looks weary and gray since his ordeal," according to all reports. I have not changed and nothing bends me, and soon the republic will see what I am made of. The army will see what I am made of. So will President Polk. And their brown claws will not touch me this time.

The *Martha* vibrated more than most river packets do, and I wondered if Captain Rolfe knew his main bearings were out of true. The hooded shores, heavy with mist-shrouded trees wearing their yellow October colors, slid by. I would need to talk to Rolfe; I would need to help Jessie out of her world and into the real one. I had left her in the gloomy stateroom, sitting in her ivory nightclothes on the bunk, crooning to Benton at her breast. The boy was dead. Sometime in the small hours his weak heart had failed. Kitty, her colored maid, had discovered it. Now the infant hung limp in her arms, while she whispered and sang and clutched the still, cold infant.

I would have to disturb her. It is not in me to flee from any duty.

I retreated from the deck rail and entered our dank stateroom. Jessie sat on the edge of the bunk, rocking softly, the child still clamped to her breast. She eyed me, and then the shadows, where Kitty sat helplessly.

"Jessie, it's time to let go."

She nodded. "He's dead, I know."

"Yes. May I take him?"

"I had him for such a little while."

But she handed the cold infant to me. It didn't resemble anyone I knew. I stood, holding it. She turned away, not knowing what to do or caring to see what I would do with the dead boy.

I found the blue receiving blanket and wrapped it around Benton. The boy should have weighed more. He weighed almost nothing. Did souls have weight? Did a living infant weigh more?

"I'll have the cabin boy bring you something. Tea?"

"It was the strain," she said. "All the while you were under a cloud, the little baby knew it. It shrank him up."

"Jessie—you are a beautiful mother."

She smiled fleetingly. "I wanted him to be like you," she said.

"Rest a while. I'll be back."

"I'll never see my baby again."

I nodded. Then I slipped out on the dewy deck and made my way forward, the bundle in my arms. Below, the side-wheeler shivered its way upstream, gliding over murky water, leaving a gentle wake behind. A quiet rhythm punctuated the dawn as the paddles splashed and the great drive piston reciprocated.

The grimy white wheelhouse was ahead. I knocked, and was shouted in, but I saw only the helmsman steering the boat's slow passage. "Captain Rolfe, please. Frémont here."

The helmsman simply pointed at a door behind the wheelhouse. I opened it and found myself staring at the half-dressed captain eating breakfast in a small galley. The man wore blue trousers and a stained gray union suit.

"It's you, Frémont. I knew you were aboard."

"Captain, we have lost our boy."

Rolfe stared at the small bundle. "I am sorry. Was it cholera?"

"He was sickly and died in the night."

Rolfe nodded. "I'll have the carpenter's mate build a box. Have you plans? We can stop and bury him . . ."

"Can the child be shipped to Saint Louis?"

"We're coming on to Jefferson City . . ."

"I would like to do it that way."

"I'm sorry, Colonel. It's a hard thing."

"Hard on Jessie, yes." That was less than I intended to say. "Hard on both of us," I added.

Captain Rolfe dabbed his chin whiskers, wiping away the remains of oat gruel, and tugged a cord. A cabin boy materialized

"Take Colonel Frémont to the shop."

I followed the youth down a gangway to the silvery rain-soaked boiler deck, and finally to a noisy room aft. It took only a moment. The carpenter's mate eyed the quiet bundle, nodded, and set to work.

I was glad to escape and headed forward until I stood at the rounded prow. This ship was heading west. I was heading west. I was going to California, but going the hard way. Jessie would meet me there, after crossing the isthmus of Panama. She had come to see me off.

I watched ahead as the river boat wound its way around lazy curves, scything deer from the riverbanks and alarming ravens. The bankside trees clawed at us. An overcast hid the sun and hushed the wind. This was level country. Far away, where the Rockies tumbled up to the sky, I would chop a hole through the wall. That was what this was all about as far as any other living soul knew. But I knew it was about much more. The West Pointers would eat crow, every feather and claw, beak and brain. They would rot unknown in their graves; the nation would decorate its public squares with statues of Frémont.

But of that I said nothing, especially not to my wife. She was my ally, prized from the Benton family by our elopement. I acquired the most powerful father-in-law in Washington, and we have put each other to good use, he in his dreams of westward expansion, and I in my dream of decorating every village square. These were unspoken but ever present. He doesn't like me, and I've never cared for him. But we make common cause.

We docked at Jefferson City, an indifferent city of indifferent people, and I watched the roustabouts heft the small pine casket ashore to a waiting spring wagon, and that was the last I would see of my son. The Bentons would bury him. Jessie did not join me at the rail, and I supposed she lay abed. I am made of stern stuff, and I watched what passed for a coffin removed from the vessel. The *Martha* did not tarry long, but it did take on some dripping wet cordwood, and then we shuddered west once again, and I would have it no other way.

I put my son out of mind.

This, my fourth expedition, had formed swiftly. It had been privately financed by that old fur trade entrepreneur Robert Campbell, along with O. D. Filley and Thornton Grimsley, but all told, they had not pledged a third of what the government would have given me. There were those in Saint Louis who saw the virtue of steel rails to the far Pacific, spanning the unknown continent, and funneling the whole commerce of the Pacific and the Orient through the gateway city. I was indifferent to that. Success would merely line other men's pockets. But I was not indifferent to other facets of this trip. I would do it without the leave of the army, without the hindrance of government. And I would do it in winter, the very season requiring the most strenuous exertions and posing the greatest risk. Let them absorb that.

I would be my own commander, exempt from court-martial, and my only judge and jury would be public opinion and my private esteem. I supposed there would be some obligation to my backers, most particularly my father-in-law, who contributed his skills and his purse to all this. And I would provide it. They would receive the cartographic results for which they anted up.

There were other things on my mind; I wished to look upon the great foothill tract in California, Las Mariposas, that had been purchased for me by the American consul, Thomas O. Larkin, from the Mexicans. It was not anything I wanted, and Larkin had violated the trust I had placed in him. So I was stuck with a huge tract of rolling land, good for little. Perhaps something lucrative could be made of it, though I wasn't sure what. I knew it would do for the grazing of cattle or sheep, because that was how the Californios had exploited it. But it might yield more under good Yankee management. I had sent an entire sawmill around the horn, knowing that sawn lumber is in short supply in that remote province. I planned to discover how best to line my pockets.

The Mediterranean climate of that far shore appealed to me, and I imagined it would appeal to Jessie as well, but it fostered indolence in the natives. She could not endure the transcontinental trip, so she would travel to the Pacific across the isthmus of Panama after seeing me off and meet me in a remote place recently renamed San Francisco, destined by geography to become a fine city someday. Thus she would accompany me to Westport Landing, where my corps of exploration would assemble and depart, and then return to Saint Louis and New Orleans, and we would have a rendezvous some unimaginable distance away, at some unfathomable moment to come.

It was just as well. She might be brimming with youth, but she was not fit.

I returned frequently to the stateroom where Jessie secluded herself. She seemed uncommonly stricken, and I did my best to cheer her, along with her maid, who was quartered below. By the time we reached Westport she was up and about, wearing gray wool, taking tours on the boiler deck, studying the ever-moving panorama as we shivered our way west.

"I am very nearly the only woman on board," she said on one of our tours, her arm locked in mine.

"The wilderness offers no closets," I said. "Men go west first."

"Oh, fiddle, Charles. There are women in the wagon trains, and no closets for two thousand miles."

I enjoyed her renewed brightness. She might have an entirely unrealistic perception of the strength and weaknesses of the sexes, but at least her lively spirit was returning, along with a healthy blush to her cheeks. She took great delight in me, which I found flattering. She certainly had her pick of men, being a senator's daughter, but all those high-bred swain were felled before they knew they had been hewn down. On my part, I prided myself in offering her the utmost consideration.

This was not her first experience of steam travel, and she eyed the roustabouts with a knowing eye. Most were freed blacks, raw-boned ragged men in ceaseless toil. The furnace required enormous amounts of wood to wrestle the packet against the steady current, and that meant that the deck hands sweated through long days, lifting three-foot logs, nimbly swinging them into the firebox, somehow avoiding burning themselves, only to draw yet another log off the great piles stacked on the boiler deck, only two feet or so above water. It was steam that wrestled with gravity and nature, but the sinewy legs and arms of men fed the furnaces that wrought the steam.

"They are so thin," she said.

"They move tons of wood each day," I replied.

"They would be good men for you to take with you."

"I have better men," I replied.

Indeed, I had assembled a fine lot of volunteers, many of them men from my old corps of exploration who knew the wilds and how to survive in it. To these I had added a few adventurers, who would travel unpaid. There was no money to pay wages, and not even enough to equip them, but my father-in-law planned to introduce a bill that would cover costs. His first efforts along those lines had been roundly rebuked, with the court-martial looming as the obstacle to any further consideration. But the senator and I thought that on the successful completion of the railroad survey, some funds would be forthcoming from a grateful Congress. So I did not hesitate to assure our company that one way or another, they would be paid, and in any case they would have safe passage to California. Thus did we finally dock in Westport, where the Missouri River bends north, and we were met by most of the men of my company, who were waiting for their leader.

CHAPTER TWO

John Charles Frémont

I grew anxious, as we approached Westport, that there should be an appropriate showing of my men. I wanted Jessie to see with her own eyes the enthusiasm of the company, so she could report favorably to her father and my backers when she returned to Saint Louis. It would suit me ill if few of my stalwarts showed up to greet us.

I was not disappointed. When we rounded a leafy bend and Westport suddenly hove into view under an opaque pearl sky, I noted the compact crowd at the levee awaiting the *Martha*. Westport was a tangle of temporary gray structures in a sea of mud; its denizens had not yet acquired the civic spirit that fostered grace. The disorder of the town reflected the disorder of their passions.

The ship's passengers crowded the rail as the shuddering subsided and the steam whistle emitted an eerie howl like a wolf's cry. Then came deep silence as the packet slid against the thumping current toward shore. Deckhands had pike poles and hawsers at the ready, and soon the stained boat would be snubbed fast to thick posts set in the mud.

This was Westport, famed entrepôt where the Santa Fe caravans and Oregon trains and most overland companies outfitted and then vanished into the unknown continent. There was a last weird silence, broken only by the slap of waves on our prow, and then the boat thumped against the piles and a dozen brawny blacks made it fast.

But my gaze was on my company. There they were, the motley crowd I had recruited over the past several months. I was gratified to find cheerful ruddy faces among them, men who had been with me during previous expeditions. Men who were in my California Battalion. Men who had climbed the Sierra Nevada with me in midwinter, proving it could be done. Some of them were ready and willing to try it again, loyal to their commander through all kinds of weather.

"There's Godey," I said to Jessie. "He'll be my second. And there's Preuss, the topographer, grouchy old German. And there's the Kern brothers. Philadelphia people. They've come to greet me. Ned Kern was with me on the third expedition. I'll have two artists this time. They'll catch every landscape. Railroad men like sketches best of all. See what's ahead, where the trouble is."

"They look very competent," Jessie said, as the sweating roustabouts slid a long gangway over a small span of water to the muddy bank.

"They are, when taking direction," I replied. "But they need to be welded into a company, and that's what I do best. Ah! There's Vincenthaler, another of my stalwarts. With me in California. Oh, and Taplin! With me on the second and third expeditions, army captain then, and I made him an officer in my California Battalion. Ah! Raphael Proue, a Creole, with me on all three of my trips. And Tableau! Morin! Voyageurs, my dear. Men born to the wild."

"They've spotted us," she said. "Oh, capital!"

I eyed her sharply. Her face had lit, and I saw a bloom in her cheeks that belied the somber gray of her stiff woolen dress. Good. She would take the good impressions back to Saint Louis and convey them to her skeptical father. When it came to Senator Benton, Jessie was my best advocate. He listens to her but expects me to listen to him, and I play the lesser part in his company.

I waved cheerfully at my men as they crowded the gangway but said nothing. I would have more than enough to say once we had alighted and our luggage had been hauled ashore, along with several leather-bound trunks filled with cartographic and navigational apparatuses.

It is my style to address people with a level tone, avoiding the extremes of passion at all times. That is a quality of leadership I possess, this steady calm that wins respect and quiets all turbulence. Such was my conduct now as we descended the gangway, Mrs. Frémont on my arm, and found ourselves surrounded by smiling bearded men of various vintages. Our servants, Kitty and Saunders, would take care of our things.

I turned at once to Alexis Godey, another of the Saint Louis Creoles and a thoroughly able man, one who understood me.

"Alex! You've paid us honor with your presence. I am honored to introduce you to my wife, Jessie."

"Mrs. Frémont," he said in flawless English.

"My wife has suffered a great sorrow, Alex, which I will make known in due course, so we will refrain from taxing her."

Godey stared, blank as to what that was about, but he would learn soon enough. He was discreet, which is more than I could say of most Creoles.

A wiry man unknown to me stood before us. "Andrew Cathcart at your service, Colonel Frémont. Captain, Eleventh Hussars, off on a little adventure." He spoke with a burr, and I disliked him on sight. I didn't want adventurers, and I don't care for Scots.

"Ah, yes, you're the one who wrote me. I'm glad you'll be with us," I said, somehow concealing my thoughts. The Scot was simply larking his way west. "Captain, this is Mrs. Frémont," I said.

She offered her hand and a curtsey.

"Honored indeed," Cathcart said. "You're the toast of the regiment."

Jessie did not smile.

I found myself shaking the hand of Ned Kern, my artist during the third expedition, and an officer in the California Battalion. A good hand. Kern introduced his brothers, Richard, also an artist, and Benjamin, a medical doctor, both the color of bread dough. I introduced them to Jessie, but without enthusiasm. These Philadelphians didn't look hardy enough to stand up to what was coming. Not even Edward, who had topped the Sierra Nevada with my company two years earlier, looked the part for this trip. Both Richard and Benjamin looked so pale I wondered if they had spent even an hour in the natural world. I decided to keep a sharp eye on them, and if they proved too fragile, I would dismiss them before we ascended the Rocky Mountains. Tough old Preuss could sketch if he had to.

We met the others one by one, even as other passengers and freight drifted away from the levee, until at last only our own company remained. Several of the company had already slid our trunks into a spring wagon.

"Let's go, Godey. You're driving, I take it. Along the way, you can tell me what's here, what's missing, and what needs doing. I want to be off as soon as it can be managed. Also, you can rehearse what you know about these gentlemen. And don't mind Mrs. Frémont. Anything private for my ears are for hers also."

The company drifted apart, mostly to the saddle mules that had been tied to a lengthy hitch rail. Westport had returned to its slumbers. It was plainly a town that woke itself up with the arrival of a wagon company or a riverboat, only to doze under the pewter skies.

"You'll take us first to Major Cummins's house, won't you now?"

"As you wish, Colonel." He slapped the lines over the croups of the gray mules, and they sullenly pushed into their collars and started us rolling. I did not like the looks of these mules and wondered about the rest.

"Colonel is it, my friend? I'm an ordinary civilian now, Godey." I said it with that certain quietness of voice I knew commanded respect.

"Always Colonel to me, sir, but I'm at your command even if you call yourself mister. It was a pity."

Had Jessie not been sitting there, and her maid on the seat behind, Godey might have called it something stronger than a pity. I never used oaths or words that gave offense and rebuke such language uttered in my presence. And that is a part of the hold I have on my men. I have studied on it.

"We will install Mrs. Frémont there; by day she will occupy a tent I will raise for her at Boone Creek, whilst we put our company together. The major has generously offered to board my wife and her servant."

Cummins was the old Indian agent there at Boone Creek, outside Westport, and had in his charge the Delaware nation. It would be a good thing; Jessie under a roof by night, in camp by day, where she would observe and take her impressions back to Saint Louis men who counted. I had brought her this distance for a purpose.

"Very good, sir."

"And Alex. Mrs. Frémont is grieving the loss of her infant."

The Creole tugged the lines, slowing the mules. "Loss, Colonel?"

"Our boy, Benton. On board."

Godey hawed the mules forward. "I'm sorry, Colonel. That is a hard thing. It's a bad omen. Should the company be told? Maybe not a word?"

"I will, at the proper time," I said.

"Then my lips are sealed."

That was Godey, I thought. No man more reliable, and none more faithful to me.

The burdened wagon creaked through rain-softened lanes, past gloomy oak groves and sullen wet meadows. West of Westport little existed except those copses and creeks where the wagon companies fitted themselves for the great haul west. Ours would be entirely a pack-mule expedition once we reached the mountains, and we would need scores of them to carry ourselves and our truck. But where I was going no wagon could go. I would take a few horses but would trade them if possible. They were no good in the mountains and flighty on the plains.

I planned to take a good look at the men, several of whom were entirely new to me. I have good instincts. It is a gift. I know in an instant what a stranger thinks of me and am prepared for him even before he opens his mouth. Cathcart, now, he might be alright even if I didn't much care for him. An officer in the Queen's hussars would understand command. But those Kerns. They would take some study. Ben's surgical tools might be a valuable asset, but the man hadn't the faintest idea what this trip would be about. Fine Pennsylvania family, privileged sons. Not a bit like their leader. I had never known a day of privilege.

I shifted uncomfortably on the seat. Would a day ever go by, in all my life, when I wasn't reminded of my origins? We drove through swelling hills clothed with tawny grass and copses of trees. The air was chill and more autumnal than it should be in October.

"Last night, Colonel, we were treated to northern lights. No one had ever seen them this far south," Godey said.

"It is a good omen," I replied. It was my habit to turn superstition to my advantage, lest it work against me. "Now, what is our condition, Alex? Are we ready?"

"Alors, non. A lot of green mules need to be broken to pack

saddle, and only half of our equipment's come in. We're lacking tack, pack and riding saddles, those India rubber sheets you ordered, some kettles and kitchen goods. Most of the provisions are here. Flour, sugar, molasses, all of that. We're not ready, and it'll be a week or two."

"That's fine. Winter passage is to our advantage."

Godey eyed me sharply, but I meant it.

We reached Major Cummins's Delaware Agency midafternoon. It proved to be an odd assortment of shabby log structures, strung in a row on a flat devoid of trees, which had all been sacrificed to the woodstoves within. The gouty old agent greeted us effusively and set several nubile maidens to work settling Jessie and Kitty in an empty cabin. I saw at once how it was with the major, whose face bore the rosy hue of dissipation. He did not lack for comforts.

"Ah! Colonel, I'm at your service. We're all at your service here," the major announced. "Whatever you need, anything at all, any little thing, you have only to call on me."

"Mrs. Frémont will be here nights only," I said. "She'll be in camp by day."

"A most admirable arrangement," Cummins said. "We will entertain her accordingly. I'm available late afternoons for libations and devote myself to my duties at night."

The man either had laryngitis or his tonsils were ruined.

We clambered to the ground while the Indian agent sent his charges scurrying about. Jessie and her servant found themselves in a primitive cabin with a puncheon floor, a fly-specked window, and a fireplace for heat. I examined it and thought it to be adequate for women.

I continued on, with Godey, to the Boone Creek camp a mile distant. It was spread through a cottonwood grove and showed signs of hard use. It had been a favorite marshaling place for wagon companies heading to Oregon or Santa Fe for years. But it was convenient to Westport; merchants could deliver the last of our equipment easily, within an hour after it was taken off the boats.

Now at last I could see what sort of company this would be. There would be no blue uniforms here; these were either civilians or else soldiers on leave, such as Cathcart. But still, many of my men were formerly enlisted, and this was a military camp, with tents formed in a square and the mule herd under guard. The men had divided themselves into four messes, each with its cook fire.

Even as Godey reined the mules to a stop, the company flocked to our side. It was grand. I am not one for displays of feeling, and these men knew it and greeted me courteously. But I could see they were pleased to receive me in camp. And with amiable handshakes we either resumed old ties or took the measure of one another. I was particularly anxious to meet the newcomers and assess their feeling for me. It would not do to have dissenters and soreheads in the company, and it was important to me that my command be acceptable to them all. So I paid close attention as I met them one by one, at least those who had not come to the river's edge earlier. Take Micajah McGehee, for instance, a Mississippi man, more literate than some, son of a judge, gentle in nature. I was delighted to see evidence of his respect for the Pathfinder, as I had come to be called, and knew that if the man's health held up, he would be a good addition to the company.

In due course I gathered them close, because I never raise my voice.

"Mrs. Frémont will be here by day, whilst we organize ourselves," I began. "She has recently suffered a most grievous loss, the death of her infant son Benton, and any courtesy extended to her at this time would be most welcome."

My company fell into deep silence.

After a few moments, I smiled. "Now, then. We'll begin. I intend to reach the Pacific coast early in the spring, having found an easy way across the middle of the continent. I understand that last night you all witnessed northern lights, a great rarity here. That is a splendid omen. And all of you will share in my good fortune."

CHAPTER THREE

Jessie Benton Frémont

He was so buoyant before the trial. He was certain the court-martial would come to nothing; the malice of General Kearny and his West Point cronies would be exposed and the charges dismissed. Was Frémont not the conqueror of California, a national hero? Had he not been celebrated and fêted in every village and city from the frontier to Washington City?

He was buoyant then, eager for the trial to begin so he could clear himself and shame his accuser. My father, Old Bullion they called him, was already roaring in the Senate, buttonholing officials, lecturing the uninformed. Between my husband and my father, nothing bad would befall us.

When we finally reached Washington to await the trial, John and I slipped away from my family for an idyllic week I shall never forget. It was heaven. For five of our six and a half years of marriage, he had been away on his expeditions, but now he was there every evening, every dawn. We slept late each morning, breakfasted in bed, hiked through red-brick Georgetown, drove in the pearl moonlight, and returned to our rooms to share all the pleasures that can ever befall a happy husband and wife sharing a reunion.

And from our joy that week, we would bring a son into the

world. But the trial did not proceed as we intended; that wall of stiff-backed officers in blue and gold and white glared malevolently at John and even more acidly at my father. And in the end, they won: they found John guilty on all three of the charges: mutiny, disobeying the commands of superiors, and conduct prejudicial to military discipline. And President Polk betrayed us by largely accepting the verdict, though he commuted the sentence. John resigned.

He has not held me in his arms since that hour. How often I held my arms open to him, invited him into the circle of my love, only to have him say in that polite, courteous way of his, that no, my illness forbade it; no, I was too tired and it would not be healthy or wise for me to surrender to my passions just then. How polite he always was, how much withdrawn from me, and how he had veneered it all with his innate courtesy. But the truth of it was that I yearned for my lover with all the hungers in my twenty-four-year-old heart. Now, at Boone Creek, I yearned for one last embrace from my husband before he once again vanished from my presence.

But he always had a courteous answer. At first it simply was too soon—too soon after Benton's birth, too soon after Benton's death. And so my beloved husband seemed to grow distant and not to need me or want me. But all this I set aside. It was more important to help him and the fourth expedition in any way I could.

I was in the presence of my rivals. For I had come to understand that John enjoys the company of men, in wilderness, far more than the company of my sex, in cities. I had been slow to come to it, thinking only that his duties took him far afield and that soon he would return to the bosom of his family. But it has never happened in that fashion. No sooner is he back among us in Saint Louis or Washington City than he is restless, his gaze west, yearning for the campfires and wilds I could never share with him.

He grew a beard after the court-martial; the clean-shaven handsome man I had married now hid behind sandy and luxuriant facial hair that made him all the more distant from me. To be sure, a beard is a utility in cold and cruel weather, but there is more to it. For the beard is yet another layer between Mr. Frémont and me; between Mr. Frémont and his company of adventurers.

If I have been unwell, as has been my case ever since the trial, it has much to do with this deepening gulf between him and me. I sense at times I am losing him, only to enjoy other moments when his old warmth and love reappear, as if rising from some ocean bottom. I have not known how to cope with this. One moment I am desolate; the next I think I must do whatever I can to advance his life and career; and yet at other moments I feel I must pull a little free of him and return to the hearth of my own family. One thing I know: Frémont has changed, and I wonder whether I play a role in his life.

But all these dark thoughts were only something to abolish from mind and heart and spirit as we settled in Boone Creek. I knew what I must do. I would help the colonel any way I could, and I would so master the nature of his company that I would make a good report of it to my father, and the colonel's Saint Louis backers.

I put Kitty to work settling us in the log cabin that the Indian agent, Majòr Richard Cummins, provided. She opened my trunks and set my clothing out to air, shook the brown bedclothes for bed bugs, and laid a small fire in the stone fireplace against the night's chill. There was a marital-sized bed with an iron bedframe and a narrow bunk for her across the room. It would have been Benton's, and Kitty would have made herself comfortable on the floor, but now it was hers.

Major Cummins had shown us in, blandly inquired after our needs, and departed, along with the colonel, who headed at once to the encampment along with Alexis Godey. The major was no surprise to me; his gouty body and ruined face informed me at once of his prodigal appetites. His bland good cheer was the patented atmospheric of a man dependent on the government for his stipend and fearful of losing it. His lithe Delaware handmaidens bespoke his appetites, and it took no imagination to see how things stood with him. But he was our host, and I would endure, so long as his gaze did not rake me too finely.

"Major, I would like some stationery and the means to write," I said.

"At your service, madam. There will be a slight charge, which I'll enroll to the colonel's account."

No sooner had Mr. Frémont settled me in the cabin than he rattled away in the wagon, and I was once again alone. This was the first moment since Benton's passage to a different place that my husband was not with me, but I always had Kitty, whose angular dark face and shrewd gaze were ever a comfort. I never mistook her silence for a lack of awareness. She seemed almost to know my thoughts and found discreet ways to tell me so. She belonged to my father, but he had lent her to me. Neither the colonel nor I believe in involuntary servitude, but I welcomed her comfortable presence, especially when I ill cared to feed myself and my mind was adrift with thoughts of the coughing and blue infant whose lips barely caught my breast before he was taken away.

"I suppose the colonel, he's at Boone Creek now, just meeting the gents," Kitty said.

"He's a shrewd judge of character. He may be meeting his company, but he's doing more. He's sorting them out," I said.

"Imagine he's got some mighty fine ones," Kitty said, gazing from the tiny glassed window across empty fields and wooded watercourses. "He'll need himself some fine ones, I do believe."

"Oh, it's not going to be much of a trip this time, Kitty. Not like crossing the Sierra Nevada."

Kitty responded with an odd sharpness. "Miss Jessie, this heah trip, that's night curtains we been seeing in the sky."

"Night curtains?"

"I never done seen anything so cold."

I didn't encourage Kitty's superstitions and turned instead to hanging two woolen dresses, a suit, several skirts, and some flannel nightclothes. There wasn't an armoire, and we would make do with some pegs driven into the log wall.

A rap at the door brought the desired stationery and inkwell and a quill, though the major had not included a blotter. It would do. I meant only to write to Lily, and a letter to a girl not yet six could not be long. I thanked the shy Indian maiden who proffered the items.

"I'm going to write a note to Lily," I told Kitty.

The maid retreated into herself. This was magic she knew little about.

"My dear Lily," I wrote. "We miss you very much and hope Grandfather Benton is taking good care of you. I know how sad you must be at the death of your baby brother. I hope you said good-bye to him when he was laid to rest. It hurts not to have a baby brother, doesn't it? But we must swallow our grief and face the future as best we can.

"Soon I will be home, and then we will take a long boat trip to a warm place called California, and there we will see about what to do with the tract of land your father purchased. Maybe we will put cows or sheep on it. It is very big. Seventy square miles.

"Meanwhile, my dear, I am daily with your father as he prepares to go to California overland. And after our sea journey we will all be together again on that distant shore. I hear it is a very pleasant place, with smiling people, and we will begin a new life there.

"My darling Lily, we both miss you and love you and hope that you are doing well with your lessons and that your grandpa is taking good care of you."

I signed it, "Your loving mother." It was the first letter I ever wrote to her, and my father would have to read it to the girl. I missed Lily terribly, but not so much as I missed Benton. I wondered fleetingly whether I was not giving Lily her due or dividing my love in a proper manner. But I can do only so much.

I slid the letter into the envelope Major Cummins provided and addressed it to Miss Elizabeth Benton Frémont, care of The Honorable Thomas Hart Benton, Saint Louis. Then I sealed my letter with a drop of candle wax and handed it to Kitty, who held it as if it were a hot potato, her fingers barely able to clasp this mysterious thing.

"I told Lily we would be seeing her soon," I said to Kitty.

Kitty nodded, slid into the late light, and returned empty-handed.

I felt trapped that evening. The major's ladies eventually brought us a meal of sorts—moist, rich corn bread and a stringy beef stew, but I wasn't hungry. In truth my mind was a mile or two distant, where my bearded husband was preparing to flee from me once more. It did not feel right this time. It felt as if he was avoiding my company.

I retired early and doused the tallow candle even before the last light had fled the western skies.

That night I had a terrible recurring dream that felt worse than it really was. Over and over I dreamed that Frémont and I were at the moment of reunion. I awaited him with opened arms, aching for his embrace and his kiss. He was in his blue army uniform, clean-shaven, young and vibrant, and as he rushed to me I took him into my arms only to have him vanish. Simply vanish. He was gone, and I would awaken briefly and cry out. But then I slid back into the arms of Morpheus, only to experience the dream again. And again.

I was awakened before full light, this time by Alexis Godey. I peered at him through the cracked-open door.

"Madam, forgive the intrusion. The colonel sent for you," he said.

"We haven't done our toilet," I replied.

"I am at your service whenever you are ready," he responded.

It took a while to shake a bad night from my body. But I am young and stronger than most of my sex. We were ready in a few minutes, though not properly washed, and stepped into a lovely chill half-light. The day was no more than a promise, with a streak of blue along the eastern horizon and not a breath of air moving. We clambered into Mr. Godey's spring wagon and were soon rolling past dewy meadows, and my heart was brimming because in a few minutes I would embrace my beloved, and he would not vanish just as my arms enfolded him.

The colonel's camp was bustling as we approached. I saw several fires blooming and knew them to be the separate messes. The colonel always assigned several men to each mess, the meals divided into small companies within the larger one.

But Mr. Godey drove us past the crowd of men, straight toward a small wall tent out beyond the camp, and then drew to a halt.

"The colonel's put you here, madam," Godey said.

We stepped down upon a grassy sward and discovered a small abode with a camp cot and canvas chair.

"He'll send breakfast over directly, and if there's anything you need for your comfort, let me know," Godey said.

"Where's the colonel?"

Godey smiled. "Here, there, everywhere."

"And will he join me for breakfast?"

Godey paused, smiled, and nodded. It seemed no answer at all. He flapped the lines over the rumps of the mules, and the wagon jarred away.

"Land sakes," Kitty said, surveying our austere quarters.

The brightening heaven did at last reveal Colonel Frémont. He was dressed in a gray flannel shirt, black woolen trousers, a blue cotton bandanna about his neck, and a flat-brimmed slouch hat.

He would come to us eventually. I loved watching him. He was compact and lean and lithe, and moved with grace and ease, unlike so many men who seemed barely to command their own bodies. I could hear nothing, for all of this occurred some yards distant, but I could read events even at that distance. I had become an expert at extracting meaning from the way people approached one another at Washington City balls. And now I could see my husband in easy triumph, quietly turning this band of adventurers into a disciplined company that would soon plunge into wilderness, mapping, sketching, observing flora and fauna, studying gradients, finding a way over the spine of the continent.

It was lovely seeing him so alive, not at all broken as he had been. And soon he would welcome me.

CHAPTER FOUR

Benjamin Kern, MD

I was expecting to like Colonel Frémont. My brother, Edward, had been with the colonel during his third topographical expedition, the one that resulted in the conquest of California. Indeed, Ned played no small role in that affair and commanded Sutter's Fort for a while.

It was Edward who lured me into this adventure with his vivid depictions of the unknown West and his absolute trust in the sublime competence of Frémont. Edward was the artist/cartographer on that trip, who along with the brilliant German topographer Charles Preuss, mapped the unknown continent.

So enticing were his tales that I was seduced. Come along on the next adventure, Edward urged, and so I did, along with my other brother, Richard, also a fine artist. Frémont had no funds to pay us, this new expedition being privately financed, so we outfitted ourselves with all the best wares and agreed to join him at Westport. We would go along for the sheer joy of it and supply Frémont with services as well. Edward and Richard would provide valuable sketches of unknown country, of great importance for a railroad right-of-way survey; I would bring my surgical tools and skills as a healer.

I was on hand when Frémont and his lovely young wife de-
barked at Westport Landing, and I watched as the pair were immediately surrounded by admiring colleagues and friends from
the previous expeditions. It spoke well of Frémont that many of
his old command had signed up for the new one. I noted at once
that they addressed him with deference and affection and that he
had a quiet and easy way with them—I'd say a natural authority,
though in this case his command did not rest on rank but simply
on his personal qualities.

I scarcely had the chance to take the measure of the man at Westport but intended to when we reached Boone Creek, because we
three Kern brothers were putting our lives and our safety squarely in
the hands of this leader. There were certain aspects of his conduct,
such as the perilous crossings of the Sierra Nevada in winter and his
actions that led to a court-martial for mutiny and disobedience of
General Kearny's orders, that invited scrutiny.

The camp itself was actually sprawled over a vast tract of lush
Missouri meadow and woodland; it takes considerable pasture to
nourish well over a hundred mules and a few horses. So I was curious as to how this celebrated conqueror of the Mexican province
would conduct himself. I should not have worried. No sooner had
he settled into a small tent at Boone Creek than he was inventorying his equipment and listening to his lieutenants about what
needed doing, always in that quiet, civilized manner that seemed
to be inbred in the man. Some men are born to command, and he
was one.

I knew nothing about expeditions and how they are assembled,
so I had the advantage of seeing everything fresh. I gathered that
the mules were a major problem; some large percentage of them
were entirely green and required breaking either to saddle or
packsaddle. Missouri may be a well-populated state, but it cannot
on short notice supply a hundred thirty trained, docile, reliable

mules, plus a few horses, especially so late in the year, after countless companies heading for Oregon or Santa Fe had depleted the market.

The mules were largely left to Frémont's old command, plus a few Missourians, who, I gathered, prided themselves in the art of reducing quadrupeds to usefulness. That would be no easy task for this gang of adolescent animals. This enterprise was, I fathomed, under the direction of Charles Taplin, late of the United States Army and a veteran of the California campaign. His able assistants included some Missouri frontiersmen, also veterans, such as Josiah Ferguson, Henry Wise, and Tom Breckenridge. Another pair, Billy Bacon and Ben Beadle, also lent a hand. They were getting some additional help from Elijah Andrews of Saint Louis and Raphael Proue, an older Frenchman. I learned later he was the oldest man in the company. I can scarcely tell an aged Frenchman from a young one.

These worthies had a formidable task: half the mules in the herd had never known a saddle on their backs, and a few were little more than frisky yearlings. The muleteers proceeded, I thought, in a no-nonsense fashion, dealing with each animal according to its nature. If the animal was docile and accepted a halter and didn't struggle against a rope, it was rubbed down, saddled with a folded blanket and a crossbuck, and allowed to absorb the novelty of weight anchored to its back. But if an animal was recalcitrant, it was swiftly thrown to earth by various devices that I marvel at, hobbled, haltered, tied to a snubbing post, and allowed to learn the authority of stout manila. What struck me most as I watched this massive recruitment of animals was that the muleteers devised a method for each mule, reading its nature in its responses to its steady subjugation. The quiet ones advanced easily; the outlaws learned about their future life the hard way. I have come to an admiration for this skill, heretofore unfamiliar to me. I saw some lessons in it for the medical profession.

But there was plenty of other work undertaken at Boone Creek. The voyageurs were expert with all manner of equipment and were inventorying kegs and cases of picks and shovels, axes and rifles and little brown casks of gunpowder and pigs of lead, along with awls and knives and hatchets and coils of rope. All these had to be counted and divided into separate packs. Since several of those on this trip were unpaid volunteers, including the Kern brothers, we looked to our own equipage. We each had good woolen underdrawers and shirts, but we found we lacked stockings and tanned leather to repair or resole boots.

It was a day or two before Colonel Frémont found time to acquaint himself with me, and this happened not at one of the messes, as I had expected, but because he sought me out. I knew exactly what to expect: an assessing gaze, absolute calm, quiet and cultivated voice, and a certain distance.

"I'm pleased you'll be with us, sir," he said. "I always worry about calamities to my men. You'll be a comfort."

"That's all I'll be, I fear. There's not much a man can do out in the wastes. But I can set a bone or amputate. And I have a few powders. I have some cathartics that may ease some distress. Edward says that's a complaint."

"They'll take heart from it."

"And you, sir?"

"I'm fit. Nothing like that ever befalls me. I thrive out there, and the farther I am from settlements, the healthier I am. I'm fated to prosper in wilderness, so I'll have no need of your services."

There are men like that, and I supposed this one was one. "Will the trip be taxing for someone like me? Or my brothers?"

"A trip is as easy or taxing as one makes it. If you learn your lessons along the way, you'll walk comfortably into California. The secret is to economize everything."

"I'll make a point of it."

"Very good, sir. If you have any difficulties, talk to my second, Alexis Godey."

With that, he drifted away. We had not gotten past the barest acquaintanceship. But of course there would be a whole trip ahead to form friendships. And yet my instinct was that this man had no intimates. Since he arrived, I had seen him address most everyone in that quiet manner but also stay distant from them. Yes, he kept space between himself and his command. His emotions were unreadable. At night he vanished into his own tent, permitting only his man Saunders to enter, and no one saw more of him until the next dawn.

He struck me as a man apart. That was just as true for his old comrades of the California Battalion as it was for newcomers like me. I found myself wondering if the man had ever had friends, men who could be called intimates or confidants, because I saw no sign of it nor did it seem obvious from my cursory examination of his character. In time I rebuked myself for invading his privacy. Whether he had friends or none was not my business. But the puzzle would not leave my mind, and the more I observed Frémont, the more curious I was about him.

I wondered what hold he had on these men. He obviously had some sort of grip on them, and it was plain that his veterans looked up to him. Was it the quietness of his voice? His civility? Was it something assumed? He expected full obedience to his wishes and received it without cavil. He used no profane language, unlike some of his veterans and his Creoles, who had their own French scatology. That was part of it. He was a gentleman from a powerful American family, and the company knew it. I thought it must be caste. He somehow let them know he belonged to a higher order.

I felt a little useless there. Save for the Kerns, every man had been put to work. Even the California Indian boys, Manuel and Joaquin, who were being returned to their people by Frémont, were assigned tasks such as leading the haltered mules or building fires for the morning and evening messes or scrubbing kettles. I noted with approval that Frémont's freed black servant, Jackson Saunders, was treated exactly the same as the rest, except that Saunders had rather less to do and spent time attending to the colonel's wardrobe.

The camp had the quality of a military bivouac, but there was that notable exception of Mrs. Frémont, sitting quietly before her tent hour after hour, absorbing the autumnal sunlight. The colonel had told us all that she had suffered a great loss en route here and was in fragile health. But he added that she would welcome us and was eager to acquaint herself with every member of the expedition. That seemed to be the case. Young as she was, Mrs. Frémont rarely drifted from her tent and was content to receive members of the expedition, one by one. And at the end of each day, Alexis Godey would harness the mules and take Mrs. Frémont back to her log quarters at Major Cummins's agency. But the Pathfinder never accompanied her. I found myself curious about their relationship and rebuked myself for it.

That seemed excuse enough, and I drifted to her each midday, eager to acquaint myself with the wife of the Pathfinder and the daughter of the most powerful senator in Washington. I was never disappointed. She mastered my name and vocation instantly and always invited me to join her for tea kept hot on a charcoal brazier. Even without being asked, her maidservant, Kitty, would pour a steaming cup of oolong and present it to me.

"Well, Mrs. Frémont, it appears we'll be on our way in a day or two. And you'll be heading back to Saint Louis?" I asked.

She smiled faintly. "Briefly. I'll take my daughter, Lily, with me on a riverboat to New Orleans, and then to Panama, across the isthmus, and meet the California steamer on the Pacific side. The colonel and I will meet in Yerba Buena, they call it San Francisco now, in the spring."

"That's a perilous trip, madam. The jungle fevers . . ."

"I have never fled from peril and don't intend to start, Doctor."

"Chagres is famous for them. You'll want to move overland as fast as you can. Avoid the swampy places."

"The colonel and I are destined, Doctor. Absolutely destined to meet as planned in that distant land."

"You see little of him here," I said.

For an instant her face clouded, but it took a sharp eye to notice. Which I have. I am insatiably curious about people, and especially these people. "It is my daily pleasure to observe him organizing this enterprise," she said primly. "I marvel at it. How rare is this chance? What woman in similar circumstances may observe a commander and his men? I count myself lucky."

"I'm glad he invited you to come here," I said.

"I invited myself. He was all for saying good-bye in Saint Louis and said my health wouldn't permit something as strenuous as this. I think perhaps he now feels a woman can travel across the isthmus without difficulty." She smiled wryly.

"What awaits you on the Pacific shore?"

"It's like Italy but scarcely settled, he tells me. Have you never yearned to see another world, Doctor?"

"Many times. That's why I'm here. Curiosity is my vice. What's it like to walk across a continent? What's between here and there? What awaits me on the coast? Who on earth would join an expedition like this? Are we all madmen?"

"Then you know the joy of a challenge. We'll be together in California, and we'll head for his estate. He's never seen it. It's called Las Mariposas, The Butterflies. What a lovely name! The consul, Larkin, purchased it, and it wasn't what the colonel wanted but we're stuck with it. It's mostly meadows or foothill forest land, you know. It'll pasture thousands of cattle or sheep. So, we're in the livestock business, it seems. We'll know more when we see it. I'm rather taken with the idea. Perhaps my destiny is milkmaid or goatherd."

"You preferred not to go overland?"

"The colonel wouldn't think of it, sir. He's fully occupied with finding a rail route, and a woman would be in his way."

"Did he fear for your safety?"

"The overland journey will be safer than passage through the jungles of Panama, sir. No, safety was not among his considerations. He did feel it would be inconvenient to be taking a wife and daughter with him." She smiled suddenly. "He says I'd put most of his men to shame."

I wanted to probe further but dared not. For a girl of twenty-four, she was as seasoned and shrewd as someone much older. She had been born into a powerful political family, had entertained presidents and secretaries and all sorts of dignitaries, and she would know instantly if my gentle probing transgressed the bounds of decorum. A pity. I really wanted to find out what sort of man Frémont was, and the truth was that I hadn't the faintest idea. And I suspected that she didn't have the faintest idea, either. I had gotten one thing out of it: he believed he lived under some sort of star and that his fate was not in his hands.

CHAPTER FIVE

Captain Andrew Cathcart

I was heading for Cathay, actually, and thought to shoot a few buffalo en route. When I heard about Frémont's expedition I signed on, thinking to have a sporting holiday. I'd been in the Eleventh Prince Albert Hussars for a decade and grew bloody weary of it, so I sold my commission. I prefer to rove. It's a habit of the Scots.

This chap Frémont, when I looked him over, seemed a thoroughly competent officer who had rambled all over the American West and pocketed California for the Yanks. Still, there were the shadows cast by the man. What sort of officer was it who could get himself in trouble on charges of mutiny, insubordination, and conduct prejudicial to military discipline? The fellow would take some observing, he would.

What I found, when I first met the man in Saint Louis, was a perfectly civilized fellow, mild of manner, who obviously didn't care one way or another whether I joined his party. I saw no rebel in him. Neither was he rigid. In fact, I saw not much of anything when I was sizing him up. It was as if he lived on some distant shore. But I saw nothing to alarm me, either. He had manners, an odd gentleness, and seemed quite at peace. I decided to ramble with the fellow and told him I'd join him at Westport, which I did. The arrangement suited me: I had made no commitment, and neither had he. If I didn't like the way he was commanding his men, I could walk away.

He told me he was going to hunt for a railway route to the coast along the 38th parallel, something his father-in-law ached to see and that some Saint Louis businessmen thought might bring prosperity to that frontier city. That parallel should take a traveler straight to the bay of San Francisco, which those visionaries saw as the Pacific portal of the American republic, but there were a few bumps along the way, according to the scanty charts available, mostly from Mexican sources. He said he knew of a way and was destined to tie the republic together.

I outfitted myself with the best that pound and shilling could buy, because Frémont would not do it. This was a private survey, he had informed me. I didn't mind. I prefer my own kit and gear. I have lived in the field and was not afraid of cold and rain, wind and sun, and misery. Those are a soldier's lot. When we all were settled at Boone Creek I saw no evidence of luxury in Frémont. His gear was as simple as the rest, though he did prize some scientific instruments, half of which I could not fathom. He had the usual sextants and magnetic compasses and thermometers. He also had two chronographs that should give him good longitude readings from the Greenwich Meridian. He was equipped to survey, with a theodolite, quadrant, transit, and Gunter's chain. He had altimeters and barometers. He also had a morocco-leather portfolio of charts and tables. I scarcely grasped the half of what he was carting west, but I knew it would burden a dozen mules. His topographer, Charles Preuss, would be well-equipped to map the rail route and all the surrounding country. If Preuss and Frémont didn't know where they were at all times, no one would.

I've known officers to bivouac with wall tents, Brussels carpets, enough ardent spirits to stock a pub, wagons to haul all their truck, camp cots, canvas chairs, and a staff of orderlies and chefs. Frémont showed none of that, and I gave him credit for it. He did have a considerable wardrobe. Some of it was simply his blue uniforms stripped of the marks of rank. He was a button-up man. If he wore a coat, he buttoned it right to the chin. If he wore a flannel shirt, it was buttoned to the neck.

Of course there was the oddity of Frémont's young wife, receiving the men as if she were the Queen herself. She had dark circles under her eyes, and I learned that on board the *Martha* she had lost an infant son. I pitied her but also admired her bravery. She put on a good front before all of us, no matter how she hurt within. Frémont rarely visited her; he seemed much more absorbed with sorting out the gear and putting his mules into service. But I was glad to see the men cosset her; she certainly wasn't getting much attention from her lord and master.

That mule operation I watched closely, drawing from my own years as a cavalry officer. We didn't much truck with mules in Great Britain and took far more time perfecting our mounts, employing a patience acquired over generations. The Yanks' methods were rough but effective, and in a matter of days the green stock had become serviceable and would probably settle into usefulness on the trail. I did see them accidentally lame a mule they had thrown to the earth, so their rough treatment was not without its toll. And I had the sense that some of those mules would prove to be outlaws. Missourians are mean by nature and that only breeds mean livestock.

I volunteered to help, being a cavalryman, but was turned down. It soon became plain that Frémont's old hands, veterans of his previous trips, were a circle unto themselves, and we newcomers were regarded as baggage. That was particularly evident at the messes. His veterans formed their own messes; the rest of us found ourselves thrown together. I could understand it. The veterans knew one another's abilities and limits; the rest of us were jokers in the deck. One thing I did learn, though: those veterans could cook. Any one of them could produce an adequate meal, without scorching the stew or spilling the oatmeal or burning the side pork. I wished we had a few blokes with such skills in the hussars.

One of Frémont's regular chaps, a Mexican War veteran named Lorenzo Vincenthaler, seemed particularly eager to isolate the rest of us, which worried me because he was one of Frémont's obvious favorites.

There were other peculiarities about this company that soon emerged as we prepared to leave. We had an array of specialists of one sort or another with us, and I was hard put to connect this with the practical business of locating a railroad route to the Pacific. Take the German, Frederick Creutzfeldt, for example. He was a paid botanist. Why a financially strapped, commercially funded expedition whose sole purpose was to establish a rail route needed a paid botanist was something that kept tickling my curiosity. Who hired him? Was it Benton, maybe? And for what purpose? Was he looking for coal, or for plants that might have crop value? Assessing timber resources? The more I studied on it, the more likely it seemed to me that this private expedition was to be staffed as closely to the military ones as possible. Here were a renowned topographer, Preuss; an established cartographer and artist, Edward Kern; Creutzfeldt, a botanist; Rohrer, a millwright; and Stepperfeldt, a gunsmith. The Pathfinder intended to explore, and railroad building was merely the scaffold for his larger ambitions. I supposed I'd learn much more on the trail, when men thrown together in wilderness usually discern the truths and realities that are masked in more civilized places.

Meanwhile, I did not at all mind being thrown in with the

newcomers. One of our chaps came from Mississippi and had the impossible name of Micajah McGehee. Now how do you pronounce that mouthful? I reduced him to Micah, and he cheerfully accepted it as long as he could call me Cap. He was along entirely for the adventure, as fiddle-footed as I am. So our mess was almost entirely adventurers, save only for Edward Kern, a Frémont veteran. I had the hunch that it was going to be better this way than if we had been roped into the other messes. The Creoles had their own mess, which included the black servants. I took that as a sign of social status here in the States.

By some mysterious process, the company completed its preparations, and on the eve of October 19, 1848, the Pathfinder announced that we would break camp in the morning and travel only a few miles, the purpose being to test our mules and packs and deal with any difficulties. I had supposed we would be at Boone Creek another week or so and was delighted at the prospect of leaving. As usual, Godey drove Mrs. Frémont back to the Delaware agency that evening, and I wondered whether we would be seeing Mrs. Frémont again, at least until we should meet on the Pacific shore. If the colonel and his lady said any private good-byes, these were invisible to the rest of us. He seemed concerned, instead, with assigning saddle mules to each member of his company, trying to gauge which mule best suited which rider.

As Godey drove Mrs. Frémont away, she turned to look at us one last time, her expression obscured by her bonnet. But I knew exactly what passed across her face; it was an inexpressible yearning and a grim determination not to show the slightest feeling. I felt an odd pity. We were her rivals. As for the Pathfinder, he seemed not to notice. And in a few moments, Godey's wagon and its cargo disappeared around a tree-carpeted slope, and I never saw Jessie Benton Frémont again.

I felt just then an acute homesickness. I have felt it often, but those smudges under her eyes set it off in me, a longing for Ayrshire, from whence I came, that I could scarcely endure. For it was there, facing the western sea, that I grew to manhood, and it was the sea that lured me ever westward and was still taking me away from my people. I don't know what makes me roam, what it was about the western seas and the mysteries beyond them that lured me away from my hearth; from the kind and sometimes reproachful eyes of my mother; from the settled world of Ayr, its hardy cattle, its sere slopes and mild winters so gloomy at the time of the solstice that a cheery fire lighting our parlor seemed like heaven. Why had Jessie Benton's departure plunged me into that secret melancholia that I have struggled so long to ignore?

I was suddenly angry at this man Frémont.

We raised camp rather late that morning of the twentieth, coping with the usual difficulties. Some of the greener mules had other notions than to haul our goods. Some of the company proved to be inept at saddling. Others discovered they had too many goods and too little space in panniers and packs. One mule bit a man's finger, and Ben Kern applied a plaster.

We arose before dawn, actually, and completed our morning mess in darkness with a steady breeze chilling us. A simple meal of gruel sufficed, and we soon had our kettles and tin bowls packed away. Frémont wandered freely, at ease, and I never heard a command issue from his lips. His veterans seemed to anticipate what he wanted. An occasional question was all it took for him to make his will known. At least among his old companions of the wilds there was great jubilation, as if this were the beginning of something sweet, a nectar that befell only the most privileged of mortals. I marveled at this.

The break-in trip was not without its mishaps. A girth strap

loosened, sending a pack of macaroni and sugar and coffee southward until it hung beneath the quivering beast's legs. But these
things were swiftly remedied, and no harm was done. Here on the
backs of a hundred-odd mules was grain for the stock, tents, tools,
flour for ourselves, rubberized sheets for wet ground, and a myriad
of other items too numerous to detail. All those mules were trans-
porting a miniature city as well as thirty-three men heading west
into the unknown to look for a place where shining rails might
span the midcontinent.

I found mule transportation much to my liking. A mule's gait is
dainty compared with the gait of a horse and gives the rider the impression of floating. It was in perfect ease that I spent my hours in
the saddle. Mules can be uncommonly stubborn, but mine seemed
determined to keep up with the rest, and I had no need to deal with
insubordination. I thought that maybe the Queen's hussars ought to
weigh the benefits of mule travel.

The five miles proceeded peaceably enough through grassy
country under a variable Wedgwood sky, and Frémont called a halt
for the day in ample time to inspect the mules for sores on their
withers and for the evidences of all sorts of troubles. It had been an
easy day's travel, wisely shortened to permit adjustments to the tack
and equipment and to break in the mules for what would be a long
haul. The hunters, Godey especially, had proceeded ahead of us and
left two does and a buck on our path, ensuring us a fine venison dinner that eve. These bloody carcasses had been loaded onto skittish
mules, which alarmed them, but eventually our parade resumed.

"Easy trip, eh?" I said to Doctor Kern, who was unloading his
truck from a mule.

"No worse for wear," he replied. "I must say, Frémont has a way
about him."

That was the very thing that had struck me through the entire day. I had never seen a commander less conspicuous or more effective. I wondered what his secret was. Whatever it was, he induced men to see to their appointed tasks without ever addressing them. It was as if he had a secret finger signal for every whim.

I chose not to raise a shelter, it being mild and with little sign of rain, and settled into my Hudson Bay blankets at some distance from the fire. I did vaguely remember that well into the night a horseman left camp in some hurry, the rapid gait conveying some urgency to me just as I drifted into sleep. I gave it no further thought until morning, when Frémont appeared out of the east, on a worn horse.

He had, it seemed, decided to spend one last hour with Jessie and had returned to Major Cummins's agency well beyond Boone Creek, awakening her and her servant in the small hours. She had welcomed him happily, he said, and had set Kitty to making some tea, and there the lovers whiled away an hour before he saw fit to return to his company.

It had been a cruel night for her, apparently. Cummins had found a wolf den nearby and knocked the pups in the head. When the wolf bitch returned and found her pups gone, she began the most pathetic howling and mewling and whimpering and coaxing the dead to return to her bosom. This dirge did not cease. The forlorn wolf did not surrender her hope but continued through the deeps of the night to lure her pups back to her breast. All of which stirred the most dire melancholy in Mrs. Frémont, who was aware that the major had destroyed the wolf pups. She felt the wolf's suffering within her own bosom, as only a mother who has recently lost a child can do, and so passed a night of torment and sadness, broken by the startling arrival of Frémont.

All of this he told us in his usual offhand way, while we listened silently. His veterans thought all the more of him for his romantic journey back to see his wife and to comfort her in her moment of sadness. My own instincts were otherwise. I wondered why he was telling us about this night passage. Frémont's trip was an attempt to salve his neglect of his wife, and the man was a bastard.

CHAPTER SIX

Henry King

We started west with great ease. The company's outfitting was so perfect that we had no difficulties and proceeded steadily along the Kansas River, making twenty-five or more miles each day across frost-nipped grassland. The whole company was at ease and in the finest of spirits. I could not have been happier myself. Just being with Frémont once again was enough to fill my days with delight. No man ever led a happier band.

Our mules were in good flesh and carried us easily as we progressed across the plains, rarely encountering any serious climb or descent. There was yellowed grass waiting for them at the end of each day, and our skilled muleteers put the mules out on it. We maintained a light but ready guard against thieving Indians but didn't expect trouble.

The timing of this expedition worked out perfectly. I was afraid that Frémont might leave a fortnight earlier, which would have been awkward for me because it would have interrupted or postponed my wedding. But it was all just fine. We married, Beth and I, and I enjoyed a few days in the bosom of hearth and home before I set off for Westport Landing, even as the restlessness in my heart was growing unbearable. I could not, under any circumstances, avoid this trip, which I had fastened on ever since I heard that Colonel Frémont was planning it. I was with him in the California Battalion, rising to captain in an irregular armed force that was composed of the army's topographic corps and civilian Yanks in Mexican California.

There were several veterans of that campaign with us now, the memory of our easy conquest of California glowing in our bosoms. Without half trying, the colonel had welded together the most powerful armed force on the Pacific Coast, drawing on a motley crowd, whether regular soldiers or Bear Flag rebels or settlers. Most of us were irregulars, but it didn't matter. It wasn't only that we took California with ease; it was that we had such a good time doing it and achieved it without much cost in blood. We were a terror, bearded men in buckskins, and I never forgot it.

I was eager to renew an old friendship. Charles Taplin had been with Frémont during the conquest, rising to captain in the colonel's irregular army. We had been through the whole campaign together. I spurred my mule forward to catch up with him. Fortunately, our mules were gaited much the same. It is next to impossible to conduct a conversation when two beasts have different gaits and one or another rider must always rein in or spur forward.

"Ah, Henry, I was hoping you might join me," Taplin said.

"This brings back the old days for sure," I replied.

He smiled wryly at me. "And you abandoned a wife for it?"

"She can wait," I said.

"I don't know that I would abandon a wife after just a fortnight."

"She's the picture of domesticity," I returned, enjoying his needling. "She's especially skilled at mending my socks. But her cooking is still wanting."

"Probably an improvement on the cooking around our campfires," he replied.

"No, sir. I don't think any woman can achieve the perfection of good cow buffalo hump, nicely blackened on the outside, or buffalo tongue, well roasted on the outside and pink within."

"I take it you're not done with adventure, Henry. I'm done with it. I'm going to settle in California. I was greatly smitten by the climate. It's like living in perpetual springtime. When I resigned my commission, I had in mind heading west. This seemed the way to do it." He touched heels to the mule, evoking a slight spurt before the sullen animal settled back to its indolent walk. "I should like to find a Californio lady. It strikes me that a diet of chili peppers yields a hot nature in them." He eyed me again. "But of course, that doesn't interest you."

I laughed. I was not going to let Captain Taplin make me the butt of this company's humor the entire trip. A bridegroom was considered exotic in this crowd.

"I love this country," I said earnestly. It stretched ahead to a distant brown horizon lost in fall haze, mile upon mile, with naught but wind and sun and cured yellow grasses. This time we would climb over the roof of the continent and make our way to the far coast again. It was that ridgepole part of it that excited me. The colonel could inspire his men to achieve anything, summer or winter, desert or mountain.

"An improvement over the fair sex," Taplin agreed.

He was not going to let go of it, so I simply grinned at him. Silence was the best reply I could offer. I knew then and there that I was going to hear about this the entire journey, and the day we topped the Sierra Nevada and beheld California, they would still be asking whether this was an improvement on Beth. The joke was going to be on Captain Taplin, once he discovered that those chili peppers he yearned for were volcanic in more ways than one.

Even as we rode, I saw Frémont's veterans taking their ease, enjoying the trip while the greenhorns were struggling, sore in their saddles and worn out by the middle of the day. I supposed they would harden eventually, and then life would become easier for them. I didn't know what a botanist was doing on a railroad survey, but maybe the colonel wanted to achieve the very thing he accomplished the previous times as an army officer, making a major contribution to science. He always had his eye on the public, like a man planning to run for president. A few more laurels wouldn't hurt. Still, since this was an underfinanced commercial expedition, I didn't quite fathom it. Every businessman I'm acquainted with wants to cut unnecessary expense, and here we had an odd German named Cruetzfeldt with us whose task was to pluck flowers. I supposed he didn't leave a new wife behind. That sort of man never marries.

I could understand Preuss. He was along on the previous trips, doing his mapmaking and reading the instruments and furiously writing notes, pretending not to enjoy himself. The man wouldn't smile. It always ended up a sneer or a grimace. I always wondered what he put in his diaries. If you're going to run a railroad, you need a map and some topographic knowledge, what kind of grades you'll be facing, things like that, and that's what he supplied. And I could understand Ned Kern, too. He was with us in California. He could sketch, and a railroad needs to have drawings of the terrain if it's going to run a line through it. I supposed I could even understand Kern's brother Benjamin. A doctor is handy to set a bone or fix a mule, but he'll not be doctoring the veterans. Only the newcomers will get snake bit or fall off cliffs or get kicked by a mule.

Some of us weren't getting paid, and I didn't know if that's because the colonel was laying out fancy salaries for these newcomers. Some things about this trip didn't make much sense, and one of them was the whole idea of a railroad to the coast. Who needed it? It would be a lot of rail to nowhere. Where were the customers? This railroad would pierce through two thousand miles of

wilderness, buffalo, Indians, and mountains, with scarcely a settlement along the way. I thought the colonel was doing this trip at
the behest of his father-in-law, who had the power and money
and also a dream about a railroad. It would have made more sense
to push it south or north of here, but I have never underestimated
the power of politics. Old Senator Benton called it the middle
route and believed it made more sense than one farther north or
south. Actually, it was simply a ploy to bring trade to Saint Louis.

Four days out we ran into a prairie fire, a wall of smoke rising
from a lick of orange flame from south to north, and managed to
get through, our keg of powder and all, without getting ourselves
blown up or scorched. The grass was high, which didn't help. It was
odd, because we'd had some rain off and on. But that day we made
twenty-five miles and camped in a little valley with good grass.
The next day we made twenty-eight miles and stopped at the
Potawatomi Mission. We got some butter from the agent, a blood-
sucker named Major Monday, and spent the rest of the evening
looking over the Pott Indians, just as they looked us over. We put
an extra guard on, but these Indians were tame enough.

We were getting into buffalo country by then, and we would
see how the greenhorns could shoot. When you have buffalo, you
also have wild Indians; the two are wedded together so tight that
if one vanishes, the other will too. We were going to have plenty to
eat, good hump meat or tongue at the messes. But I expected all
that to disappear when we hit the mountains. There would be
deer and elk up there, not the big shaggies.

The colonel said he'd follow the Smoky Hill branch and then
cut down to the Arkansas River and stop at Bent's Fort, where he
hoped we could improve our livestock. We had a few laggards and
one or two half-lame, and maybe we could trade them off, along
with the horses, which are no good in high country because they
panic.

There was one thing I was noticing and that was the cold. The wind was tough on some of us, and we weren't seeing much sun, either. The pools froze up at night. No one was complaining. The cold was better than summer heat and horseflies. I didn't mind the cold so much, but the wind got mean and there was nothing here to slow it. There was hardly a tree between here and the British possessions.

I heard some shots, and pretty soon Godey came back to us. He had been ahead, hunting, and shot some buffalo bulls. I didn't look forward to the meat. Bulls are tough and sometimes stringy and not good for much except some stewing if you've got the time to boil the meat senseless. But at least we were getting into buffalo country, and we'd have us a cow or two now. Still, it would be entertaining to see how the greenhorns dealt with some bull meat, so I decided to join their mess.

That was morning, and it was up to each mess to hack meat for supper, so I kept one eye on the greenhorns. It was a sight, alright. Chopping meat out of an old bull was about like sawing the trunk off an elephant. Ned Kern knew enough, but his brothers didn't, and the rest had never seen one and hardly knew where to begin. But Ned began slicing into the hump, and it took a deal of work even to open up a hole. Not even the surgeon was doing much good. Of course the rest of the messes had gone for the tongues; not much else worth putting into a cook pot. By the time the greenhorns got enough meat for supper, they had put hatchets and an axe to the task and were plumb worn out. I could hardly wait for supper, when they would get another lesson.

That eve we camped in the shelter of a clay cliff beside Smoky Hill, and a few of Frémont's veterans lent a hand to the greenhorns, getting a big fire going and getting that sawed-up meat on green sticks to broil on the lee side of the flames. I think the doctor, Ben

Kern, figured it out long before they began to chomp on those slabs of shoe leather they were about to down for dinner. When the moment came, he tackled one or two bites of the brown ruin on his tin plate, sighed, and gave up.

He never complained; I'll give him credit, but McGehee was whining.

"Fat cow's what we want," I said to the doctor.

"The other messes have tongue. I think I'll remember that."

"Say, whiles I'm here, do you have powders for anyone bound up?"

"Salts, yes, purgatives. I have ample."

"That's good. I get bound up on buffalo. Sometimes we go a week without seeing a green, and then it's misery."

"See me, Mister King."

"I guess a doctor's worth something after all," I said.

A faint smile spread across his face. "I have my instruments. If you break a leg, I can amputate. A saw cuts right through bone, and I imagine your leg would be a good bit more tender than this old bull." He was smiling blandly, obviously enjoying himself.

"I'm a young bull, alright."

"Watch your tongue," he retorted.

I had to admire the doc; he had some wit.

It was getting colder than I wanted. The wind smelled like December. It had a whiff of the Arctic in it. But the chill was nothing compared with the sheer pleasure in being hundreds of miles from the nearest shelter. That was the plains for you. A norther could blow out of the north and there was nothing to slow it down, and sometimes it plowed clear into Mexico.

We set off the next day in cold weather, a mean wind adding to our misery. I thought that pretty soon we'd hear some whining, but the greenhorns didn't emit a peep, and we made our grim way west through an increasingly arid country, broken now by gullies and slopes but utterly treeless. Ere long we'd be using buffalo chips for fuel.

The colonel seemed oblivious to the lancing wind and everything else and simply led us along a route that he did not share with us, content to let nature supply us. And it did. Godey shot a cow, and we feasted on good hump meat, plenty fat, and this time the greenhorns got a taste of prime buffalo meat. It made an impression on them, for sure. The whole trip, Frémont had scarcely given a command, and the slightest suggestion was all it took to remedy or achieve anything he wished. I didn't know, and probably will never know, what the man's hold was on others.

The Delawares left us the next morning. They had agreed to accompany us a way but didn't want to tangle with some of the tribes we were facing ahead. The colonel continued up the Smoky Hill fork for the next days. These were exposed stretches, with a howling wind that burrowed into a man's clothing and chilled him fast. The temperatures were mostly in the twenties and thirties, but it felt worse. There wasn't a tree in sight most of the time, nothing to break the gale that whipped through our straggling party. Despite good cured shortgrass, some of the mules were weakening, and I wondered whether the colonel was aware of it. He wasn't stopping to let them recruit. Sometimes one day on good grass is all they need. But the colonel plunged on, through increasingly barren country, in weather that did nothing to lift the mood of the company. If the greenhorns needed hardening, they were getting it sooner than expected.

At least there were buffalo. For some reason, our hunters continued to drop bulls instead of good cows, but we made do with tongues and boiled bull stew, at least when we could find enough deadwood to build fires. There were places where the plains stretched to infinity and not one tree was visible. The messes were fed with some antelope and even some coon meat the hunters felled here and there, but the staple was bull meat, boiled until it surrendered.

Then one day Frémont turned us south, and we headed over a tableland that divided the drainages of the Missouri and Arkansas and plunged into a lonely sea of shortgrass that probably would take us to the Arkansas some hard distance away. But the winds never quit, and now they brought bursts of pellet snow, which settled whitely on the ground and on the packs, shoulders, and caps of our men. It was early and wouldn't last, but it was snow and it brought on chill winds that never quit and drove me half-mad. I just wanted to find a hollow somewhere, an overhang, a cozy place where that fingering wind didn't probe and poke and madden me. For the first time, I began to wonder about this trip. It made no sense at all to travel this time of year.

The colonel didn't seem to notice the cold or the wind. He rode without gloves and didn't hunch down in his saddle the way most of the men were hunched, trying to rebuff the cruel wind. I wondered what sort of god-man Frémont was, riding like that, as if he was unaware of the suffering around him, unaware that others were numb and miserable. But he didn't choose to see what I was seeing. He had no eyes for the hunched-up mules that stopped eating and put their butts to the wind and hung their heads low. We sheltered where we could, sometimes under a cutbank, other times in a gulch, but it didn't help much. The wind always found us. The wind found everyone except Colonel Frémont. I swear, the wind quit dead when it came to him; I swear he rode in an envelope of calm warm air, never knowing what other men, mules, and horses were going through.

CHAPTER SEVEN

John Charles Frémont

We reached the valley of the Arkansas River in perfect ease, and I was satisfied that the exploration would proceed without difficulty. My outfitting had never been better despite limited funds, and we were proof against the worst that nature could throw at us. We entered the wide sagebrush-covered valley and found it largely denuded of trees on its north bank, so we crossed at a good gravel ford and then the travel was more comfortable and there were ample willow and hackberry and cottonwood to feed our fires and build our shelters. The road was excellent, not so churned up as it is on the north bank, where the Santa Fe trade had wrought quagmires.

I was satisfied that we had located a good rail route across the prairies, and Charles Preuss was, too. I trusted the man, dour as he may be, simply because he drafted excellent maps and kept unimpeachable logs during my first two explorations. His readings, both at high noon and of the polestar at night, were finer than any before attempted, and he could tell me within a few feet how high we were above the sea. Now he was daily advising me about how far we wandered from the 38th parallel. He had a certain irony in his eye, knowing full well that by all Hispanic accounts there is no practicable route over the Rockies at this latitude or even anywhere close by. South Pass on the Oregon Road offers an excellent route along the 40th parallel and is much used now by the Oregon bound. And of course, the Sangre de Cristos peter out off to the south, offering unimpeded passage west. But we had been commissioned by men who want to run rails straight over the top, so we would find a route for them, even if it meant turning high mountain saddles into benign passes and impossible chasms into placid valleys.

The visionaries in Saint Louis thought there might be a practical route and had set me to find it. Preuss just shook his head, an ironic gleam in his eye, saying nothing and yet telling me everything on his mind with little more than an arched eyebrow. I tended, privately, to agree with him but could not confess it publicly, nor did I wish to refute my father-in-law or bring him bad news. Better to find a route of some sort and let them decide whether it will break the United States Treasury or bankrupt all the merchants of Saint Louis to build it. In any case, it is my fate to achieve the impossible. I have known all my life that I am destined to do what other men cannot do. It is out of my hands. If it is my fate to find a new route west, through the middle of the continent, then it will happen no matter what I may choose to do.

No sooner had we reached the south bank of the Arkansas than we ran into an encampment of Kiowas, old Chief Little Mound's people. Their tawny lodges were scattered through cottonwood groves. They seemed entirely friendly, and I saw little menace in them. And some of them were handsome, which pleased me, for I take them to be a noble race. But I did halt my company and let them know that I had the utmost respect for Indians, and I required that all my men treat the savages with kindness and discernment. Of course I doubled the guard, not wanting my mule herd stolen.

They seemed an impoverished people, and I imagine they were verminous. Certainly they were unwashed. They mostly stood beside our trail, examining us one by one as we rode past. Who knows what thoughts were festering in their heads? When we camped that eve, there they were, collected silently around our perimeter looking for something to lift when we were occupied with other things. I brought few trade items because trade was not our business, which meant I could engage in little commerce with those people. And now I wished I had a few gewgaws.

But, oddly, Doctor Kern came to the rescue. They found out that he was a medicine man and were soon seeking him out. Godey and other of my veteran Creoles are pretty good sign talkers, and so the consultations proceeded. Kern hung out his shingle, examined the patients, and prescribed from his cabinet. In one case he compounded salves for some skin lesions. The Kiowas watched the compounding with wonder and took away these ointments as if they were gold. That made Ben Kern a very popular man among the Kiowas. The good doctor told me later than many of the Kiowas were flea plagued and he dreaded any contact with them because fleas are hard to get rid of.

The next days we traveled with the Kiowas, who were our constant companions, all of them curious about our ways and observing our every act. Apart from losing a saddle blanket, we suffered no losses, but it took constant vigilance to keep what was ours. I was especially zealous in protecting my instruments, which we needed to measure latitude and longitude as well as elevations and temperatures. We had several instruments whose sole purpose was to give us an altitude above sea level. The mercury barometer was the simplest, but it was variable in its results because of shifting air pressures. It was a fragile device, a thirty-inch glass tube partly filled with quicksilver, and we took special care of it. So I put these things under guard at all times and kept the mules under watch.

We had lost several mules en route, and I intended not to lose more. It was a puzzle. None of our stock was so heavily loaded as to give out, and all fed themselves nightly on the nourishing grasses that stretch endlessly in every direction, and yet some of our animals faltered, stumbled to earth, and would go no farther. I ascribe this to bad blood. There is bad blood in human beings and bad blood in animals, and the weak are constantly being culled out, both by nature and by man. I see even in my company some bad blood, men whose weakness will tell on them. I have good blood, and passage through hard country is as easy for me as a stroll down Pennsylvania Avenue in Washington City is for my father-in-law. I can't help those who cannot help themselves, and if any feel foreboding about our passage across the mountains, I hope they will withdraw from the company and not wait until they become a burden and liability.

We were well supplied with meat. Godey and several others are expert hunters and discovered a few buffalo in most every ravine, taking refuge from the wind. One could wish that we could feast on cows, but that was not to be our fortune this trip. We ate bulls. There was always ample meat for us and plenty to give to the Kiowas, who were tagging along with us. It seemed a good way to preserve a tenuous peace, but the constant presence of these half-starved people did not elevate the mood of my company. It didn't help either that it snowed off and on and that the thermometer swung wildly up and down. Give us a southerly wind and we rode in comfort; give us a northerly one and the weaker men in my company wrapped themselves in their blankets and grumbled.

The farther upstream we progressed, the more excited the Kiowas became, and I could not fathom what was exciting them until we arrived at a large camp of Arapahos, and among them was my old friend Tom Fitzpatrick, Indian agent for these southern plains tribes. He was in the midst of a great gifting of the tribes, a peacemaking process intended to secure their friendship. Major Fitzpatrick (all agents receive that honorary rank) was well known to me as Broken Hand Fitzpatrick, a veteran of the fur trade, a mountaineer without equal, a man who had survived numerous scrapes involving Indians, weather, animals, starvation, and cold. Indeed, he had been a part of my company on the second expedition when we made a winter foray over the Sierra Nevada into California, refurbished our company at Sutter's Fort, and returned to Saint Louis unscathed except for one small loss. He had done his work without complaint, constantly using his experience and skills to help the distressed.

Were he not employed by the government as agent, I would have approached him about the prospect of guiding us over the mountains ahead. But that was not a possibility, especially since my party had no official status and I had no way to loosen him from his duties. I thought to ask him who, in his opinion, would be the ideal man to guide us over the mountains lying to the west. If anyone would know, he would. But whether or not I could find a guide familiar with the country, I never doubted that I would succeed. I knew my fate, and I knew I would reach California no matter what lay ahead.

We had clearly arrived on the eve of a powwow of some sort. There were smoke-blackened lodges scattered through the bottoms, amply supplied with firewood from the groves of hackberry and cottonwood scattered across the valley. Some of the lodges had gaudy medicine art painted on them. Fitzpatrick, and an assistant who was probably a breed of some sort, had a wagon loaded with gifts from Uncle Sam, which after some treating with these chiefs and subchiefs would be dispensed. There would be something or other for every lodge. These were simply bribes. Don't attack white men and stay at peace, and your father in Washington will give you these things. A blustery wind blew through the valley, scarcely broken by the copses of trees. I smelled snow on the breezes.

Major Fitzpatrick recognized me at once as we rode through the loose-knit campground, and he waited patiently. I was glad we were not in blue uniforms, which might have upset the tribesmen. Plainly, the lot of us were ordinary citizens. We seemed a larger force than we were because of the hundred thirty mules and a few horses, most of them bearing our provisions neatly stowed in the reinforced duck-cloth panniers I prefer for mountain travel. The major eyed us knowingly, perhaps even recognizing a man or two, especially the Creoles.

"Colonel Frémont, I believe?"

"So it's you, Tom," I said. "I see you're busy."

"Oh, not so busy that we can't delay matters. I heard you were coming. Moccasin telegraph."

"Then you know about our mission."

"I do."

The response was so abrupt that I eyed the man sharply, aware that this was not the usual effusive greeting of this veteran of the mountains. Fitzpatrick had made his name in the beaver trade and had been a partner in some of those companies. He had guided me on my second venture into Oregon and California. Indeed, he was with me at the time of one of my most celebrated moments, a December crossing of the Sierra Nevada that we attempted, with great success, even though the local Indians warned against it. Broken Hand Fitzpatrick had roamed across the West, but from that trip with me he acquired a knowledge of country previously unknown to him, and I fancy he appreciated it. Now he was an experienced Indian agent.

"Railroad survey, thirty-eighth parallel."

"It's rather late in the season," he said.

"That's the object. Trains run year around."

"But summer's the time to look for a route."

"I do things my way, Major."

He nodded and motioned me off my roan. My company was drawing up, studying the Kiowas and Arapahos, tribes that were not exactly friends in other circumstances. The Indians were wrapped in bright striped blankets and brown buffalo robes, and sometimes their breaths were visible. The major himself had a buffalo-hide coat wrapped around him and a heavy scarf at his neck.

I dismounted and shook, careful to grasp his undamaged hand, and I clasped it awkwardly. The hand was cold.

Fitzpatrick introduced me to the assembled headmen, using tongue and hand signs I could not follow. The chiefs stood gravely, acknowledging our presence with a nod.

"This isn't the best time to visit with you, actually," the major said. "But I tell you what. Tomorrow we'll be through here and heading for Bent's Fort. I suppose you'll lay over for a time?"

"We will, sir. I want to do some trading."

"There's not much in the place. It's late in the year."

He was saying that the Santa Fe wagon companies had depleted the fort's stock of goods, but I had hope of improving my stores anyway.

"We're well provisioned, except for stock," I said.

He smiled wryly, his gaze on our herd.

"I tell you what, sir. I'll see ye at the fort before sundown tomorrow, and we'll palaver. Just now, you see, I have a deal of work. We're going to powwow, and I'm going to hand out peace medallions, a few muskets, some powder and lead, some red blankets for the blanket chiefs, lots of knives and awls and trade beads, and five hundred plugs of tobacco. And for that we want friendly treatment for the wagon companies. Now I'll see ye off."

This interview was more abrupt than I had hoped, but we would have a time to talk things over on the morrow.

"Very well, Major. Until tomorrow, then."

"Oh, and by the way, Colonel. When ye get beyond the trees yonder, ye'll have your first view of the western mountains."

"I'll tell the men."

"They stretch like a white line across the western horizon. A lot of snow, sir, this early in the season. I'm told that no one has seen the like." He stared evenly at me.

"It's nothing I am worrying about, Major."

"Nothing to worry about, then." He lifted his beaver hat, smiled, and waited while I boarded the horse I hoped to trade for a mule at Bent's Fort.

I signaled my company, and we rode west once again, while several hundred bronze faces observed our every move. Pretty soon we passed through the entire encampment and found only a few squaws beyond, collecting firewood. And then we were free.

Alex Godey rode up and joined me at the van. The column had assembled behind us and was snaking its way up the valley along a trail hemmed by the silvery sagebrush that grew rampant in the area.

"Did Major Fitzpatrick have any news, Colonel?"

"No, but we're going to have a good talk at the fort tomorrow evening."

"He was busy."

"He was something more, which I intend to get to the bottom of. He did not seem eager to see us. Oh, and he did make a point of something. There's a lot of snow ahead. More than anyone's ever seen this early. It seemed important to him. It doesn't worry me, but it troubled him."

"Alors, he's a man to listen to," Godey said.

"If I'd listened to every caution well-meaning but timid men offered me, I'd not be here now, leading my own expedition. I'd not be known."

"Ah, bien, sir, but you have the lives of many men to think about now."

"They have signed on voluntarily, and I will see them through, Alex. Now that you've raised that subject, I am hoping that the fainthearted will abandon us before we begin the ascent into the mountains. In fact, I plan to invite them to do it."

Godey smiled. "I doubt that anyone will, sir. They have their eyes on the history books, eh?"

"Well, I don't. What the world thinks of me is of no consequence to me. What I think of myself is all that matters."

We rode silently, following a river trail that gradually rose from the valley to the open plains. And there, when we topped out on the plains, lay a white wall far to the west, a brooding blue and white rampart barring our way.

CHAPTER EIGHT

Thomas Fitzpatrick

I am not very good at concealing my private opinions, but when it comes to John Frémont I make the effort. He is well connected. He is also a national hero, idolized everywhere for his contributions as an explorer and as the conqueror of Mexican California. It behooves me to keep my silence, especially because his father-in-law is the most powerful man in the Senate and can do me mischief.

Indian agents serve at the whim of presidents and with the consent of the Senate, and an agent's security rests on the most precarious of platforms. So is the case with me. I happen to like my office. I am at ease with the Indians, many of whom I know well and count as friends. I am able to mediate the conflicts rising between the advancing tide of white men and the tribes, and so far, at least, I have preserved the peace and made allies and friends of these people. I think a less-experienced man in my office would cause mischief.

All of which is my way of saying that when Frémont showed up with yet another exploring company and a large mule herd, I chose to conceal whatever lay within my bosom and deal with the man as best I could.

My own views were formed during the second expedition, the one in which he first invaded Mexican California. I was a well-paid guide on that one, along with Carson. Frémont's instructions were to proceed out the Oregon Trail, mapping it thoroughly, and then link up with Naval Lieutenant Wilkes on the Pacific Coast, in order to link the two explorations by land and by sea. Those were his instructions and what I thought I had contracted to do. He did as much but then struck south from the Oregon country, contrary to any army instruction but probably with the connivance of Senator Benton, until he came to the eastern flank of the Sierra Nevada. Then, on January 18, 1843, he attempted a winter passage of the Sierra Nevada, a course so reckless that he narrowly averted disaster. He managed to invade Mexico without leave of their authorities, risking an international incident, and eventually refitted at Sutter's Fort on the Sacramento River. From there it was a relatively easy journey home. Never did the man have a more reluctant guide than I, and I count myself lucky to survive a winter passage of the Sierra Nevada. I was duty bound to complete my contract with him, and I did. But I never again permitted myself to be engaged by him.

It was all portrayed in his subsequent report as a triumph, and the perils he exposed us to were blandly bridged with cheerful rhetoric. I knew better.

Even by the time he reappeared in my life, that November of 1848, I still remembered the starved, cold, miserable, and desperate hours high in the Sierra Nevada, in the dead of winter, in which our lives depended not on Frémont but the merciful cessation of the storms constantly rolling in. We were spared from the man's folly by a random turn of weather, but at terrible cost in terms of the ruin of men and animals. I believe that the miraculous respite in the weather only strengthened his belief that he is fated to succeed at whatever he does.

After we had topped the Sierra Nevada and were heading into mild California more or less unchastened, I chanced to remark to him that we had been extremely lucky that the weather held.

"It wasn't luck; it was destiny," he replied.

That alarmed me then, and it still does.

But how could one find fault with a brave national hero? His journals were published by the government itself and became the guidebooks of westward expansion, and the young topographic commander became a celebrated and rising man. But I would never celebrate him. Ever since that journey, I knew I was living on borrowed time.

And there he was once again, wandering into my powwow, as powerful and protected in 1848 as he had been in 1843, despite the court-martial and conviction on all counts and his resignation from the army. Standing behind him were the most powerful men in Washington City.

I am not very good at hiding what lies within me, but I put a good face on it and welcomed him. There is no man alive who is more obsessed with the opinion of others. Frémont looks into the eyes of others not to see what others are about but to see what is mirrored back to him. And so it was with me. We met there, at the hour of my council, and he was not so much interested in me or the tribesmen but in my view of him. I had not seen him in the intervening years, and he was eager to fathom my perception of him. I fear I did not conceal my private thoughts adequately.

If I was a bit chilly, I don't doubt that he registered it instantly.

However the case, I reluctantly agreed to see him at Bent's Fort as soon as I was done with the Indians. If he was still unsure about my approbation, he would not be unsure when we had finished there. I concluded my business with the Kiowas and Arapahos and started to the fort with my hired boy, Tito, and the empty wagon, from which I had distributed a goodly number of muskets, blankets, knives, awls, and trinkets, along with peace medallions.

The unsettled weather turned into yet another snow that evening, and we rode the wagon through six or seven inches of fresh white powder. That was an uncommon thing so early in the season on the southern plains. But maybe it could be used to promote some prudence in the Pathfinder. I would try, both for his sake and mine—or rather, for the sake of those men he was about to put in harm's way. Even as the tribes dispersed, going off to hunt buffalo and settle into wooded river bottoms for the winter, so did we ride wearily west along the sage-carpeted valley, well bundled against bitter winds. It was my hope that these very winds might impress themselves on the explorer, but I somehow knew they would do just the opposite. The promise of adversity was the siren song in John Charles Frémont's bosom, and that was how it would play out.

Two miles east of the fort and south of the river, I spotted their camp, located in the shelter of trees. Three campfires glowed. Frémont had chosen a good place, and judging from the messes he was keeping nearly all of his men there to guard the mules and supplies, which was wise. In the early twilight, the orange fires wavered through the spidery screen of brush, under a cast-iron sky. The adobe fort with its generous fireplaces would be a good place to stay this wintry night, and I welcomed it.

We raised the post as we rounded a low shoulder. The tan adobe rectangle on the north bank welcomed me with its promise of warmth and safety. That's what civilization was about. There were never-used bastions and a portcullis leading into a yard surrounded by warehouse and living quarters. Since the twenties, it had served as a great entrepôt on the Santa Fe route as well as the depot where southern tribes traded thousands of robes and tongues for blankets and pots and arrowheads and knives and sweets. As lavender twilight engulfed us, we could see that the post was worn and ill kempt. It had seen its day but still was the great comfort of the southern plains. Where else was there so much as a roof? or safety?

Frémont was waiting for us, standing alone in the yard. Whatever passed between us would be unknown to his company, I supposed. That was fine. Tito looked to the four mules and harness, and I stepped down to the clay yard wearily. I was not so young as I used to be, and a life outdoors had settled rheumatism in my bones. Still, I was far from the grave, or so I supposed.

The place seemed oddly empty; the post was ill manned now, almost as if the Bents had lost interest in it. And that pretty well summed it up. Charles Bent, governor of New Mexico, was murdered in a Taos uprising in early 1847; his brother, William, didn't much care about his great post anymore and had let it deteriorate. Maybe it was only age filtering through William, just as it had filtered through me.

The Pathfinder greeted me cordially, and I motioned him to the billiard room upstairs, a sort of observatory that once was filled with good company but now stood silent and gloomy. The place was William's stroke of genius. He had a billiard table hauled clear out the Santa Fe trail and put in there, and then added plenty of Taos Lightning and some imported beer, and for a few bright years that upstairs billiard room and its crowds of rowdies and drifters and mountaineers and hunters and tradesmen were the center of the whole universe.

We ascended creaking wooden stairs, trekked around the fort's perimeter, and then entered the chill room, protected from the wind by tight shutters. The billiard table was gone but some chairs, remnants of more hospitable times, remained.

"I've been wanting to talk to you, Tom," he said while I laid a piñon fire and lit it with a lucifer. The kindling caught, and small yellow flames began to lick to sticks of wood. The room would warm soon. "This is my good fortune. You're the one man here who knows this country. I tell you, Tom, out there's the future of the country, the road to Cathay."

"Well, I have in mind some talking," I replied. "Let me show you something."

I threw open the shutters on the west side, exposing a twilight panorama that embraced vast distances. Off to the west, lit by a blue band over the horizon, the remnant of the day's light, rose the Rocky Mountain front, a stern white wall as far north and south as the eye could see.

"That's where you're going?" I asked.

"Straight west, as close to this latitude as I can manage."

"You see any notch or gap ahead?"

"Well, those Wet Mountains are no great obstacle. It's the ones beyond that might give me some trouble. We'll be hunting for a good pass. All I need from you is some direction. You've been through there. Where can you take wagons? If I can find a wagon road, I can find a road for steam cars."

"There might be a wagon road. I don't know the country as well as Uncle Dick Wootton. He's a hunter here, and, if anyone can steer you across those mountains, he can. But that's not what I want to talk to you about."

Frémont had already guessed my mission, and his wry amusement was a dismissal even before I plunged in. But I would anyway. I would because lives were at stake. I had been with this man through a January crossing of the Sierra. One small change in weather would have destroyed Frémont, his topographic corps, Kit Carson, and me.

"Worst snow in memory," I said. "No one here's seen anything to match it."

"All the better. If I can negotiate a route through the roughest winter known, then there'll be no argument about it back east."

"Is that what they say back there?"

"Well, not exactly. They say that we need a practicable route. I'll give them one."

"You plan to find coal or timber this time of year? Steam engines need fuel and water."

"I'll find the route, grades that steam locomotives can handle, and worry about that some other time."

"You want to locate a route that might be under twenty feet of snow now? Where you can't see the true bottom or whether it's rock or marsh or talus?"

His wry amusement was all the answer I would get. But I pursued it.

"What can you report? That you've found passage to the Pacific but haven't seen the terrain itself because it's under drifts?"

"I'm not concerned about that. We can use poles to measure snowpack and terrain."

"And you expect to find coal seams in the dead of winter?"

"I'm not concerned about fuel in the mountains."

"Well, what do you expect to report?"

"That there is, or there isn't, a way west on the thirty-eighth parallel."

"So you're going to look just where the Rockies are highest and widest?"

"All the better, wouldn't you say, Tom?"

"And the most lethal?"

"There's not a man on earth who would attempt what I am attempting."

There it was, and it didn't surprise me. This wasn't about finding a rail route.

"There's a way around the Sangre de Cristos below Santa Fe," I said. "There's South Pass on the Oregon Trail. Neither of them would cost much compared with laying rail over trestles and gulches and rivers and canyons out there." I waved a hand westward.

"I told my backers I would do it."

The billiard room had heated well now and recovered some of the cheer it possessed back when Bent's Fort was a great oasis and men from all over the West collected right there in that room to share a cup, tell yarns, exchange vital information, and plot out great enterprises. The great stone and adobe hearth threw light and cheer into this haven, and with every degree of additional warmth Frémont's determination expanded. He wanted to achieve the unheard of.

"It's not the railroad, it's the challenge, isn't it?"

"What do you mean, Tom?"

"I mean that even if you succeed in getting over the top, three tops actually, in snows and weather like this, you still won't give them a rail route along the thirty-eighth parallel."

He shrugged. "I'm on my way to California. Jessie's probably headed for Panama now. We're going to meet in Yerba Buena on the big bay out there. I've got some property to look at, and this is the way to get there."

"What's beyond the San Juans?" I asked.

"I imagine we'll find out," he said.

"Well, let's see now, Colonel. You make it to the valley of the Rio del Norte after scaling two ranges in winter, and the first thing you'll hit is sand dunes, dunes everywhere. And if you continue, you'll cross miles of barren land without a tree for firewood. There'll be snow. And when you cross that, assuming you still have your company, you'll face maybe the roughest country in the region, and all of it under the worst snow in memory. It's no place for a railroad. I don't think a transcontinental railroad will ever be built there."

"You know it well enough to say that?"

I hesitated. "Not well enough. But there's a man who does, and he's around here. That's Richens Wootton. He's run wagons up in there. He told me once there's a place he calls Cochetopa Pass that takes a man across a northern corner of the San Juans. You have to know where to turn off from the Rio del Norte, some stream called the Saguache, a tributary of the Rio. You find that, maybe you have a route in summer. In summer, John."

"And winter," Frémont said.

"You won't find it without a guide. I've been in those mountains, and I can pretty well tell you, one creek looks like any other, and one peak like another, and that's in the summer. It'll be worse when everything is white."

"But Wootton knows?"

"I don't know of any other. He's hunting meat for Bent, but he pretty much steers his own course."

"I want to talk to him."

"The kitchen, I suppose," I said.

"You lead the way," he said.

"I wish I weren't," I replied.

CHAPTER NINE

John Charles Frémont

We made our way down the stairs, the treads hollow under our boots, and into the vacant yard. Bent's Fort had an eerie silence about it. The great doors had not been shut for the night, and I wondered whether they would be.

"Where's Bent?" I asked Major Fitzpatrick.

"Who knows? Probably with the Cheyenne."

"Who's running the post?"

"No one is. There's a dozen engagés here—Mexicans, Creoles mostly."

"Wootton?"

"I wish I knew, Colonel. He's a meat hunter and a trader here, and that's all I know. Bent's not the same. Charles was murdered, and then George died. He's buried just outside the walls. William's Cheyenne wife died in childbirth. Cholera's cut the Cheyennes in half."

"Someone must be running this place."

"Unofficially, I am."

I wondered why the major was so reluctant to say it.

We crossed the somber yard toward the sole source of light, which bled from a small window on the south side. Within, several men in buckskins and rough wool sat around a plank table. There were Anglos and Mexicans and breeds, all so weathered a man couldn't tell them apart. Some had bowls of stew before them. Most were done eating and were smoking pipes. The change in mood was palpable. Here was fire and cheer and comfort. William Bent's melancholia had not reached this corner of his great fortress.

"Major," said one, eyeing me.

"Colonel Frémont here," Fitzpatrick said.

They looked me over, their gazes neither friendly nor hostile. No one was introducing himself, but they were curious about me. I took them to be laborers mostly and wondered whether there was a trader around. It was plain that none recognized the Pathfinder.

"I'm looking for Richens Wootton," I said.

"Wootton here," one replied. He was a big fellow, with a pulpy nose and an unkempt look. "Stew in the pot. Not much to eat around here except buffalo."

"I'll have some," I said. I hunted for a clean bowl, found none, and finally realized one served one's self here. I espied a kettle of water, found a dirty bowl, scrubbed it clean, and then ladled stew from the iron pot suspended by rods over the fire at the hearth. I repeated the process with a metal spoon. Fitzpatrick pursued the same agenda, and we settled at the table with the rest.

The stew proved to be corn gruel with some unknown meat in it, probably boiled bull.

"Not much to eat here," Wootton said. "I haven't shot a buff for three days and we're down to old bull."

"You're the man I want to talk to," I said between bites. "You know the country west of here?"

"No, I wouldn't say that. A man could spend a lifetime out there and not know it."

"But you've cut through a few times."

He shrugged. "Pretty rough. I go through there to get to the Utes and trade for pelts."

"You know the passes."

"What passes?"

"Through the San Juan Mountains."

Wootton looked faintly amused. "Twelve thousand foot peaks and a few saddles is all. I wouldn't call them passes."

"Streams flow from there. Water goes downhill."

"Through canyons. I hear you're looking for a railroad route. Forget it."

"I'll find a way."

Wootton turned silent on me, so I ate quietly and assessed the rest. There wasn't a man among them I would want with me. They were mostly inscrutable, their faces masks. They struck me as a little slow. I wished I could follow their thoughts, if they had any.

"This is the worst place on the continent to run a railroad," Wootton said. "Three ranges of mountains and where are you? A land of canyons, and then more mountains, and then desert—and all that before you hit the Sierra Nevada. You run rails up grades and over trestles, and then down the other side over more trestles, and you hit canyon lands, trenches so deep and wide you can't bridge 'em. It makes no sense. Anyone could tell you that."

"Do you know the entire country?"

"Not by half," he replied.

I smiled. His response was answer enough. But he wasn't through. Wootton was a stubborn cuss.

"Suppose you find some sort of pass. Does it make sense? What about all those trestles and bridges and tunnels and grades, eh? You could run a rail line to the coast south or north of here for what it'd cost to do these mountains."

"I welcome skeptics," I said.

"And why do it in winter?"

I started to give him my stock answer, but he rudely interrupted.

"You can't get through. Don't even try. The Indians, they're saying this is the worst. Snow's higher than a man in those ravines."

"I don't base my decisions on faulty memories and superstition."

Wootton seemed aroused, as if some anger were simmering just below the surface. "You want a guide? You got one. I'll go take a look. If I don't like what I see, I'll quit and walk out. Maybe I can help, maybe not. You can pay me in advance. If you get trapped up there I'll never get a dime."

The offer was so startling after all his truculence that I barely could digest it. I didn't agree to it, though he was the only man around, apparently, who had even been in the San Juan Mountains. But he looked like trouble. The sort who wouldn't take direction. I marveled that he didn't see opportunity and public esteem when it was placed before him. The less ambitious weed themselves out of the race.

"I'll consider it," I replied.

"What are you paying?" he asked.

"I haven't said I would pay you anything."

He laughed suddenly, his truculence a thing of the past. "I'll go to Pueblo de San Carlos with you and see what they're saying. Believe me, they'll know. Maybe I'll hire on, maybe I won't."

"You won't persuade me to stop," I said. "I don't stop."

Wootton simply chuckled and stretched.

That was how I acquired a guide, or so I believed. Fitzpatrick had remained as silent as the rest of Bent's crew. The whole lot seemed to be unmanned. My very presence had plunged them into wariness. Wootton seemed to be a boor, but I didn't doubt I could reduce him once we were underway.

I turned to other matters. "We've some worn-out stock to trade, three saddle horses and two lame mules. We're also looking for provisions."

I waited, wondering who was in charge, who might be the post trader, and it turned out to be Wootton. "We've some small Mexican mules in good flesh. Left behind by the last company through, eight, ten days ago, and pastured a few days. I'll trade three for your five. But provisions, we've got none. We're scarce on fodder here. And the buff, they've hightailed out. We're about reduced to eating pack rats."

"Anything else for sale or trade?" I asked.

Wootton smiled. "Cupboard's empty, but have a look if you want. You want some trade beads? How about Green River knives?"

"I'm well equipped, but for some staples."

"You'll be eating mule meat," Wootton said.

He was no fool after all. I was taking my commissary with me, on the hoof. A hundred thirty mules could feed thirty-three men for whatever time it took to cross those mountains. Mule rawhide could build snowshoes, keep feet shod, yield caps and vests and pantaloons. These ruffians knew all that but had talked themselves into huddling around the fireplace in a comfortable post. I wouldn't have hired a one of them.

I thought that Bent's engaged men were a debauched lot, especially Wootton. The rest had the good sense to remain silent so as to preserve my respect for them. As for Fitzpatrick, I wondered where the man's reputation had come from. He was just another frontier soak. The red veins in his nose told me all that I needed to know. None of them had the vision to see what I was about. Carson would have. He thinks highly of me and has no envy in him. I thought for a moment I should send for him. He was in Taos, not far away, and I could have summoned him and he would have come at once. But Carson knew less about the barriers ahead than Wootton did.

I headed back to camp alone, crossing at a ford just below the fort they showed me. It was a taut moment, pushing my roan into inky water that threatened to sweep him, and me, downstream, but soon he clambered up a gravel beach, and I rode toward the distant orange dots of my camp with the bitter wind at my back.

Godey was waiting up for me; the rest had built barriers against the wind and settled as low to the frozen ground as they could get.

"Any news?"

"The usual. Don't go. Too much snow. Bad winter. No place for a railroad."

"It's all true," Godey said, and laughed.

"I agree with them. It's no place for a railroad," I said.

"Then, why?" Godey asked.

"To prove that we did it," I replied. "If I'm going to say no, don't go that way, I've got to show them why. I've got to walk the ground. So we're going."

"You are very peculiar," he said. "A human locomotive."

"Maybe it's not in my hands," I said.

Godey stared at me and smiled slowly.

I traded stock the next day. The new mules were tough but not in good flesh as promised. They proved to be small and wiry and they looked useful, no matter that they were skinny. As for the horses, I didn't want them in the mountains where they would spook at any cliff and bolt at the sound of a hawk. I don't have much use for horses in any country higher than molehills. We left Bent's Fort on a raw morning, straight into a mean wind. Wootton came along, driving a freight wagon drawn by four mules. The man meant to do some hide business for Bent, one way or the other. I intended to ask him a few things en route. I didn't even know where he hailed from or whether he had a wife and family. It seemed unlikely.

That was an easy leg of the trip despite icy winds that never quit, day or night. We were following the Arkansas River, where there was ample wood and shelter. My efforts to find out more about Wootton came to naught. Instead, I was the one being interviewed.

"What's the good of this trip? You'll be chest deep in snow. How do you find a roadbed for the railroad under twenty feet of white stuff, tell me that, eh?"

"I leave that to engineers," I said.

"Even if you get through, and I'm not saying you can, mind you, you won't have a railroad line. What can you tell anyone about a canyon whose floor you never see because you're walking on twenty feet of snow?"

"I agree, Mister Wootton."

"Then why? The senator, is that it?"

"That, sir, is neither here nor there. I'll engage you if you know a way; if not, it's time to dissolve this arrangement."

We sparred like that off and on all the way to Mormon Town, as they were calling the place. Some Mormons were farming it. Some old mountaineers had settled there, along with their Mexican concubines, and were living far beyond the reach of law. Wootton ended up learning more about me than I about him, which nearly decided me to look for someone else.

In the final stretch, as the Rocky Mountains loomed whitely before us, I settled again beside Wootton. We needed to come to an agreement.

"You see that snow?" he asked, pointing upward. "You see it's smooth and white and nothing is sticking out of it? No rocks, no trees, just white? That's the sign of a lot of snow. Lighter snow, there's gray and blue spots all through. It's sort of speckled. But not up there. See how the wind's whipping snow off those peaks—a regular plume, like a cloud? That tells me the snow is cold and powdery and not melted in."

"I've worked through worse," I said.

"So I've heard," he said, eyeing me.

"What would change your mind?" he said.

"You mean, at what point would I quit? I can't answer that because I have no intention of quitting."

"What if it becomes plain that no railroad can go through, eh?"

"I'm on my way to California, sir," I replied.

"That's a dandy place," he said. "If you can get there."

We reached the pueblo midday. There wasn't much by way of lodging for thirty-three men, but we finally sheltered in an adobe house with a good hearth, and my men could enjoy four walls, a roof, and some warmth. Pueblo wasn't what anyone could call a town, not even a village. It was just a disorderly patch of adobe houses with snow-covered squash gardens, full of heaven-knows-what sort of people, all male except for a few leathery ladies of Old Mexico. But people crowded around, unbidden, eyeing us, our string of burdened mules, and our armaments, which largely consisted of Hawken's mountain rifles. The arrival of thirty-three travelers and a hundred-thirty-odd burdened mules was the social event of the season. The only question was whether they would dance with us or massacre us.

These poured in until the house could hold no more. They were rough cobs, old mountaineers with Hispanic wives and a few Mormons who had settled only recently, many of them dressed in farm dungarees.

When they scouted out my intentions, it didn't take them long to come to a unanimous conclusion, and to advise me of it. "Worst winter we've ever seen, and it's a death trap. You go on up there, and we'll find your frozen carcasses in the spring, what's left after the wolves have done you."

That was the consensus, as expressed by an old trapper named Ephraim.

Wootton looked me over and announced his pleasure: "I can

see what they see, and what I see is snow and cold. I'm not going to leave my bones up there, and I hope you don't either, Colonel. Count me out. A man needs to take heed of the way things are."

I had expected as much and nodded. "You know of anyone who's a competent guide here? I'm going ahead, and I'll hire the right man."

"There's one, and only one. His name is Williams. Old Bill Williams. He's an odd duck, living alone too much, but he knows that country," Wootton said.

That was bad news. I knew the man all too well.

CHAPTER TEN

John Charles Frémont

I could scarcely imagine a worse choice for a guide. I knew the man. Old Bill Williams had signed up for my third expedition, lasted two months, and quit. I had employed him for a dollar a day, and he seemed glad enough to get it. I supposed I might employ him now for the same amount, and he still would be glad enough to get it, being an improvident sort who was always out of pocket.

Old Bill Williams was memorable. He was a tall beanpole, well over six feet, all whipcord and without an ounce of fat. He had lived a lifetime out of doors and was weathered to the hue of an old saddle. His private toilet was nonexistent, and he apparently wore whatever came to hand until it fell off. He was bent at the waist so that his nose preceded his toes. He walked with an odd wobble, almost spastic, and shot his rifle in the same manner, but with deadly effect. The old border man, who was probably in his sixties, was no one's fool when it came to surviving in wilderness.

"Where do I find him?" I asked Wootton.

"He's around here somewhere."

I cased the crowded adobe house, examining a wild collection of mountaineers and their concubines, but I did not see him.

"He's not a man to get into a crowd," one of these people said. "Try over at the Paseo, yonder."

The Paseo was the closest thing the pueblo had to a store. There was a plank bar of sorts, a few shelves of goods, and plenty of benches. Sure enough, Old Bill was perched on a log stool all alone and not wanting company, his face caught in shadow. A dying fire at the hearth supplied the only light. I waved away the others, wanting to talk to the old mountaineer myself, without the crowd.

"Colonel Frémont here," I said, extending a hand, which he did not accept. He was sipping something amber from a tin cup he held in hand. I took it to be aguardiente, Taos Lightning, which had a way of scouring a man's pipes.

"Do you think I don't know?" he replied. "I was doing my best to be scarce."

"I'm not interested in the past," I said, although I had found his previous conduct instructive. "I'll get right to it. I'm taking a company to California and need a guide. We're going to cross right about here, thirty-eighth parallel."

"No, no you's not gonna do that," he said, and sipped at whatever was in his tin cup. "You're gonna go around, like any other sensible man. Thirty-eight parallels, what is it? Why not forty parallels, or twenty-three? Is thirty-eight your age, maybe? I don't care if it's parallels or rectangles or triangles, you ain't going straight over."

"Up and over. As close to this latitude as I can. I'm looking for a rail route." The man seemed abysmally ignorant. "Parallels from the equator. Invisible lines marking distances from the center of the earth. It's round, you know." I waited to see whether he knew that. Men of his station couldn't imagine the earth as a globe.

"They's no such thing as a straight line," he said. "God slides a curve into everything."

"You have some theology?"

"I'm a minister. I've got the Good Book measured and weighed and sawed into parts, ready for a sermon or a funeral."

I scarcely knew how to deal with this vagabond. "You know this country, and I need someone who'll show us the right pass."

"I know every square foot, but I'm not agoin' so you better think of someone else."

"We've a large company; we're well equipped."

"Those are big mountains and I never seen such snow. And what sense is it? That's no place for a railroad. You go around. Me, I'd take her south of the Sangre de Cristos. You can cut through there, not much trouble."

"Up and over, without you if I must. But that's where I'm going."

That was bravado, but I intended to do it. If I could not find a guide, I would proceed without one. It wasn't so hard, really. There were some ancient Mexican charts to guide me. Follow the Rio del Norte north until I found the Saguache River, and go up it and over Cochetopa Pass. If I missed the right creek, I'd try the next one.

"My bones hurt just thinking on it," he said. "I'm too tired."

"I need you. A dollar a day would fatten your purse."

"What good would that do? All I'd do is leave my frozen carcass up there."

"A dollar a day and a ten-dollar bonus when we got past the Rocky Mountains."

He stared morosely into his cup.

"You're the devil is what," he said. "I'm glad I didn't go get myself froze and shot on your last one."

"It's snowy, sure. But with good mules and good men beating a trail, we'll be over the top in a week or two."

He grinned malevolently. "You wouldn't know that pass from a piss ant's jaw."

"That's right, but we'll find a way no matter what, and you can earn some good money or not."

He grinned, wiped his mouth, and said nothing. I am a close observer of men, and I knew he would soon come around. Even now, he was looking past me and at the opened door, where Alexis Godey and several others waited.

"Not me, no way, you don't even know what cold is. How are you going to feed all them mules up there? You think there's one stick of grass? You think there's one cottonwood they can chew on? It's under fifty feet of snow."

"We'll be looking for grain here."

Williams sipped, coughed, and cackled.

"Go on, get away," he said. "I'm warm and I'm not about to freeze my butt, not for some . . . old railroad."

He turned his back to me, his dismissal.

I fired my parting shot. "We're going to bed down here. We'll raise camp here before sunup. You'll join us or not. Try God. He'll tell you to join up."

He presented me with his full back, which wasn't much wider than a fence post.

I signaled I was done, and the rest flooded in. If they could buy some brandy here, they would. They wouldn't be seeing spirits for a long time.

Godey pulled me aside. "Did you hire him?"

"He'll come around. I told him we're leaving before dawn, with or without him."

"He didn't like the snow, oui?"

"He says grass will be fifty feet under it."

Godey laughed, but uneasily. "He's right, Colonel. You'll find out soon enough. The trick is to turn around and get out when the moment comes."

I didn't reply.

I had things to do. I wanted fodder of any sort. Grain, corn, whatever I could get for my mules. If I couldn't get Old Williams, then I wanted Wootton to draw me some charts and tell me where to turn off. I was headed for Cochetopa Pass, but I'd heard that there was another pass, slightly higher but with better railroad grades, called Leroux Pass—or Williams Pass. Maybe Wootton could pencil it in for me.

The whole mob was rushing in now, abandoning the little adobe I'd rented for the night to house us. An old gap-toothed mountaineer was pouring from a small cask behind his plank counter and raking in whatever he could. I watched coin, bills, a knife, a blanket, and a box of precast bullets cross the counter. I wanted to stop this but thought better of it. Let them enjoy a sip. It would put them in good spirits for the struggles ahead. They lit up pipes, and soon a blue haze hung over the place, disturbed by gusts of icy air pumping in from the open door.

I made inquiry about fodder and discovered that the denizens of this pueblo were an improvident and lazy lot, barely staying alive with household gardens and constant hunting. It was probably too much to ask of an old mountaineer to work his land and make it bear fruit. And even at that, it was the Mexicans who were providing for themselves. I retreated into the icy night to peruse the area, letting a quarter moon be my lantern. But a considerable walk on snowy ground revealed little agriculture here. I spotted no corncribs, but I did see some haystacks. Hay would be of little service to me.

I would need to do what I did in the Sierra Nevada: find open southern slopes to graze the mules. These slopes caught the sun, melted off the snow, and exposed grass. If the tactic worked in the Sierra Nevada, so would it work in the southern Rockies. By the end of my foray, I noted that my company had already retired to their bedrolls, with which they filled the little adobe house. A rank odor marked their presence. I chose to bed at the store, where I was welcomed cordially.

"Would you know of any place we can obtain feed for my mules?" I asked the keep, a grizzled veteran named Whipple.

"You shouldn't be crossing them hills without it," he replied. "They've got some corn in cribs up to Hardscrabble."

That was promising.

I awakened my company well before dawn that November day, and they lazily made themselves some corn gruel in a fireplace pot and packed their blankets. It was another blustery day, the sort that would pump cold down a collar or up a sleeve or up a pant leg no matter what. I didn't mind. I had discovered that I am made of tougher stuff than most men, an accident of birth.

Williams was nowhere to be found, and I imagined we would vault the Rockies without a guide. I had maps and counsel enough. I had the old Mexican charts. Carson knew the country and had shared all he knew with me. This was the plan he proposed: find the Saguache River, a tributary of the Rio del Norte, head up it to Cochetopa Pass, and descend into the Colorado River drainage. I didn't need a guide for that. Godey hastened my men through their morning rituals and into the icy predawn darkness. There were, after a few trades, one hundred thirty sound and healthy mules to load.

We raised camp about nine, and only then did Williams show up.

"You can't top those peaks without a guide," he said.

I was in no mood to haggle and ignored him. He peered at me slack jawed. I steered clear, if only to avoid getting louses.

"Day wage. You pay me every night," he said, "and you got a guide."

"So you can run when the going is tough?"

"You put your digit right on her. You is going to leave your bones up there, frozen up solid until it all melts come June, and I'm not gonna leave mine there. One dollar each night."

I shook my head. No deal.

"Why're you going up there now? It's a head scratcher," he said.

"We will do what no one else has ever dared to do."

He cocked his head. "That all, is it?" He yawned. "If I go, I go. If I quit, I quit. If I come back here, I come back here."

I had him. "You lead the way," I said. "We'll follow."

He grinned, never said yes, but hightailed to a grimy bedroll and a scabrous old rifle he had stacked nearby.

"Can't let you go freeze your arses," he said.

I didn't trust him and intended to correct his progress if he steered too far away from the route. Just by staying with the Arkansas River we could put ourselves on the west slope of the Rockies without difficulty, climbing some benches to avoid a gorge. That would put us on a grassy valley leading to an easy pass to the Colorado River drainage. It had been traversed by Stephen Long and Zebulon Pike, so I wasn't interested in it. We wouldn't go that way. Why follow others' footsteps? And we were already too far north.

We reached Hardscrabble without difficulty and found plenty of dried corn in a crib. It took little to persuade its owner, a Mormon named Hamel, to part with it. The only trouble was that it was dried ears and the man didn't have a sheller. But I put the men to the task, which they undertook eagerly, knowing that corn would feed man and beast alike in the high country. They set to work with their skinning knives, and ere long we harvested a hundred thirty bushels of good feed, ample to keep the mules in good condition during our week or ten-day crossing of the three chains of the Rockies. All this golden treasure was carefully loaded into panniers, and I made sure each pannier was tied shut and the loads were balanced.

Hardscrabble was as miserable as the pueblo farther downriver, a shantytown full of lazy mountaineers plus a few hardworking Mormons. It was also hard against the flanks of the Wet Moun-

tains, the first range we had to negotiate, and stood at the confluence of the river and Hardscrabble Creek. It was here that I made
my first decision. Once again I rented an adobe house and once
again my men slept warm. It would be the last time they would
see walls and a roof for some while. The next morning, we loaded
early. I was itching to be off.

"We're going up Hardscrabble Creek," I told Old Bill. "And
then over. There's a pass there."

Williams blinked at me so long I thought maybe he was slow
witted.

"Huerfano Road. Mosca Pass," I said.

"Oh, is that what you call it," he said, slouching so much he was
actually staring up at me, even though he had six inches of height
on me. "You wanting to make a railroad there?"

"It's closer to the thirty-eighth parallel."

"Why this parallel, eh? You bought this parallel from Uncle
Sam? There's a lot of them parallels."

"It's where we're going."

"Why don't you run your railroad where it's halfway level, eh?
Follow a buffalo trail. The buffalo got it all worked out."

I smiled and turned away. I'd heard enough of that.

On the afternoon of November 25, we finished with the corn,
broke camp, and Old Bill led us up the creek, through a deepening
snow-packed canyon. We were now headed straight south, in the
direction of the pass I had heard much about. But we were also
running into snow. Half a foot at first, no trouble.

Then we were pushing through a foot of it, even as we gained altitude. Williams rode a mule we had given to him, his old rifle
across his arms, his body slouched so deep in his saddle he looked
bent in the middle. He wore an odd cap made of skins, with earflaps
he could pull down if needed, but the temperature was mild.

Some of the men thought the cap made him look like he had fox ears. The rest of his ensemble was just as odd, but I decided not to worry about him. He'd spent a life in the mountains, and he would see us through. I wondered why I didn't really believe it.

CHAPTER ELEVEN

Micajah McGehee

We abandoned the Arkansas River valley the afternoon of November 25, having loaded the mules with shelled corn. We had all enjoyed pumpkin and chicken and sheltered beds that night, a luxury we would be dreaming about the rest of the trip.

Colonel Frémont was taking us south, up Hardscrabble Creek, to some pass he and the new guide, Old Bill, knew about. I didn't know the route and was a simple foot soldier on this trip. Back in Saint Louis I discovered that the colonel was recruiting for a California expedition, and I thought to join it. I was footloose and California intrigued me. I have that itch. He said there would be no pay, although his father-in-law would introduce legislation to subsidize the trip. A rail line at midcontinent would satisfy both the North and the South, Frémont said, and Congress might come through. It sounded plausible enough.

Most of the recruits thought that the government would eventually pay them, but I never took it that way. The way I calculated it, I should be shelling out a few coins to the colonel for a guided trip west. This would be my ticket to California, and that's as much as I needed. So I had signed on. I found myself enjoying the company of the three Kerns, Andrew Cathcart, and Frederick Creutzfeldt, all well-educated men like myself, and so we made something of a party to ourselves.

Hardscrabble Creek soon plunged into a gloomy canyon lined with white oak and pine as well as cactus aplenty, and as we veered westward toward the Wet Mountains the snow increased. Still, it wasn't bad, and I saw that once a trail was broken through the pillows of soft snow by the leaders, the rest of our heavily laden mules followed easily enough on the packed snow. If this was winter, I would have no trouble with it, even though I had been reared in Mississippi. We were all in fine spirits. The corn did it. That golden wealth stuffed into sacks and panniers was, for us, more assuring than metallic gold.

There were storms aplenty just before. En route to Hardscrabble, an overcast sawed off the mountains, and we no longer could see the snowy reaches of Pike's Peak. That and the brutal wind made that leg of the trip worrisome and hard. There's no way to fight the wind. No matter what a man wears, the wind finds its way through, shooting icy fingers down your neck, pushing up your trousers, bullying in at the waist, and nipping at ears and noses and chins. The men made rawhide throatlatches to keep their slouch hats from flying away and eventually made their own leather caps with earflaps. We hunted for momentary relief any way we could, pausing under cutbanks, stopping in a copse of trees, hunkering low behind a rock.

Darkness caught us only three miles from Hardscrabble, but it was a start. We made a good camp under a cliff, out of the wind, where there was plenty of dead pine to fuel our fires. We could find no grass, but put the feedbags on the mules and gave them all a quart of shelled corn, something we had to do in shifts because we had only twenty bags. One quart went down those mule throats in a hurry, and they looked just as hungry when the bag came off as before. But there wasn't a blade of grass in sight. Frémont introduced us to his rubberized sheets, big tan waterproof affairs that let us settle into our bedrolls on top of muck or snow without getting soaked. The colonel divided up the watch, two guards, two hours apiece, and so we settled down. The night was mild enough, though I could never sleep outside in a bedroll as well as I could on a good stuffed-cotton mattress in a house. In that I was lacking, for Frémont's veterans were soon sawing wood, their hulks quiet near the several wavering watch fires.

Before dawn Godey was rousing us, and we shook the sleep out of ourselves, packed our kits, huddled around the breakfast mess fires to down some gruel, and began harnessing the mules. I yearned for some golden johnnycakes fried from cornmeal, but those weren't on the menu. The flour was already gone, and we would be surviving entirely on game soon. We were low on grains.

Now Godey was a man to inspire confidence. I pegged him as the more sensible of the two leaders, and I knew I wouldn't start worrying until I saw Godey worry. The veterans of Frémont's previous trips didn't share my views. For them, Frémont was a man of uncanny destiny. I can't say why I distrusted Frémont's judgment, but I did. As long as Godey thought things were alright, I would, too. I supposed my views were colored by the court-martial and conviction. I had followed the case closely.

It had turned cooler, and soon we were trudging up the canyon, still on foot, past giant red boulders topped with snow, following a twisting path ever higher. We had the drill down now, even without the colonel's orders. A few of us would break trail until we wearied and then fall back, and a few more of us would pick up the lead, and so on, as we rotated the hard work and spared the mules as much as we could. The mules had enough to worry about on slippery ground with a heavy load on their backs.

The only peculiar thing about all this was that this wasn't a route for a railroad. There was evidence of a crude wagon road out of Hardscrabble, but it forded the creek constantly, and I suspected that during certain spring months the whole canyon bottom would be flooded.

I spurred my mule, Betsy as I called her, up to Ben Kern.

"Do you think a railroad could run thisaway?" I inquired.

"I'm a doctor, not an engineer," he replied. "But it's a mystery, isn't it?"

"It's the thirty-eighth parallel, that's what it is. Frémont's going to stick with it. What's so sacred about it, do you know?"

"You know what it is?" he replied. "It's a golden highway across gentle grades with tropical weather to either side, coal seams every hundred miles, ample water, and easy connections. I hear it runs straight to California, without any detours. Once we're on it, friend Micah, we'll just race right along. You just ask the colonel, and he'll tell you."

That's what they called me. Micah McGee is how they shortened it. I was used to that; it had started about when I was old enough to notice. Doc Kern was smiling.

But what we were getting into was no tropical highway. The creek had swung west and was tumbling out of the Wet Mountains now, splashing over boulders, and we were breaking through two feet of snow. We were climbing through gloomy pine and aspen woods. Word came back to us that we should dismount, save the mules, which were burdened with all that corn. I slid down into the snow, hoping I had used enough neatsfoot oil to keep my boots tight against leaks. Up ahead, I saw Frémont shifting leads. He would put one group of men and mules up front for a while, and then another, thereby spreading the hard work of making a trail among as many men and animals as he could. I supposed he would call on me soon, though so far he was using only his veteran men.

The man was the least like an army colonel as I could imagine. Did he bark orders, demand instant obedience, dress down fools and knaves? No, he never raised his voice, never even seemed impatient, and somehow won the allegiance of his men. Not least, he broke trail himself for a spell, off his mule, kicking open the snow. Old Bill, I noticed, did no such thing, but hung back in the middle, staring amiably at the rest of us and hawking up great gobs of yellow spit now and then. For that he was earning a wage.

I'd come to admire Frémont, in a tentative way. So far as I could tell, he was a gifted man in the field and a natural leader whose very presence seemed to make this journey easier and more secure. And yet something nagged at me and wouldn't let up. Maybe, someday when I knew Doctor Kern better, I'd ask him why I kept pushing aside doubts that swarmed like horseflies in my head.

The men ahead of me showed signs of wearing down. But we continued, one step at a time, and because most of the party was ahead of me I was less worn than most. Still, I had to admit that we were making progress. Snow or not, we were snaking through the Wet Mountains, a lengthy line of men and animals.

All in all, we made good time that day, maybe nine miles, and darkness caught us near the summit. I suppose one could call it a pass. But I just kept wondering how you'd get twenty tons of iron horse up there, especially if that horse was drawing a dozen steam cars.

The next day we started downslope, which was harder because the snow was heavier on the western side of the mountains. Men kept stepping into the unknown and taking a tumble. We were wet and cold ere long. The canyon narrowed until its walls vaulted up on either side of us and we were caught in a creek, fighting through pines and white oak. Giant red rocks hemmed us, and I thought that a railroad company would be detonating tons of powder to break through all that. We made only a few miles through deep snow and finally retreated up a side canyon and camped away from the gorge we were descending. We fed the mules more corn, since there wasn't a blade of grass in sight.

Colonel Frémont seemed perfectly relaxed, as if all this were the most ordinary passage in the world. And somehow the men seemed just as relaxed. He had a way of pacifying our worries. We boiled up some beans, having trouble keeping heat under the kettles because the wood was so wet and we were so high up. The mules were restless; a quart of corn a day didn't appease their hungers a bit, and they were primed to cut and run toward anything that looked like fodder. It was hard to drive them through an aspen grove, because they had a hankering for the smooth bark of the younger trees and could peel it off with their teeth.

Frémont's veterans taught me something one night when the wind had died. They built pole racks next to their campfires; stripped out of their soaked and cold duds, right to the buff; and then hung their wet, water-stained clothing next to the roaring fire to dry out. They wrapped their blankets around themselves for the hour or two they were drying their duds. Most of them had woolen undershirts and drawers, and these absorbed campfire heat and some smoke too. But they dried. When I tried it, the first in my mess to do so, the Kerns eyed me askance, but they saw the merit of it. After a couple of hours beside the cook fire, my duds were bone dry and felt good when I clambered back into them. I marveled. The dry clothing lifted my spirits. It took the Kerns a few more nights to attempt it, but Captain Cathcart saw the merit and soon was drying his clothing whenever he could.

I did notice one thing. Frémont himself never toasted his underwear. In fact, he stayed buttoned up in that blue overcoat he wore constantly, a military coat without any insignia on it. His conduct was entirely private. He had his own tent, and inside that canvas, shielded from our eyes, he did his toilet, arranged his clothing, slept, ate, trimmed his beard, read his law books, and hid from us. I gradually realized he was a true loner, and this nightly retreat from us was a need in him, just as staying buttoned up to the chin was a need in him. He didn't want us to see anything of him but his dressed-up self, even in the worst weather. Dry clothing was so valuable to me I marveled that Frémont didn't dry his. But his manservant, Saunders, never brought any duds out of that tent to dry by the fire, so either the colonel's clothing never got wet or he chose to wear wet clothing. It sure set him apart from his veterans and also from those of us traveling with him for the first time.

The weather was mild enough, and little wind caught at us that night, so I didn't hear much complaining. Indeed, Frémont and his vision of a new path west seemed to have infected us all, and we could only think of the magical railroad that would be constructed in our wake. The only worrisome thing was that Godey and the hunters weren't finding any game, not even a track in the snow. The deer and elk had retreated to bottomland for this hard winter, and we were working through a silent country without so much as a crow above us. I thought little of it, because we were heading down the canyon and at its foot we would find game, and the thirty-three men in the company would enjoy some elk or venison.

We could not see what lay below the snow and kept stumbling over hidden logs and rocks and obstacles we could not fathom. The burdened mules were lamed by sudden plunges into the snow, when there was no footing. Sometimes we had to dig one out. Mules virtually vanished, plunging into snow so deep that it was all we could do to keep their heads clear so they could breathe. Then the company would halt while the few with shovels dug around the trapped mule until we could drag the wretched, overburdened beast out of its snow prison. Thus our progress came nearly to a halt, and we lost precious time.

But then we reached the western foothills. The canyon widened out, the snow lessened, and the worst was over, or so it seemed. Ahead lay an arid anonymous valley, and beyond its broad reaches, another white wall, which we understood to be the Sangre de Cristos, which stretched from this general area deep into New Mexico. We gathered on a plateau for a rest, having utterly exhausted ourselves and our mules in that miserable canyon, and our mood was not lightened by what we beheld. Those brooding peaks presented a wall much higher than the range we had just traversed, and we understood that beyond these lay yet another range, wider and higher and more rugged than the one that was evoking such dread in our hearts.

We had managed one range, fed out half our corn, and there was not a blade of grass anywhere to be seen. Colonel Frémont seemed to think nothing of it. After a brief rest, he set us on our course once again, and we descended the rest of the way to the intermountain valley without great difficulty.

The weather turned warm, and we were heartened by an occasional bare patch covered with sagebrush. Never had bare earth looked so friendly. We were further heartened when Godey's hunters shot a deer; we would have meat for supper, which somehow gave rise to our hopes. This wasn't so bad; the colonel's calm was entirely justified. The Pathfinder knew exactly what he was about. The valleys were full of game; we would stock up, find grass, recruit our mules between assaults on the slopes, and so pass through the difficult country.

By the time we had reached the valley floor, an icy wind was billowing out of the northwest, and that stung us to hasten along. Old Bill Williams had taken command here, and he steered us south.

"Why do you suppose he's doing that? Just to keep his back to the wind?" I asked Doc Kern.

"He knows of a pass, easy as a hot knife through butter. Robidoux's Pass is what they're calling it. And we'll slide across this range as if it hardly existed."

I stared at Kern, wondering whether he believed this monstrous proposition, and caught a wry turn of his lips.

"That's what they're saying up ahead," he added.

The Sangre de Cristos did not look very hospitable.

"You see any railroad prospects here?" I asked.

"Here, there, everywhere," Kern retorted.

We camped in a wind-sheltered spot in the valley. Godey's hunters fanned out, but I knew beforehand they would come back empty-handed. There wasn't an animal track to be seen. The next day was arctic, and between the bitter wind and the low temperatures, I wondered how I would endure. The valley had snow up to four feet in some places, bare ground in others, and no feed for our mules. What looked like grass here and there proved to be the tips of sagebrush. They couldn't find a thing to eat except a little cottonwood bark where we camped. It was odd, watching them gnaw at green limbs of the younger cottonwoods, peeling off the tender bark with their big buck teeth. The mules had thinned badly; they had no flesh left to burn off and nothing to fill their empty bellies.

I wondered whether they would survive the next mountain range. The only people enjoying any of this were the colonel and Bill Williams. The guide meandered through the camp, pausing at the various messes, saying nothing. I had the distinct feeling he was enjoying our anxiety, and maybe even plotting ways to make the trip as miserable as he could manage it.

I dismissed the notion as the sort of thing that didn't deserve serious consideration, but the notion kept burrowing into my head, until it lodged there. Old Bill scared me.

CHAPTER TWELVE

Captain Andrew Cathcart

I was much intrigued by our guide, Williams. He affected a rustic-
ity that was belied by his command of English when he chose to
display it. I learned that he had intended to become a preacher but
had long since digressed from that goal. Still, he was a man who
had mastered the scriptures and sometimes resorted to them. I
learned also that he had taken up Indian religion, though I could
not discover which beliefs, since each American tribe seemed to
possess its own theology. I gathered, from campfire talk, that
Williams believed he would be incarnated as a bull elk with white
chevrons on his flanks and had cautioned all and sundry never to
shoot such an animal, lest they shoot him.

But if there were remnants of a high calling in the man, they had
largely vanished as a result of a quarter of a century as bloody border riffraff, trapping, roaming, somehow avoiding the worst of the
perils that afflict those who venture far beyond the safety of civilization. Here was the man in whom this company was placing its
trust. He had proclaimed his knowledge of the country and told us
that he knew every pass and river on sight. We could blindfold him
and he could take us west.

So of course I was interested in this odd ruffian who dressed in

layers of gamey cottons and wools and in an even gamier leather tunic and britches that held his ensemble together. He was subject to
both silences and voluble moments when one could scarcely stop
the flow of words issuing from him. But on this trip he remained
silent, never doing any work he could avoid, and making the passage
as easy on himself as possible. Unlike the rest of us, who dismounted and walked our burdened mules through the worst drifts
to spare them, Williams rode steadily, his long frame dwarfing the
mule that bore him, so that his moccasined feet sometimes dragged
in the snow. He sat hunched, incapable of straightening the bends
of his body, but I did not make the mistake of thinking that his bad
posture signaled an oafish man. He took in everything, with a keen
eye.

One of the things I noticed from the beginning was his fascina-
tion with the company's equipment. Preuss's instruments absorbed
him. Frémont's field equipment, including surveying instruments,
intrigued him. But Williams never asked a question about any of
it; he simply meandered through the camps, observing, and vanished as silently as he appeared.

These particular days we were on a southerly course, having
worked through the Wet Mountains, and we were now heading
toward a gap in the Sangre de Cristos known as Robidoux's Pass,
which I was given to understand was the only one of consequence
through the formidable cordillera before us. Williams avoided Colonel Frémont as much as possible, or was it the reverse? The man
might be guiding us, but rarely did he consult with the colonel. And
Frémont seemed content to let Williams steer the party his own way.

We were traversing the valley between the two ranges, but the
going was little easier than it had been passing over the first range.
We encountered snow up to three feet in places, which wearied
the company. We were so exhausted that we often didn't break
camp until nine or ten in the morning and surrendered to our

weariness by three or so in the afternoon, when we all hastened to gather firewood before the December night engulfed us. The temperature varied from pleasant to bitter; Doctor Kern told me that one morning was eight degrees on Fahrenheit's scale. Add wind to that and not even a Scot like me could enjoy the day. But for the moment, no storms engulfed us with snow, and so we made our way, hour by hour.

Doctor Kern's boots gave out, and the experienced men in the company showed him how to create moccasins of rawhide, which they said were better in snow anyway, and so the Philadelphian was able to continue with us. Loss of footwear on a trip like this is a serious, even fatal, calamity. He would repair the boots with an awl and thong when the chance came to him.

As we struggled through the valley, with the Sangre de Cristos forming a grim white barrier on our right, I thought maybe Frémont would let me hunt. I had superb English steel and powder. I had come to North America to hunt. I wanted to try my hand at buffalo and elk. I had sold my commission in the hussars and set out to see the world, and here was the world. Frémont obliged me at once, and I found myself with a small hunting party that included Alexis Godey, Raphael Proue, and Antoine Morin, all Creoles, as they were called in these parts, and all of them veteran hunters.

We spurred our mules ahead and drifted off to the left, where the bottoms of the frozen and unnamed creek wound along. If there was game, it would be sheltering there in the red willow brush, close to whatever feed might be found amid all this bloody white. They all spoke English, but so accented and ruined by Yank perversities that I could hardly make out what they were saying. Still, a smile or two was enough. We would make meat for the whole company here in this snowy valley, where every hoofprint would lead us toward our quarry.

Our mules soon exhausted themselves in belly-high drifts. We separated, spacing ourselves two hundred yards apart or so, giving us a wide sweep that should drive the beasts before us. They wouldn't get far, weakened by starvation and fighting drifts. I wanted meat badly. Unlike some of the others in that company who were more trusting, I had calculated what it would take to feed thirty-three men over two more mountain ranges, and the sum of my calculations became my inspiration. Ten buffalo would not suffice.

Our mules gave out all too soon, and we found ourselves walking, fighting through drifts that sometimes reached our waists, keeping our rifles high and out of the snow and wet. We reached the creek and found it mostly frozen, but with an occasional open rapid. But worse, we found not a single hoofprint. I spotted plenty of bird tracks, rodent tracks, and the tracks of small creatures I could not identify. If there was game in these thickets, it was laying low, not moving an inch. But there was no game. I was keenly disappointed. I had thought to line up a fine shot or two. Where had the game gone? Had it all been driven to some sheltered valley to graze peacefully whilst we toiled by?

"Alors, we will soon boil shoe leather," Godey said.

"Are you serious, sir?" I asked.

He laughed. "Mule meat, mon ami. It tastes like smelly shoes."

I hadn't given much thought to dining on mule for breakfast, lunch, and supper.

The mules were hard to handle in the thickets because they tore at cottonwood bark and wouldn't be led or spurred or whipped. I thought to let my mule get himself a mouthful and then tug it ahead, but the beast was planted next to a green-barked cottonwood and was gnawing that bark as neatly as if it was a beaver, peeling it off and downing it. So were the rest. This was the first meal they had enjoyed for days. A quart of corn each day had been their entire sustenance, and a poor one at that. I had kicked apart their pitiful spoor and found most of the yellow kernels intact, having passed through with no effect. That bloody guide Williams had better find a pasture soon, or there would be a price to pay. If he knew the secret havens of game of this country, he didn't show it but plodded onward, oblivious to the suffering around him.

We hunted as late as we dared, fearing the early December dark would engulf us before we could find our company. We had not seen an animal. This accorded exactly with what the hunters had faced the previous days. The game on which we depended was somewhere else, perhaps driven by those north winds to some sheltered refuge far to the south.

This trek was proving to be more adventure than this Scot had bargained for, but in for the ha'penny, in for the pound, as they say. I should be trusting the Yanks. They knew the country and knew how to get through. Only the whole business gnawed at me. Frémont expected to find game and knew that his company would suffer without it.

Godey found a relatively barren patch that led back to the company, and we forced the mules along. They were all ready to break for the bottoms where they could feed on bark. What I was mulling in my head was to suggest to Frémont that he camp there, put all the mules into those thickets, and let them put some fodder into their gaunt bellies. I don't know what stayed me, other than professional courtesy. He was a lieutenant colonel, albeit a slightly tainted one, and I a resigned hussar captain, and it didn't seem to be my office to counsel him. This was his fourth expedition, and he knew what he was about.

Or so I hoped. A man needs some flexibility. If there's no pasture at hand, one heeds the mules' own signals, and what our mules were telling us as we fought them was that we were stealing their dinner from them. By the time we caught up with the company, they had built fires and were setting up tents and were unburdening the mules.

It turned out to be an odd moment. Every man in that company stopped whatever he was doing to study us as we rode in, and what they saw was our empty hands and empty saddles. We had hunted most of the day and returned without so much as a rabbit.

I suddenly felt their gazes studying me, their hunger visible in their faces. It didn't seem right; we had meat on the hoof, a hundred thirty edible mules if we should get into trouble. Mule meat was, I knew, stringy and unpalatable, but it would boil into stew, and it would sustain us. So why, then, was I seeing a hooded bitterness wherever I looked? These were bloody veterans of the wilds, and they could conjure up a meal from roots and things I could not imagine.

I made my way to Frémont's mess, past men who were pulling off soaked boots and setting them to bake next to roaring fires. Others were scraping snow away and raising tents. It seemed a pleasant camp, with mild air lifting spirits. There would be a corn stew this night, I learned. Boiled up maize with some crumbled jerky thrown in. Off to the west, the sun dropped below the white lip of the brooding mountains, plunging us into a fearsome lavender shadow that crept across the ground like death.

I found the colonel on a log outside his tent, working neatsfoot oil into his boots.

"Why, Captain Cathcart, it's my pleasure," he said.

"And mine, sir. I don't wish to intrude on your plans, but I did have an idea cross my mind, sir. A mile and a half from here, where we were hunting, a lot of willows and cottonwoods and box elders formed thickets along the creek, and I noted that the mules thought the bark was a repast worthy of kings. They took right to it, colonel, and we had a time keeping them in hand. I just thought it might be a chance to feed the whole lot, sir. Put them in that bottomland; let them feed all night."

Frémont smiled easily. "You're an observant man, and a cavalryman, too, captain. That's not very good fodder, and the animals don't profit from it, which is why it's not worth the trouble. A mile and a half through these drifts is no small trip. No, we'll give them their ration, good feed."

"They're looking gaunt, Mister Frémont."

"Ah, you have eyes for the animals. I've noticed that, too, Cathcart. But here's something I've learned from my previous trips. There's always south slopes, cleaned off by sun and wind, where the animals can feed all night. We haven't come upon one because our route hasn't taken us to the right sort of slope. But I assure you, sir, when the moment arrives, I'll call a halt and let the mules recruit themselves on the grass."

"As you wish, Mister Frémont. I wonder if you'd permit me to take my own mule and put him out on that feed."

"You're free to do that, captain. I'm not a commander but simply an organizer of a private company. But I would strongly suggest that you stay here. There is safety in company. If a storm should blow up, we'd not see you again. This country swallows people."

I saw how this was going and left the colonel to his oiling.

I passed the depot in the snow where the saddles and panniers were collected and noticed that many of the corn-stuffed saddlebags were now empty. And we weren't a third into our passage. The mules had been herded into a piney woods where they could shelter from night wind, but there wasn't a stalk of grass in sight, and nothing edible in those woods. I thought they would have been better out in open country, where they might paw down to a little grass. I wondered about the keep of mules here. In the British Isles, where livestock is scarce and keeping them is costly, every beast is fussed over and fed as well as possible. But these Yankees seemed content to wear the mules out. It didn't rest well with me. There were chances not taken.

I joined my mess, where the Kern brothers and McGehee had

put things in good order, collected ample wood for the night, and were relaxing comfortably on sheets impregnated with India rubber, one of Frémont's better ideas. If passage could be no worse than this, we would clear the Rockies in a fortnight and enter what Frémont called the Great Basin, which supposedly had level, grassy valleys.

"You see any hoofprints today?" Micah asked.

"If we had seen even one track, even an antelope track, we would have followed it and kept on following it until we caught up with the game."

"Where did the game go? It just doesn't disappear from country."

"I've a theory," Ned Kern said. "When it snows, they stand still. It costs them too much to plow through snow, and what they find to eat doesn't make up what they lose getting there. So they just stay put in thickets. You just have to stumble on them, and you'll have meat."

"I wish I could believe it," I replied. I was thinking of the way our mules had bulled into the thickets, quite beyond our control, to gnaw at bark. They did not stir up any game.

The hunt had left me soaked. I changed into my reserve drawers and tried to dry my duds, but the wind and blowing snow and fickle fire defeated me. Tonight, I would crawl into my bedroll wet and cold, and so would every other man, excepting maybe the colonel himself.

I meditated before the wavering fire, for the first time wondering whether I had played the fool, signing up with these Yanks. I was consoled at last not by Frémont's studied ease but by Godey, the calm voyageur, used to grave hardship. If Godey wasn't worried, there was no need for a displaced Scot to be worried.

CHAPTER THIRTEEN

Tom Breckenridge

I'd been with Frémont in California, and when I heard he was heading west again, I signed right up. So did lots of others who had been with him. That's the sort of man Frémont was. Old John Charles did more to win California than the whole U.S. Army and Navy together, and we had a smart time doing it, too. I always figured the West Point brass couldn't stand it, and that was what got him court-martialed and convicted. Well, hell, a Frémont just don't come down the pike every day.

This winter trip was turning into some real mischief. But I like to grab a tiger's tail. So does old Frémont. So do all his veterans, those rough cobs like me. We even got that old kraut Preuss back, even though he had moaned and groaned and muttered through the two previous jaunts. He was just as addicted to Frémont as the rest of his old hands, even if he liked to sneer at him behind his back. Preuss was the topographer, always out there with his bulky black instruments, squinting at the polestar or the sun and consulting his chronograph and his barometer and his thermometers, figuring the height of every goddamn molehill and tit, and jotting it all down with a pencil.

But old John Charles, he wasn't content with just having one scientific genius along. He went and got him a botanist named Frederick Creutzfeldt. Now go ahead and ask yourself, what was a leaf collector doing on a midwinter trip like this one? Anything he could botanize about was buried under ten feet of white stuff. Unless he planned to study the tops of trees to look for bark-beetle damage, he was without a task, and extra baggage. But that's old Frémont for you. If you're going to have yourself an expedition, you're going to equip it in the latest style, so we had a botanist from Germany along for the ride. If old Johnny couldn't nab Alexander von Humboldt, Creutzfeldt would have to do. That plain tickled my fancy. When we got up to the summit of those mountains, yonder, I planned to ask old Freddie what sort of lichen he's scraping up.

I thought some of those new gents would quit, with all the cold and wet and heavy going, but they were game. I'll say that for them. Maybe they didn't break trail, the way we did, but they plugged along behind us breaking wind, and I never heard a whimper. But some day, maybe I'll get a peek at their diaries and see whether they wrote out their whines.

All of those new people, they didn't know much, but we showed them the tricks: how to build a snow cave to get out of the blow, how to stay clean, how to cook your drawers on sticks beside the fires until they're hot and dry, how to grow a full beard to keep your ugly snout from freezing.

We all looked pretty grim at times, with icicles dangling from our beards like chimes and ice collecting in our eyebrows and a rime of frost around our nostrils. They learned quick, those artists and botanists and hoity-toity farts like that. That settled a wager or two. Half the veterans were betting the artists and pansies would hightail south at the first chance, but that didn't happen. We all were looking shaggy after a few weeks of cold, but all that hair kept us halfway comfortable. If you don't want a frostbit chin, you grow some fuzz.

Old Bill Williams, he was a card, slouched on his mule and letting the rest of us do the work. He was being paid for what was in his noggin instead of what his muscles could do, though I sometimes think there wasn't any difference between his brain and his belly. He wasn't wearing himself out any, and that made for a little grumbling. But I didn't care. The man had roamed these parts for a quarter of a century and knew every trail and every pass and every bear's den on a high slope. So he claimed, anyway. On the borders, reputations grow faster than a pecker in a parlor house. I always figured that if we got into trouble, he'd lead us straight to a denned bear, and we'd get meat, fat, a pelt, and shelter out of it.

On December 3, after weathering a bitter night with ornery temperatures and an unsociable wind, we pushed into the canyon that would take us up the road and over Robidoux's Pass and into the valley of the Rio del Norte. Or so they said. Me, I just tag along. What the hell? For days we had been pushing south, the forbidding massif of the Sangre de Cristos looming on our right like a jailhouse wall. Those shoulders formed a rampart such as I had never seen before, the cloud-wrapped peaks forbidding us passage westward. Even old John Charles kept staring at that white wall, while icicles dangled from his beard and eyebrows. Our burdened mules didn't like that wall either; they might be dumb beasts, but they knew enough to shy away from those fatal highlands, and the slightest westward passage brought them all to a halt. Only curses and whips set them on our path.

When we did enter the yellow canyon, everything improved at once. We were out of that icy wind. The creek had snow piled along its banks, but back a little there were bare patches we could traverse without trouble. The mules beelined for every spidery cottonwood and quaking asp to gnaw at the bark, and it made me aware how starved they were. We could barely keep them on the trail. I was all for letting them gnaw a meal out of the bark and twigs and leaves for a day or so, but old Frémont, he would have none of it. It was almost balmy in there, with sun heating the south-facing slopes and making the sun-heated rock friendly for an hour or two midafternoons. But later on, snow showers skidded over, wetting us and making our passage treacherous. Still, this was easy, and our spirits soared as we gained altitude.

We made the divide about noon, and were once more exposed to the howling wind, which stole our hats until we treated it with more respect. Doc Kern, he had to toss his rifle onto his hat or he'd have lost it forever over a precipice. I spotted Herr Preuss trying to set up shop on that barren ridge, with the wind battering him so violently he could hardly stand. I knew what he wanted: the altitude of the pass, and he was not going to get it in that gale.

"Hey, you old bastard, you want some help?" I asked.

He unbent his bundled body, stared up at me through wire-rimmed spectacles, and glared. "If I vant help I ask for it, ya? If I vant help, I make every man here help me. I don't vant help. I do this myself."

A touchy sort, I thought. Me, I don't know Germans from Spanish and barometers from sextants. But I'm good with a Hawken. I braved the wind, curious about how the topographer would deal with it. He scraped away a crust of snow until he found bedrock and then set an instrument on it. The device was little more than a long upright glass tube full of quicksilver.

"What's that, Herr Preuss?"

He glared at me. "Mercury barometer, that's what it is called, and not a good way to do this. Wind bad. Air pressure, ach!"

He got on his hands and knees, ignoring the icy gale, and studied the mercury in the glassed column, muttering to himself.

"How high are we?" I asked. I wanted to skedaddle off that ridge fast, but curiosity got the best of me.

"Stupid Yankee question," he said. "Where you from? Missouri? With wind like this, we could be below sea level, ya?"

I laughed. Old Preuss, he was one to make some sport.

He pulled off a glove, extracted a notebook, and began making calculations in it with a stubby pencil. "Nine thousand seven hundred seventy feet, give or take," he said. "Don't ask any more questions."

"That's why I'm out of breath," I said. I wanted a lot more air in my lungs than I was getting.

He stuffed his instrument into a rosewood chest and hurried away. He had converted barometric pressure to height above sea level, all he could manage there. He didn't look happy with himself.

I hastened off that ridge myself and hurried down a barren blue rock slope, with mules in front of me, finding precarious footing. Every living creature among us was in a hurry to get off that damned ridge and into some shelter, any goddamn shelter. We followed a vee downward, with Old Bill steering us as if he knew what he was doing. I saw no trace of a wagon road, but that didn't mean much. Railroads could go anywhere. Railroads could climb Mount Everest, right?

So far, we hadn't had much trouble on the alleged road to Robidoux's Pass, and I told myself that Old Bill, he knew what he was about. He wasn't just making this up. We were sailing right along. Up high, on that saddle, I saw naught but white, grim, and desolate ridges and peaks with a plume of snow streaming off of them. And of course no game. Animals had more sense than we did.

That was a moment of elation. There we were, midway on our passage across these chains of the Rockies, the divide of the middle range, and nothing more than some hungry animals were plaguing us. The canyon on the west side of the pass had been cut by a rill that sawed furiously into the mountain slopes, and we hurried into it, wanting to escape that gale. This was different. For one thing this canyon was choked with snow. I thought maybe we were walking on top of fifteen or twenty feet of it. Truth to tell, I had no idea how far down we would strike rock. One moment we would be carving a trail through snow; the next we would be stumbling over cross-hatched deadwood, giant logs lying every which way a foot or so under the snow, which halted us and stymied the burdened mules. This here was no cakewalk.

This was a twisty, narrow defile, filled with giant boulders and slabs of rock that had tumbled down from above, gray and red barriers we had to work around.

"Some road, eh?" King said. "Robidoux must have been three sheets to the wind."

"There's no wagon road here," I replied. "Impossible."

"I wouldn't take Bill Williams's word for anything. The stupid bastard. Maybe this isn't Robidoux's Pass at all," King said.

We were, at that point, trying to ease one mule after another through log-strewn narrows, when the slightest misstep sent a mule to its knees. Sometimes we had to pull off their packs before they could get themselves up and out of those miserable little holes hidden by benign-looking snow. Now, too, the snow showers increased. The sky would darken and spill thick flakes, and then the shower would blow off and we would enjoy a moment or two of bright sun, which hurt our eyes. Every time the snow blew, I'd get a dose of it down my neck.

I swear, some of us had so many icicles dangling from our facial hair that we rattled and chimed with every step. If the trail up the east slope had been easy and warm, the trail down the west slope made up for it. We plunged into snow so deep we had no idea of the contours of the gulch beneath our feet. Our lead men broke the crust, and those who followed stamped a deepening trench in the enormous drifts, until we were progressing through a virtual tunnel whose walls reached many feet above us. I dreaded what a cave-in or avalanche could do. The mules didn't like it and had to be goaded ahead. Old Bill Williams, he just nodded and let us do the work.

Still, we were out of the goddamn wind, which counted for plenty.

The rill we were following twisted every which way, and once we got below timberline we faced new obstacles—heaps of dead-wood, logs, and brush—that frustrated our descent. Snow show-ers added to our tribulations, but we worked grimly forward until we rounded a bend and caught a glimpse of a vast, arid, naked valley ahead.

"It's the Rio," Godey announced. He actually slapped old Johnny Charles on the back, which I've never seen done before or since.

That was a cause for rejoicing. We had conquered the second range. Ahead would be grass prairies, warmth, escape from wind, comfort, and game. I could hardly wait to climb onto one of those mules, Hawken in hand, and go after some juicy red meat. We might even find some big shaggies down there, and surely plenty of deer and elk.

The rest of that blustery day we fought the narrow defile, work-ing around tight corners, staring up at giant orange rock slopes, which were often sawed off by clouds. More and more, we could glimpse the peaceful valley ahead, looking like the promised land, and that inspired us to move our hundred and thirty mules and our-selves with haste. After a tough descent, we reached the foothills.

Godey settled us in a willow grove not far from some giant gray sand dunes that formed an unexpected barrier to our passage. But that would wait for the morrow. We turned the mules loose in cot-tonwoods, where they began gnawing ravenously on bark and leaves and whatever roots they could pry out of the frozen earth. I watched those wretched animals do everything in their power to feed themselves. They worked at bark and twigs frantically, as if they knew that worse would follow. It troubled me some. Them mules knew more than we knew, and no one was paying them any heed.

It was snowing again off and on, but this would be a comfortable camp, and we rejoiced. By dusk we had ample deadfall at hand for the mess fires, and we settled down for an evening of rest and recovery. Two ranges down, one to go. Men built towering fires and dried their outfits as best they could, but blowing snow didn't help none. A man would get his drawers half baked dry and a gust would pelt fresh snow into them.

I discovered old John Charles before his tent and thought to ask him a question that had been burning in my bosom.

"That's no canyon for a railroad, is it?"

"No, of course not. This pass won't work," he said. "I'm not sure it's Robidoux's Pass. There wasn't a sign of a wagon road."

"Herr Preuss told me the ridge measured almost 9,800 feet."

"He did, did he? I'll talk to him about it."

"Do you think maybe Old Bill got himself turned around?"

The colonel didn't like that and stared at me for an answer. I was getting into some kind of politics there.

I drifted back to my mess. This would be a macaroni night. At least we had some of that to feed ourselves. But later I discovered that Frémont had lit a bull's-eye lantern and had settled himself in front of his tent with a book. A book! What manner of man would park himself outside of his tent on a wintry eve with a book? He had pulled his spectacles on and was quietly reading away.

I edged up to him and discovered a massive tome in his hands, with dense type on every page.

He gazed up at me and fathomed my curiosity. "It's Blackstone's commentaries," he said. "Common law and cases. I should like to practice law when I reach California."

I stared at the book, at him, at the whirling snow that blew across its pages.

Later, when I was back among my mess mates, I told them that the colonel was reading Blackstone, and they marveled at it.

"Other men would be looking after the animals, checking supplies and all," King said.

"It's all for show," Vincenthaler said.

But Godey objected. "Why would a man of his repute do anything like that, mes amis?" he asked.

CHAPTER FOURTEEN

John Charles Frémont

All my life I have been cognizant of the impressions I have made on others. There were multiple messages in my reading of Blackstone. I could just as well have pursued the jurist's ideas in the privacy of my tent, but that would have accomplished nothing. So I settled myself outside, where my study would be seen and considered. I wanted my company to draw proper conclusions, and I don't doubt that I succeeded.

They would marvel, of course. There we were, deep in a snowy wilderness, where common law was the last thing on the minds of these men, and there I was, toiling at my book by the light of a bull's-eye lantern. I considered it a most efficacious moment.

It signaled, of course, that my thoughts were now on life in California and that our present problems were surmountable—indeed, nothing to dishearten good and valiant men. It was an acknowledgment that we were two-thirds through the cordillera that had posed the principal barrier to our westward progress. It expressed my calm, and my utter absence of anxiety. To be sure, we were in some peril, but it was important to let the entire company know that these perils would be dealt with. It was never far from my mind that we had a larder of one hundred thirty mules, meat on the hoof.

So I chose to read the Blackstone, knowing the galvanic effect it would have on my men. They would cease their fretting and be well armed in spirit for the final assault on the Rocky Mountains. Ahead lay the vast, arid valley of the Rio del Norte, whose head-waters collected near where we were camped and wound their way south and east, clear to the Gulf of Mexico. We were not far from settlements. Down that drainage lay Abiquiu, northernmost of the Mexican hamlets, and below these, Taos and eventually Santa Fe. Ahead lay a fertile river bottom chocked with game, filled with grasses and brush and a few trees. By the time we were ready to as-cend the San Juan Mountains, we would have fresh meat, the mules would be well fed and even fattened, and we would be in prime condition for the last alpine assault.

To be sure, just west of us was a bleak sea of sand dunes, mostly covered with ribbed snow, but the wind had whipped against their sides, exposing a desolation devoid of all vegetation. We would need to cross that wasteland, and I supposed Bill Williams would know where to do it. I had found myself less and less sure of the man. Was that really Robidoux's road he took us over? I didn't see any sort of road at all, especially on the west side, which was deep in snow and crosshatched with fallen timbers, making wagon pas-sage impossible. The grades were too precipitous for a wagon road in any case and were probably beyond what was acceptable for a railroad.

A dark suspicion of the man flared in me. Maybe he was an utter knave. But I set it aside as unworthy. He might be unprepossessing, but by all accounts he was the foremost master of this country. I didn't need to like the man; I needed only to respect him.

The dunes ahead would have to be skirted. They were constantly in a state of wind-driven flux, and no rails could be laid across them. It was plain that the 38th-parallel route was not practicable unless it strayed considerably from the parallel. But it was my duty to finish what was started, and I would continue to pursue a rail route as close to the 38th parallel as possible. If the passes ahead proved to be as difficult as those we had traversed, I might be forced to disappoint Senator Benton and his colleagues. But I had no intention of doing that. I planned to force a passage by whatever means, and this of all my expeditions would be long remembered for going where no company had gone.

I set the book aside, blew out the lantern candle to save tallow, and returned the Blackstone to its oilcloth case. Then I hurried through the bone-cold night to Godey's mess and found him unrolling his blankets atop one of those rubberized sheets that were the salvation of my men.

"Alexis, tomorrow you take the lead. Straight across the dunes. If I ask the guide to steer us, he'll take us around to the north."

"I'll do it, sir."

"There'll be neither food nor fodder nor water in those dunes, and that will be Williams's argument against the direct route."

"We can save a day or more, colonel."

"That's how I see it. And Godey, kindly put your best hunters out. I don't suppose they'll find anything in those dunes, but put them two or three hours ahead of us, and they'll reach the valley floor in time to make meat. That's what I have in mind. When we reach camp tonight, I want the men to discover some elk haunches roasting for them all."

"I'll send our best hunters, colonel. But it doesn't look like game country to me, sir."

"You're quite right, Alex. But it's something that must be done. The men expect it."

"As you wish, sir."

"The mules are feeding well tonight on the bark. They should be fine tomorrow."

Godey's hesitation told me he disagreed. I have come to read men well and can sense disagreement in them almost as fast as ideas form in their heads. But he smiled. "We'll have them on good pasture soon," he replied.

That's what I liked about Godey. He read my mind. He understood my deepening disillusionment with Williams. And he accepted my instructions without cavil.

The weather cursed my designs that night. A wind arose out of the north, bringing snow squalls with it and severe discomfort to my men, who could not stay dry. The icy blast rattled canvas shelters, raked cook fires, chilled the mules, drove men to cover, and even whipped the mules farther and farther from our bivouac. By dawn there was a thick layer of white upon us. Men were numb. Mules had vanished. The dunes to the west had a new layer of snow over them, to make our passage harder. But I set an example, expressing good cheer, even amusement at our plight, and soon enough a thoroughly chilled party was out, wading through snow, to recover our strays. Others were attempting to ignite cook fires, without much success in those Arctic gusts. And once again, icicles dangled from beards and eyebrows, and a rime from our breaths covered our leathern coats.

I heard that Ben Kern was both frostbitten and attempting to treat some frostbite in others with stimulants. Some of the wretches had stockings frozen to their feet, and getting flesh and cloth thawed and separated was no easy task. They should have known better than to let themselves suffer needlessly. There are canvas shelter cloths and blankets for all. But some men just won't perform the tasks that would spare them trouble. Later I would find out who had let himself suffer frostbite and keep the lapse in mind.

But it would all work out. By noon of a blustery and bitter December 4, with the thermometer's mercury hovering low inside its bulb, we set out across the sand hills, the hunters well ahead of us, the balky mules fighting our whips and kicks. It was all we could manage to drive them into that blast of air, and they fought us as if their life depended on it. It was odd. The mules clearly did not want to leave the protection of that cottonwood and willow forest, which offered fodder and warmth, and this time they resisted frantically, looking for any opportunity to turn tail and head east. We had to maintain utmost vigilance.

"Drive them ahead of us," I suggested to Godey, but that didn't work either. They all simply quit. I am always one to learn from my mistakes, being flexible in nature, so we put several men and mules in the van, to clear a path through the drifts, and in that manner we won the reluctant cooperation of the rest of the mules. But they were not a happy lot and trudged with head down, brushing as close to one another as their packs would permit, for the sake of whatever warmth could be gotten that way.

We saw not the slightest sign of game, but neither did I expect to see any in an area of shifting sands. In all, we made only five miles that day and camped in the lee of a great dune, which gave us a little protection from the furious wind. I was disappointed. I had planned to reach the river. It would be a miserable camp, without water, save for whatever snow we could melt, and without much fuel for our fires. The mules would be hard to contain, and I decided to double the guard. One slip and the whole lot would head back to that grove.

Bad as the camp was, it was better than what lay ahead, a featureless plain covered with snow, without shelter or wood or feed. Beyond, looming in the West, was the jagged white wall of the San Juan Mountains, the last great barrier we faced until we reached the Sierra. The tops were sawed off by cast-iron clouds, but I knew that the San Juans probably contained peaks in the fourteen-thousand-foot range, if my informants were right. I scraped away snow until I reached naked sand and put up a tent, feeling the heavy canvas flap in the Arctic wind. I hoped my tent stakes would hold in the soft sand, and I drove them as deep as I could, not liking the softness beneath my feet.

Nearby, my men struggled with firewood. There was naught but sagebrush, which they harvested ruthlessly. It would barely heat water, and their porridge or macaroni would be tepid, more glue than food this evening. I didn't mind it myself, but I had long since learned that I am more resilient than other men and can endure most anything. I ascribe it to good blood. The mules lost no time crowding east and had to be checked forcibly. I feared we would need to picket all of them. I watched my Creoles and California Indian boys, Manuel, Joaquin, and Gregorio, wrestle with the animals, finally picketing some in the lee of the dune where there was a little brush. I was returning the boys to California; the army had brought them east as curiosities and to let them get a glimpse of civilization and the great father in Washington. They had been docile and useful to me on the trail.

I was not yet settled when Old Bill materialized. He was permanently bent and walked with his northern half leaning forward and his southern half backward. But now he hunkered down on the balls of his feet, a form of rest common among mountain men who knew no chairs in the wilderness. Carson often did it. I could never find comfort in it.

"Hard night on the mules, no water or feed," he began. When addressing me he spoke a fairly educated English; among the men his inflections were rustic, even quaint.

"They'll eat snow," I replied.

He snorted. "Warming a mouthful of snow costs them more heat than they can get from eating," he retorted. "And they hardly get a spoonful."

"I know that."

He stabbed a crooked index finger west. "See that? It's death. It's plain death to anyone that goes into there."

"I know a pass," I replied. "Cochetopa. It's on the Mexican charts."

"So do I, and it's death, I'm saying."

"We have come this far without loss, Mister Williams."

"There's a way around. I've taken it plenty of times, just ease around the south of this range here. Cuts some foothills, plenty of valleys likely to have game and grass. Takes an extra day or three, but I'll put you all beyond those hills yonder, and you'll be glad we did."

"There's a path heading north; that's the one I plan to take. It leads to Cochetopa. It cuts off of Saguache River. It's an old Spanish route, and it's where we're going."

"It's where you're going to get into trouble like you never did see before, Colonel."

He was riling me, so I smiled pleasantly. I cared less and less for the oaf. He squinted at me and began an amazing monologue.

"You see the Rio del Norte out there, that winding bottom? Well, that's all sagebrush flats, not grass, and there's no feed worth a damn. You think you'll put some iron back into these mules? You'd better take stock. You're about out of corn and they're about to start stumbling and tumbling unless you get them on some good pasture.

"It gets worse, even before you start into that wall." He paused dramatically. I enjoyed his theatrics. He could run for the Senate and win. "Beyond that river, where those brushy flats lie, that's the strangest country you ever knew. It's where all the waters off those mountains have collected, just a little under the surface. It looks like naked arid land, don't it, sir? It is, for sure. But just below, it's wet like a sponge, like a hidden marsh, and if you think it's tough to pull and push mules through a lot of snow, wait until you push them through that. They can't hardly step without each foot sucking up and oozing in. If you take off their packs, maybe you can help them a little, but that means the men'll be carrying the load on their backs through the same swamp. This time of year, Colonel, they'll soak their feet and their boots; they'll freeze, and their feet will be so frostbit you'll likely perish the whole party, men and mules, before you even reach them hills you're planning to leapfrog over. I'm saying, Colonel, it's not the way to go; you'll be wearing the last out of the mules before you even step into the first gulch taking you up to where the gales blow constant and kill a man in five minutes."

"I don't want to stray from our plans, Mister Williams." I smiled, wanting him to see there was no hard feeling between us.

"Yes, sir," he said, unbending his hairpin frame until he was upright again. "I suppose it'll be for us to see."

That was an odd observation.

It was something I was very familiar with, the undertone of people trying to deflect me from my plans. I would have the honor of crossing the Rockies in December and intended to see to it no matter how much carping I had to endure. No one had ever done what I was about to do. I would alert Godey to be aware of conspiracies and disloyalties and to report these to me in confidence.

As the day waned, I could see the cook fires blooming, perfidious light and heat that would vanish for lack of tinder even before the supper was warm. It was something for them to endure; it would strengthen their manhood and prepare them for the travail ahead, when we toiled across those subterranean wetlands on the other side of the Rio del Norte.

CHAPTER FIFTEEN

William Sherley Williams

That man Frémont, he was the serpent that tempted Adam and Eve, no doubt about it. I reckoned it when I looked him over close. I can sometimes see right through, to the inner spirit, and inside of the colonel was the serpent himself, same as got Eve to eat the apple.

That next day, mean cold and blowing again, we raised camp late and worked out of the sand hills through some gray snow, and I climbed up on a ribbed dune to watch until the wind blew the heat out of me. It was the serpent all right, snaking through a trench in the dirty sand-topped snow, single file, the head of the serpent out front, and the tail most of a mile behind, one hundred–some worn-out mules, a hairy man here and there, all in a snaking black line. The corn was most gone, so the Creoles had adjusted the loads, but them mules were still hauling heavy goods, canvas shelter cloths, and all of that, and now they were looking like scarecrows, caved in, muscles ridging on their flanks like hogbacks.

They knew their fate, I could tell. I can see right inside an animal, and they knew they was about finished and soon they'd die. They knew that, so they didn't much care. They stopped fighting the wind and snow and just didn't much care, and I knew they'd all but given up on this earth, anyway. Maybe I'd see them down the road apiece. I have that vision so I know I'm coming back as a bull elk. Animals got no clock; it's all here and now. Only us mortals got time. But animals know what's coming where we don't.

There was a lot of nothing to eat in that naked flat of the Rio del Norte, just a little sagebrush poking from the dirty snow, and the mules toiled past it, knowing they would die soon. I got inside the skull of one of them, and he was saying he was worn out and cold and he hurt and no one cared and pretty soon he would stumble and die. I have the ability. I can even get myself inside the head of a squirrel. I can converse with a chipmunk if I'm of a mind. I told that mule I was going to cash in, too, mighty quick now, but not this trip. I plain knew. Once you get to talking with animals, you see how they think. I picked up on it.

This was a solemn day, mean black clouds, mean wind, mean sleet spitting in our faces, and the serpent's men had froze-up beards again, icicles dangling and clanging off beards, and eyebrows pasted with ice. They was all cold and wet down inside, round the waist, over the belly. The colonel never took the lead, never broke a trail himself, but let shifts of his men do that, busting up the crust and making a path. It was all done without an order. The men seemed to know when to quit, and another bunch would bust up crusted snow and the serpent would snake along, heading for the river that ran betwixt naked banks where the wind never slowed or quit. If the serpent thought to feed the mules there, he would be surprised.

Ahead loomed the worst heights a man could fathom, a white death so high it vanished into the cast-iron sky. I knew that country; it was bad enough in the summer, and now I couldn't tell one part of it from another. White canceled out everything. I would go in there as much a pilgrim as the next fellow. But it didn't matter to the serpent. He would go in there and drag the whole company to its doom. And what for? Not a railroad. No. He was looking for the tunnel into hell, is what he was trying to find. The more I thought upon it, the more I thought I should help him to the tunnel of hell. Why would a sane man do this?

We proceeded out on that vast flat, with nothing but snow and sagebrush and greasewood and wind. They told me it was Thursday, December 7, but I never know one day from another. For once we made good time, though the wind was bad and the temperature was worse and the air scraped heat out of me. I entertained myself by watching the spirits of the mules hovering just above them. When animals are fed and healthy, their spirits climb back inside of them and stay there, but now their spirits rode their backs along with the packs, and that told me what I wanted to know. The mules plodded listlessly, but we made time anyway.

Godey sent hunters ahead, but I heard no muffled shots on the wind and doubted that we would feast on deer or elk that night. Most of the day we were wrapped in a gray cocoon, with ice crystals stinging our faces and melting down into our beards, where the moisture froze, until we clicked and clanked as we progressed. We could not see the looming mountains, except at rare intervals, and our only companion was silence that day.

We camped on an open plain that night; there was absolutely no shelter for man or beast, and the miserable mules huddled together for warmth. Occasionally the mules on the outside burrowed into the center, for a moment of warmth. The mule herd seemed to understand this process, and periodically there would be a great shifting as mules on the outside, exposed to icy blasts, would burrow toward the middle of the herd for respite. We laid our bedrolls on iron ground and pulled stiff canvas over us. There was no fuel for fires, so we went nearly hungry, but for a few pieces of jerky the colonel had stashed away for moments like this. I never heard such silence. The company said nothing, each man caught in his private thoughts.

My thoughts were on the mules, which declined to eat snow for moisture, knowing somehow it would only chill them worse than the icy gales were chilling them. Men lay restlessly in bedrolls, which did little to stay the cold, and the night passed interminably, each man awake and locked in his private thoughts.

I suppose the serpent slept. Like the rest of us, he huddled in blankets underneath flapping canvas. He knew no suffering, saw it not in others, and blamed all suffering on the sufferers. A true Beelzebub, I thought. Parson Williams, as I am known, saw the man through and through and saw the need for exorcism. By the light of a gray dawn there was another few inches of snow on the ground. The company, without firewood for coffee or food, trembled itself together, threw packsaddles over the wretched mules, pulled the cinches tight, loaded the panniers, and departed on a compass course because it was impossible to fathom direction. I've been fair uncomfortable, but that night tested my endurance and made all my wounds and scars howl at me. I loathed the serpent, who acted as if everything was normal, and contemplated shooting him where he stood. Instead, I took some satisfaction in the certainty that he would do the job himself.

Once again, wordlessly, we slogged west through crusty drifts and treacherous mounds of grimy snow, a giant serpentine string of men and animals coiling toward the Rio del Norte, which we struck in the middle of the day. Here the serpent sent us north along the east bank, thereby signaling to me that he would not bring us safely around the southern flanks of the mountains, as I had proposed. I saw naught but horns on his skull and spent the day conjuring up ways to shoot him in the back, one wobble of my rifle, and thus to prevent what soon would befall us.

But I didn't. It was odd how I didn't. I would fix it all up in my head and had it exact. I'd ride forward a piece, wait for a ground blizzard to veil me, and plant a ball between his shoulder blades. I thus kept myself entertained for hours, whilst the company stumbled toward hell and finally dropped into a thickly timbered pocket beside the river, a haven for man and beast. That was December 8, 1848, and it had snowed in fits all day. The famished company made haste to free the wretched mules of their burdens and turn them loose, and I watched the beasts head for the river, there to slake a cruel thirst, and then to the willows and cottonwoods and red brush, where they tore at the bark and twigs and anything organic they could put their buck teeth around and strip free. It was poor fodder and would not put an ounce on any of them. But it would comfort them, the sticks and bark in their gut.

The hunters brought no game in; I knew they wouldn't. I have the vision, and I warned away the deer. "Make haste!" said I. "The serpent wants you." I watched them hasten away and watched the snow swiftly fill their hoofprints until not a dimple remained. I saw it as clear as other men see a rock or a tree. Two does and two yearlings warned away, and now the serpent would never touch them.

We would eat more macaroni. It would do. If the mules might enjoy cottonwood bark, I might prosper on pasta. I watched the company drag deadfall and shake the snow off of it and build huge mounds of it. There was no lack of firewood in this forest. Somewhere above us, the wind raced, but in this wooded pocket under a cutbank we found a little peace. Then I saw fires bloom, bright orange in the lavender light, yellow in the gray darkness, and not just the usual three mess fires, either. They were building bonfires at every corner, fires to drive away darkness; fires to vanquish the serpent; fires to turn this cold wild into a bright parlor for a night; fires to soak heat into the frozen ground, heat a man's backside while another fire heated his front; fires to dry out their soaked duds. And now they were talking, too. I heard shouts and cheer and relief. I have hardly heard better in a saloon, with a dozen men enjoying their cups and a good fire warming the pub. Fires circled the camp, and it was better than having a wild woman.

There would be no guard this night; no two-hour shifts. Those mules wouldn't stray from the bottoms and would eat all night, never pausing. Me, I drifted toward the dark river, which tumbled out of the mountains and flowed south and east. Snow lined its banks, eerie in the half light. I saw where an elk had descended its banks and crossed only recently.

"Go on, escape the serpent," I said. "Old Parson Williams will have you for supper some other day."

The next day, the serpent marched us up the Rio del Norte, but snows choked our progress and we made only three miles, finally camping in a piney wood. The mules would have nothing to eat once again. They never touched the resinous pine, which was poisonous to them. Godey spotted the elk tracks, got his five best hunters, and took off after the elk, which had retreated upslope into foothill forest. It didn't take long for the hunters to return dragging two elk over snow.

"So you stayed to feed the serpent," I said, angry with the elk. "But now I will feed my empty belly on you and be glad because you were stupid."

"Meat!" cried Stepperfeldt. "Meat tonight!" The man was a gunsmith, no hunter but handy to have around.

The elk, two young bucks, lay quiet in the snow, even as fresh flakes fell on their still-warm bodies. One had been shot through the neck; the other in the chest. The company rigged hempen ropes over limbs and slowly tugged the great four-foots up where they could be gutted. It took a gang of men to hoist an elk. I saw the elk spirits hover for a moment, and then gallop away, never looking back. It made me angry. Expert butchers soon peeled back the supple elk hide, which would be valuable, especially for men whose boots were falling apart. I wanted the little two-point antlers. A bit of elk antler could make a man lusty. In time, every mess had thick elk cuts broiling or stewing, and the smell of it drifted through the air. But the butchers never stopped, because they wanted the elk cut up before it froze, and the rest of the meat would be carried with the company.

Old Parson Williams was well fed that night, in a camp scraped out of four feet of snow and surrounded by pines. Once again the mules were fractious, wanting to retreat downriver to the cottonwoods and a meal, so the serpent posted two-hour guards to check the poor beasts. It would have been better to let the mules feed and collect them in the morning, but it wouldn't make any difference. The serpent would snake up the mountain, and the mules would die.

I suffered that night from fits of Christianity, and the next morning when the serpent showed his face, I squatted next to him. "Cross the river here, and go back down, and I'll take you around these peaks safe and sound," says I.

"That's a detour," he said.

"It be more like a safe passage," I replied, full of holy righteousness.

"Take us to Saguache River, and then up Cochetopa Pass," he said blandly. "That's how the Spanish did it and how we'll do it." He smiled kindly. I thought maybe to kill him on the spot but decided to wait.

I saw how it was with him and nodded. I had me some elk shoulder and coffee for breakfast, put a well-cooked piece in my possibles bag, and hied me down to the mules, which were standing in snow. Their backs were coated with the latest snowfall, and icicles dangled from their manes and bellies, jaws, and tails. They hadn't been grained and were gnawing on one another's manes and tails.

But even as I stood there, some of the serpent's Creoles began doling out a little maize and putting a few mouthfuls in nosebags and feeding the animals twenty at a time.

I watched one mule, one I fancied because it was plainer than most, sigh, eye me wearily, and stuff his hard-frozen snout into the bag, and soon I heard the quiet crunching of corn succumbing to molars. Half of it would go down that throat and emerge untouched a few hours later. That old mule's spirit hovered there and told me what I wanted to know. It wouldn't be long now.

It was cold again, that morning of December 12, but clear for a change.

This time the serpent sought me out. "You know the way to Saguache River?"

"I've walked over the hull country," I said.

"This is the most important day of all, then. We must find it. I'm depending on you."

"Well, it's not so hard. Just go wherever a railroad would go."

He laughed softly. I don't reckon I'd seen him laugh much. I had made a good joke, I thought.

There were no thoughts of railroads these days. We took off late, but in sunlight, with intense blue skies overhead for a change. Serpent's luck, I called it, as we worked up a deepening canyon that would take us once again into mountains.

CHAPTER SIXTEEN

John Charles Frémont

The guide was steering us ever westward instead of northwest. I pulled out my brass compass and checked, not liking it. We were leaving the headwaters of the Rio del Norte, a place of pine-clad hills and sloughs, where creeks and rivers tumbled together to form the great river.

By some mysterious fashion Old Bill had assumed the lead, working us away from the larger stream and up a branch I knew nothing about. I had sketches to work from. So had Preuss. Some came from knowledgeable mountaineers in Saint Louis and Westport. The most recent one had been drawn by Richens Wootton, who knew this country as well as Bill Williams.

This was a tumbled and rocky land, with giant gray outcrops, steep slopes, somber pine forests, groves of spidery cottonwoods and aspen, fierce, cruel creeks. And snow lazily smothered the country. It had caught and settled in every valley and dip, so that we were crossing spots that were ten or twenty feet deep, perilously working upslope in a tamped-down trench that reached over our heads.

This creek was not the Saguache River. I was sure of it. That stream was formidable, according to my informants, and had carved a broad valley that could support a wagon road—or a railroad. And it ran north and west, not straight west.

Yet there was Old Bill, perched on his bony mule, putting the beaters to work pounding a trail up this creek running within a narrow defile guarded by gloomy slopes. It was no easy task, and progress was slowed by steep grades, deadfall, giant boulders blocking the way, and a perilous drop to our right, which threatened the lives of our burdened mules.

I pulled aside until Preuss drew up.

"Do you know where we're going?" I asked him.

The topographer smiled wanly. "All I have is rough maps, sketched by men with bad memories."

"What do you call this creek?"

"I don't call it anything. How should I know? Maybe we should call it Old Bill Williams River, eh?"

"I need to know. I need to stop this."

"Why don't you talk to him, yah?"

"Where is Saguache? The river?"

He shrugged. "It is maybe twenty miles north. But that is a guess."

"And where is Cochetopa Pass?"

Preuss grinned evilly. I had the sense that he was enjoying this side excursion and maybe enjoying my discomfort, too. I have a way of reading men.

"It's not here, that much is what I say to you. It's off that way." He waved a hand in a vaguely northwestern direction.

I wheeled my mule away. I would never again hire that man. He couldn't even say where we were. Map makers were a dime a dozen. I waited in the snow while more of my company rode by single file, and then pulled Creutzfeldt over.

"Where are we?" I asked.

"We are proceeding up an unknown valley with slopes of fifty and sixty percent on each side. I am thinking we will enjoy an avalanche."

"Have you a name for that creek down there?"

He smiled blandly. "I will put it down as Frémont, yes?"

I laughed softly so that he might know that I appreciated his humor, but only mildly. I would prefer that the Pathfinder's name be used sparingly and to good effect.

"We might climb to that ridge and see," he said.

The ridge was five or seven hundred snowy feet up. I shook my head. It was already too late to do that. We must either proceed where the treacherous old guide was taking us or turn around at once. It was time to confront Williams, but the trail was narrow and the snow-trench in which we walked did not permit me to work forward, so I pulled into the middle, between two weary mules, whose every step betrayed exhaustion. They were receiving one pint of corn morning and evening. My hope to find grassy south slopes to feed the mules had so far been dashed by the heavy snowfall this year. We were lucky on this day, the first in which we had not suffered yet another dumping of snow.

The company halted ahead at some stony shelf where the forest parted, and I carefully worked my way around the drooping livestock and reached a bench where Williams had paused.

There was little in sight but snow: snow climbing the valley walls, snow burdening pine trees, snow capping giant claws of rock that had tumbled from above eons ago. Just off to the right was a steep abyss and a creek tumbling below, mostly ice-capped but here and there open.

I waited for a moment while the old man relieved himself.

"What is this place? That's not the Saguache River."

"Never said it was," he replied.

I smiled and bit back a retort. "The Saguache River is where we're going. I want you to take us there. If that means turning around here, we'll turn around."

He sighed. Breath steamed from his nostrils. "I don't think that's the way to go. It's an extry three or four days, and this is some shorter."

"What place is this?"

"Mexicans, they call it Carnero Creek."

"Why are we here; why didn't you consult with me?"

"We're here because we're here, and I brought us here."

"We're climbing a tributary. We're climbing a cleft in the mountains. That could be fatal. What's on top?"

"Saves two days. Mules there are mighty poor, your honor. How much corn's left? Three, four days?"

In truth I couldn't say exactly.

"So ever' day counts, don't it now?"

"Where does this creek take us?"

"Up and over, then we're coming onto Cochetopa Pass to the other side."

"Are you sure? How do you know?"

"Getting higher. Lot of snow around," he said.

His evasiveness was maddening, but I smiled. Somehow, I had to deal with this renegade.

"The route I wanted was a wagon trail," I explained with great patience. "The Mexicans could wagon over to the far side. It's in their records. That's important. Railroads follow old wagon trails."

"Yep, that's right. It's a wagon road, and it'd take rails, maybe. I don't know why not. But this here's shorter, and I took it to save time. That all right with you?"

I found myself facing the most anguished decision of my life: go ahead or go back. He stood there insolently, solemn, but I could read that man's heart, and I knew he was enjoying it.

"It's what you want, isn't it?" he asked. "Snow, heaps and piles."

The question puzzled me. "I'm sure I could do with a lot less."

"But then it wouldn't be a challenge, your honor."

I didn't like the tone in his voice. He meant to reduce me. "In my own humble way, sir, I am seeking a rail route across the middle of the continent. And that's all. And this narrow defile is not a place to run rails."

"I reckon I showed you one around the south. Waved my finger right toward it. It weren't to your liking."

I heard the amusement in his tone. I also knew I was utterly at his mercy. He knew the country, and I didn't. I had only one choice. Stick with him or turn back. "All right, we'll go straight up and over. Show us the way, Mister Williams. When we get to Cochetopa, we'll be back on the rail route."

He grinned slowly, and I sensed he had somehow bested me, though I couldn't say how or why. He clambered back on his mule and sat more bent backed than ever, as if sitting straight in the saddle would give offense.

It was now out of my hands. Whatever fate befell us would be laid on him alone. I intended to make much of that in my reports.

We fought our way up the narrow gulch, which rarely exceeded two hundred feet in breadth, working back and forth across the icy creek, wherever the trail might take us. The mules so resisted stepping into the icy torrent of water and making their way over the treacherous rock that we had to drag them by the nose through each crossing. But the guide paid no heed and imperturbably proceeded ever higher. We were climbing the streambed, there being no other trail, and often we were caught in drifts several feet deep, which required breaking a trail for the burdened mules.

This was a piney canyon, not a quaking asp in sight, and the mules feared it, unwilling to move forward, which put a great strain on the company. Sometimes the thick snow covered holes, into which mules tumbled and had to be dug out. Other times the snow covered a perfect cross-hatching of downed timber, over which each mule had to step delicately, one hoof at a time, sometimes faltering on a slippery grade.

I eyed the steep walls uneasily, noting the burden of snow lodged on them, snow that our very passage might unloose as an avalanche. There were great escarpments of snow just waiting to roar down on us and carry us all into the gulch below. One good thing was the clear blue sky above us, which promised no new snows for the moment. We labored in constant shade, because no sun penetrated to the floor of this defile on this twelfth day of December. We made only a few miles that day and eventually camped late in the afternoon on a steep slope, there being no level ground anywhere. We were well above the creek, on a timbered shoulder that made no proper campground at all, but time was against us and we could see no level place ahead as the darkness thickened.

The mules stood trembling, unable to go farther, as my men stripped the packs and saddles off of them and stowed them on the upslope side of trees to keep them from tumbling into the gulch below us. Men made level beds only by felling trees and setting the logs on the downslope side and covering the scaffolds with pine branches. There was naught for the mules to graze on, and they clung to the slope, the very picture of dejection, too weary to roam. The men attached the feedbags, with the pitiful pints of corn in them, which some mules ate at once, while others barely seemed to care. Most were up to their bellies in snow, trying to find some small comfort on that cruel slope. At least there was no wind in that defile, and as the icy stars appeared, it was plain the enemy that night would be bitter cold instead of a gale. Even as we prepared to endure the night, we could feel a draft of heavy air slide down the gulch, numbing every creature.

We could not manage shelters or cook fires in that snowbound place, so men wrapped themselves in canvas and struggled to find

a little warmth as the night settled in. I stumbled past men, looking for Godey, and found him near the rear of the column. There
were no messes this night, and I could not find half the men I
needed.

"Sir?" he said, peering up at me from a mound of canvas and
blankets, nothing but his beard and a pair of eyes and a red nose
showing.

"Alex, how much corn is left?"

"One day. Tomorrow we run out."

"One day! What about our food?"

"We still have some frozen elk. Macaroni. Jerky. Sugar, coffee,
salt."

"How long will the mules endure?"

"They're chewing on one another's manes and tails, sir."

"Tomorrow, work ahead as much as you can. Find a south slope
for the mules."

The night was thick enough to hide his face but not his skepticism. He didn't respond. We had seen not the slightest sign of a
meadow or hillside in this defile. Trees crowded the creek bottom,
only to give way to heaps of talus and blocks of rock, vaulting upward and plastered with snow. The chances of putting the mules
on grass were so poor that I found myself casting about for other
prospects.

"Look for quaking asp or cottonwoods or any soft-bark tree."

Godey did not reply. There would be none at this altitude, barring a miracle.

"We'll make it," I added. "Call it Frémont's luck."

"Round the next bend, who knows?" Godey said.

Did I detect amusement in his response?

I was getting chilled and hurried forward to a hollow I had found,
a tiny cavity located in the slope that afforded me some comfort.
I cleaned away the snow, settled some pine boughs in the hollow,

used some limbs to create a sort of hut when I draped my tent over them, and crawled into my nest. I permitted myself two sticks of jerky, which I wished to eat privately from my personal stock, and settled down for the night.

I wondered what all those diary keepers were scribbling this night. When I commanded an army exploration party, I forbade diaries, but I could not do that with these civilians, and I suspected they were scribbling things about this camp and this expedition that would not please me. Preuss was keeping one in German, and probably it was riddled with his own sour comments. I didn't care what the man thought. But I wished I might see what the Kerns were writing about Old Bill. I felt sure they wouldn't fault me for taking them up this anonymous gulch.

I had been too occupied on this trip to keep my own diary but had made mental notes along the way, which I would form into a record when I had the chance. I might need it to correct the impressions of those greenhorns, who had no experience of the mountains and might suppose that we were embarked on a foolish or dangerous course. I would, of course, set all that straight later.

The camp was very quiet, very cold, and a certain foreboding hung in the icy air.

As I lay huddled under the canvas, I reached toward something just beyond the horizons of my mind, and then it came to me: this was Frémont's providence. We'd be up and over in two days, hit that Cochetopa Pass in three, get down to feed and game in four. Saguache River might take a week. A week of starving, dying mules, and hardship. Old Bill had delivered me.

CHAPTER SEVENTEEN

Benjamin Kern, MD

We broke camp about eight thirty the next morning. A brutal west wind was ripping straight down the gulch, but the sky was azure, what little we could see of it in that mountain trench. A certain foreboding had grown within me, a feeling that I did not wish to share with my brothers for fear they would think I was pusillanimous. But the behavior of the mules was evoking alarm in me.

They were now so worn they simply stood mutely, as if they had surrendered to fate. We groomed and saddled them as usual, while they stood with bowed heads, no longer caring. I had seen that all too often in my practice: mortals too far gone to struggle, too worn to breathe, too weak to grasp at life.

That is how the mules struck me as we slipped the feedbags over their muzzles, each filled with a pitiful handful of corn. Yet, one by one, we blanketed and saddled them, slung their burdens on their frosted backs, and slid icy bits into the mouths of those we would ride and halters over the heads of those we would lead or drive. They had not watered that night, and those who had gnawed at the caked snow had only drained a little more heat from their gaunt bodies.

As I studied them, with the growing dread that we were getting into grave trouble, I wondered whether the others were feeling the same thing. I eyed them sharply, but to a man they were cheerful and brimming with confidence. Was I the only one in the company filled with foreboding? Was I the coward, dying a thousand times before my death? I dared not reveal my anxiety to anyone, least of all Ned and Richard, who seemed oblivious of the plight of the mules and eager to proceed.

We managed to boil a little macaroni, which took a long while at that altitude, and so got some nourishment in us before we began, but soon we had the mules and the company lined out and were struggling upslope once again. We encountered a steep hill, maybe three hundred yards, slick with snow, and the mules could not manage it. We pushed and tugged. We removed packs and skidded them upslope through heavy snow. Then we yanked and whipped and shoved the mules up. And once we reached the top, we loaded the packs onto the mules. What should have been an easy three hundred yards of climbing took hours and left us diminished and weakened.

But the climb had brought us to the lip of a hanging valley. It lay broad and open and level, with receding slopes. There were noble prospects in all directions from here, including one back to the Rio del Norte, far behind. I should have been elated. Instead, I fell into the most painful sort of melancholia. The mules clustered in the snow, at least on level ground, not wanting to move at all. I saw nothing for them to eat, not even brush along the creek. There were only needled branches poking through the snow.

We had consumed the morning wrestling the mules that small fraction of one mile, and we spent the rest of the bright day working up the valley, and then a low hill, to a second broad valley, where we would camp. These hills were snow choked, but we would be able to scrape snow away and make a level camp and feed some roaring fires with deadwood.

But all I could think of was the mules, which would this evening receive the last small bait of grain. I thought that it was still not too late to retreat down to the Rio del Norte and the cottonwood groves along its banks, where the mules might rip and chew some sort of miserable living, though bark made poor fodder. That icy eve, the company fed out the last of the corn as if no one had a care in the world. The mules ground the kernels between their molars, sipped at the creek, nipped at the few stalks of brush poking from the blue-shadowed snow, and then stood stock-still, their heads low, awaiting their fate.

Did no one notice? Did no one pity these animals? Did my companions fear to reveal their true feelings to the others? Was Colonel Frémont so forbidding that no one of them might approach him? There was, in a few of those panniers, a good bit of macaroni the colonel had brought along. I didn't doubt that the mules would make a feast of it. There was also some sugar, which might be poured into the feed bags with the last handfuls of corn. Maybe feeding them hot water laced with sugar would help. Maybe on the morrow I would see about these remedies.

I found myself waiting for something. I thought surely some of the company would at least consult with the colonel, tell him how it was with the mules. But not one man did. His authority reigned so supreme among his veterans and retainers that not the slightest dissent manifested itself in the purple twilight. I cursed myself for being as subservient to him as all the rest.

Maybe the harbinger of bad news ought to be me. Maybe I ought to brace the colonel and give him a medical opinion about the mules and urge him to retreat to safety whilst he still could and before his mules and maybe his men perished. I sat before the crackling pine fire pondering it, phrasing words in my head, making arguments, urging him in my mind to do what was needful. And yet I didn't. I will never know why I didn't. Nor will I know what sort of magical hold Frémont had on the rest, so that not one of us approached him with a warning. What was it about Frémont? I gazed at my brothers, who seemed perfectly at ease, though they were as aware as I that the mules were about to fail. Fail! That's a weasel word. They were about to die. I believed that on the morrow, with no breakfast in their bellies, the mules would falter, one by one, and tumble into the snow, too far gone to rise up.

The fires that evening were particularly cheerful. The pine knots snapped and shot sparks into the firmament. There was warmth enough to warm our front sides or our backsides, mend clothing, dry our underclothes, apply an awl to our boots and moccasins, and bring a kettle of macaroni to a cheerful boil.

"I imagine we'll be having mule meat soon," I said to Ned.

"It's not an improvement on elk," he replied. "It's on the menu, though."

"We've seen our last elk until we're off the mountains," Creutzfeldt said. "No game here."

"I haven't seen a crow for a week," my other brother, Richard, said. "I could eat crow."

He thought it was amusing.

But we did fill our bellies that night with boiled macaroni spooned into our mess cups. It tasted remarkably good for something that was nothing but boiled-up wheat.

I could not stand my sense of foreboding anymore and restlessly cleaned out my cup and packed it in my kit, and then I worked through the snow, past the other messes, toward Frémont, all the while rehearsing what I wanted to say. It was an odd thing: no one was alarmed about anything. I was the sole worrywart in that camp.

I found Frémont at a well-executed camp, with three feet of snow carefully scraped aside, a bright small fire warming the tent and the earth before it, and Frémont sitting in a camp chair I didn't know he possessed. He was fiddling with an instrument.

"Ah, so it's you, Doctor. You're just in time to see me take a measurement with my barometer. Actually, I'm taking two measurements, and I'll compare my observations with Preuss."

I recognized one as a mercury barometer. It contained a tall column of mercury that would rise or fall in its glass cylinder with variations of air pressure.

"A barometer," I said.

"An altimeter. Air pressure declines with height. This other device measures altitude another way, by recording the boiling temperature of water."

Indeed, this metal cylinder sat on legs just above a small kettle of boiling water, and baffles caught the steam and steered it through a jacket around the cylinder.

"There's a thermometer inside that cylinder. The cooler the steam, the lower the boiling point of water, and the higher the altitude. It's all calibrated on the Celsius scale, of course, and so is the mercury instrument, which makes it easy to calculate heights."

"Subject to weather, temperature, and so on."

He smiled. "Your science serves you well. I always am glad to have learned men with me on these little trips."

"And have you reached any conclusion?"

"Why, tentatively, 8,742 feet above the level of the sea, if the mercury device has it right, and I am waiting for the boiling-water device to heat the thermometer beyond all possibility of error, apart from climactic variations. It requires a little patience, does it not?"

"We're very high. No wonder I grow so weary, with air so thin."

"We'll be going higher, my friend. The pass will be close to ten thousand."

I dreaded the very thought of it, and it must have shown in my face.

"Cheer up, my friend, we'll be up and over in just a few hours, let's say forty-eight at the outside."

I found myself unable to say what I wanted to say, which is that some of the mules would not survive even that span. What was it about Frémont? Why could I not raise the issue that was causing me great anguish?

"But of course you didn't come here to talk about altitude, I imagine."

"The mules are on their last legs," I blurted.

"Of course, of course, Doctor, and some will perish."

"I was hoping that wouldn't be necessary."

He smiled softly. "They are our commissary, Doctor. There will be mule steaks, boiled and fried and roasted mule over the top and down the other side, and we'll keep our bellies full no matter what."

"Yes, surely."

"That's why we have so many."

"I imagine you've answered my questions, sir," I said, feeling a great need to escape.

"Well, have a restful night, then. Preuss and I'll keep on with our measurements. Altitude is a tricky thing to get right."

I nodded and hurried into the bitter night. Away from his fire I felt the flood of icy air that was quietly settling over this camp. I made my way back to my mess, sat in the warmth of the fire, and pulled off my rawhide moccasins. My stockings were frozen to my feet because of the snow that had worked in. I dared not pull the stockings loose, for fear of tearing my own half-frozen flesh, so I carefully laid my feet close to the crackling fire, which my brothers watched silently. In time I felt a tingling in my feet, the sign of life returning to them, and after an interval I was able to draw my stockings off and warm my white, frozen flesh in the radiance.

"I am lucky," I said to Ned. "A while more and I would be disabled."

To be disabled there, at that time and place, would have been fatal.

I endured the prickly sensation in my feet as life returned to them, and then put on my spare stockings while the others were laid close to the wavering orange flame to dry. I was heartily sick of winter, sick of hardship, and worse, I didn't know why we were here in this cold place or why we needed to be.

"You went to see the Colonel?" Ned asked.

"He told me about his instruments and altitude and barometric pressures."

"About the mules," Ned persisted.

I nodded, even more melancholic than before. "They are, it seems, our dinner."

"It's been in the back of my mind," Ned said.

"The Colonel said we'd be up and over, descending the west slope in forty-eight hours. That's how he put it. In hours rather than days."

"To make it seem shorter. How many mules will survive that long without a bite of food, carrying us, carrying loads?"

"They're so starved now that one mule can't feed thirty-three men. Not even one meal," I said.

But all this talk about mule meat didn't sit well with me. As I warmed my feet beside that cheerful flame, I knew that the source of my melancholia was pity. Poor, dumb beasts dragged where they would not go, yanked across streams, whipped up slopes, mauled and pushed and pulled and burdened. And now all of the hundred and thirty faithful and trusting beasts were so famished, so empty in their bellies, they could hardly make the heat that kept them alive. I knew all about cold, how cold kills warm-blooded things, how cold this night would be ten times worse for these mules because their bodies couldn't make enough heat to keep them alive.

I also felt embarrassed. Other men cared little about the comfort of their animals; they were simply beasts to be used, discarded, eaten, pitched aside. But there I was, wondering what sort of man John Charles Frémont was that he could be so indifferent to the suffering of animals. I realized then that a man who had no sensibility about animals could have little or none about other animals, namely the human animals who were the beasts of burden of his insatiable hunger for fame. How many living creatures would be sacrificed on the altar of his ambition?

CHAPTER EIGHTEEN

Captain Andrew Cathcart

I could scarcely remember a worse night. Sleep was impossible. A bitter wind tormented us, piercing through every fragile barrier we had erected, crawling under canvas, probing through caps and mittens, making a mockery of blankets. I had never known such cold, relentlessly fingering me as I lay abed. I wanted to be anywhere but there, half-frozen, my body as wretched as my soul, my mind filled with black thoughts.

It wasn't my plight alone that haunted me but that of every other man and the miserable mules, which had started to give out. Yesterday they stumbled, and we could scarcely put them on four feet. This morning there would be not a stitch of feed to warm them after a night of brutal wind that would steal life from them. I wondered, as I lay there in that bitter dark, whether we would see one mule alive at dawn.

A plague on Frémont. We should have retreated from this icy mausoleum long ago, whilst we could. In the dawn, if I lived through the rest of the night, I would watch. There was yet one remedy for the mules, a great deal of sugar the colonel was hauling to flavor his tea, I imagine. In the British Isles we knew all about sweet feeds and how they perk up an animal. This dawn I would see whether Frémont would spare his mules or let them perish. He had enough sugar and some macaroni, too, to fashion a hot meal for them, a meal heated up with boiling water. I could show these Yanks a thing or two. We'd see.

I tugged blankets this way and that and dug into my kit for more woolens, only to find I was wearing all that I possessed. I wanted more gloves, layer on layer to pull over my numb hands, and more stockings to cover aching feet, but there were none. I could lie still until dawn or brave the subzero air and walk and stomp about and maybe bring some prickles of life back to my aching limbs. I chose to lie still. That bloody wind would kill me if I left my bedroll for long.

Dawn came slow in that time of year, but the men didn't wait for it. They were in the same condition as I and chose instead to build fires under the flinty stars and warm themselves. It took some doing to start a blaze with wood so cold, but a little gunpowder and some pine shavings and a lot of shelter from that gale finally did the trick. But it was as if we had no flame at all. The wind raked away the heat faster than the fires could burn, and the whole predawn exercise was a worse misery than lying in our icy robes. I was no warmer after a half hour beside the roaring fire than I had been in my miserable blankets.

We could not see the animals, and as we sat about trying to boil water for tea, all of us keeping our thoughts to ourselves, I grew aware of their silence. No coughs, no snorts, no wheeze or shuffle in the blackness. I wondered if most were dead. When the reluctant dawn did finally arrive, and we could gaze through the murk into the pinewoods where the mules had attempted to shelter from the gale, we could see that most lived. But here and there were dark lumps half-buried in snow, the gale swiftly burying them. I counted five. Several of us tramped through the thick snow to look the herd over. Those that lived stood stock-still, heads lowered, and most of them jammed together to share whatever heat they could offer one another.

The dead mules were frozen solid. So much for mules as a commissary, I thought. We'd have to kill a living animal for food. The dead mules were rock-solid, and cutting meat from one would be like cutting steaks from a bronze equestrian statue. With saws and axes we might whittle away some meat, but I knew that if it came down to sawing and hacking a dead mule or slitting the throat of a live one for dinner, these weary men would take the easy way. The colonel's much-heralded food supply in extremity was not a good supply at all without live animals.

This morning we would saddle these half-dead animals and make them carry us up a wintry slope until they dropped. It took an hour to get some water boiling for coffee or tea, and I hoped the first act would be to give these animals a hot drink. But the Americans simply ignored the stock, as if the mules didn't exist, and went about readying themselves for another assault on the mountains.

Frémont appeared, smiling, restless, enjoying his morning coffee, saying little. I soon realized he would do nothing, absolutely nothing, for the mules this morning except grind them to death. I was too cold to hate the man but full of schemes to give a furtive handful of sugar to the beasts, preferably with hot water. In the end, I did nothing. Old habits of command prevailed. It was not for me to give orders or to disobey the man in charge. It haunts me that I did not rise up and do what I had in mind, without the leave of Frémont. I had been in the hussars too long.

The bitter wind never quit, and I knew this would be one of the worst days of my life. And yet the camp was uncommonly cheerful. We stood at the very base of the ridge that would take us into the drainage of the Colorado River and ultimately the Pacific. The ridge was not half a mile distant, though this last assault would be steep and cruel. There was, among the company, a sense of victory. Beyond, we could tumble our way west, into warmer climes, where grass grew and a man could pull off the layers of leather and wool that now kept him alive.

So we saddled the mules, which stumbled stupidly as we brought them in one by one, brushed the snow out of their coat, and threw packsaddles and loads over them once again. One mule simply went down, and no tail twisting could wrench him up. He had played out, lying inertly in the snow, too worn to resist the bullying. I watched it lying there, its lungs pumping irregularly, its neck arched back, its mouth open. And then with a shudder, it ceased to breathe. And even as it died, snow was filtering into its hair.

No one came to butcher it while it was possible to do so.

I saw Ben Kern staring, mutely, and he saw me, and a faint shake of his head told me his every thought. I felt an inconsolable sadness. The mule had died even before we raised camp and tackled that terrible grade. What would the hard day ahead do to the rest? So there they were, the Creoles and Missourians and the rest, offering not even some heated water to these miserable beasts and loading them with all the tons of gear and our own remaining fodder before leading the stumbling creatures up the valley once again, one slow step at a time, the men in front wielding giant clubs made of deadwood to hammer a trail through thick snow that sometimes reached the shoulders of men sitting on those mules.

I counted it a miracle that the mules walked at all. They are noble beasts and were giving their last breath to the task. But as soon as the grade rose dramatically, they could go no farther and simply stood in that trench cut into the drifts, heads hanging.

"We'll pull them up. Then it'll be downhill," Godey said, so we dragged out our hempen ropes, fashioned cruel halters over the snouts of the mules, and tugged them upward, one step at a time. But the mules were beyond walking and simply stood where they stood. It became a great exercise of force, men in front of and behind each animal, pulling and pushing, yanking and shoving, as we climbed the last few hundred yards toward that treeless summit not far ahead.

Then Godey's own mule, Dick, gave out. He had treated it more severely than the rest, and now it folded to its knees and would not budge, its half-frozen body blocking the trench trail. Godey saw at once it was over for Dick and swiftly unsaddled the animal, and we pushed it into a drift, where it expired, one last sad rush of air, and then lay inert, its mouth open, tongue hanging out, neck crooked back. Godey said nothing, which was the only decent thing to do, and set off on foot, dragging the mule that had stood in line behind Dick. And so we spent a whole morning and midday struggling up the last few hundred yards to the barren summit.

And when we got there, we saw grass, a whole slope of it that the wind had whipped free and clear. But when we finally emerged on that great cap of the world, the subzero gale blew heat out of us so swiftly that no living creature could survive there for more than a few minutes. To put the mules on that grass would be to kill them all within the hour.

We paused up there to look about. There we were, on top of the world. The distant valley of the Rio del Norte was behind us, and beyond it, the white peaks of the Sangre de Cristos. To the north and south, range after range, peak after serrated peak whitened the landscape, beneath a bold blue sky. I saw cirrus clouds to the west, heralding another storm, and knew we were in for worse than this cold day. But that is not what stopped my heart. To the west, some miles distant, stood another wall of mountains, with a notch in them well above the one from which we all gaped at this alpine world. We had not crossed the divide. The valley into which we would now descend was yet another drainage of the Rio Grande and led to the Atlantic.

But in this bright, eye-smarting place we could not tarry, not for an extra second, because the icy gale was plucking the last heat from us and further destroying our mules. We studied the mountains and hastened across the ridge, dropping into a gulch so steep we could not keep our footing, and floundered our way downslope through giant drifts higher than we could stand, amid yellow pines. And there more mules simply halted, too worn to proceed, but we could not stay there in that awful place and hurried on, needing all that was sustaining about lower altitudes and escape from wind and perhaps fodder for the mules, which were now clearly in extremis. My own mind was filled with terrors now. We had not crossed the divide, as Frémont had promised us, and we could see nothing to the west or north that suggested descent or cessation of this towering range. It was as if, up there, we were witnessing our death warrant. Or so I thought. We were all too numb ourselves to say a word to one another. We slid and stumbled and plowed our way down that steep slope for as long as we could endure, never reaching any sort of bottoms that might yield feed for our wretched animals or game for ourselves. I felt trapped.

Finally, in the last hour of December light, the colonel decided we would camp in a wind-sheltered bottom, in four or five feet of snow. There would be plenty of firewood but not a bite for the mules. We unloaded the mules and heaped the tack in a single place were we could get at it in the morrow. We had to keep our tack from the mules, which were gnawing at leather and canvas and rope and trying to break into the panniers for whatever would fill their bellies. Most of them had lost manes and tails, which had been gnawed away by other mules.

Some of the men attempted to dig out a camping place, while others wearily spread a rubberized sheet over the snow and collapsed onto it. I had never experienced such silence in a bivouac, each man among us entirely private. If their thoughts were similar to my own, it was no wonder. They dared not utter what they were thinking. So deep was Frémont's grip on his veterans of previous journeys that they would follow Frémont to their doom rather than wrestle him or set themselves loose from the rest of us. I could not fathom it, and yet I was doing the same thing. There I was, in probably fatal circumstances, meekly accepting my fate.

The mules stood stock-still in the bottoms. A little brush poked through, and a few of them found the energy to nip at stalks and twigs. But most had given up and numbly awaited their death. No one seemed to care. I was weary, but I made my way to the bottoms and flailed away with a piece of deadwood, gradually exposing more brush for a few mules to masticate. I was satisfied to see several of them begin to nip and chew. I hoped that my example would stir the others to open some of the snow fields to the forage, but I made no progress there, though most of the men had watched me carefully, and all of them knew my purpose. It was as if they needed a command from Colonel Frémont to undertake the labor, and that command was not forthcoming.

In time they did complete a makeshift camp, and mess fires burned in holes in the snow, their heat glazing the walls of the pits. The company could find warmth in those protective circles, which reminded me of the walls of an igloo, and there the men congregated as a lavender darkness descended, and along with it an icy downdraft from that ridge above, which was ladling killing air down that draw, air that would murder the weakened mules.

Some men, it turned out, did go upslope, and they recovered eight of the beasts and herded them down, arriving in camp at dusk, the mules stumbling and sliding so slowly that they barely made it while daylight lingered. These eight were simply herded in with the rest, to live or die as fate saw fit. I once again felt a great loathing for men who would not make every effort to sustain their beasts. And yet these same men were so weary they could barely sustain themselves, so I supposed my judgment was harsh.

The bright fire down in that snow pit cheered me that night. Our mess had the greenhorns, the ones who had never been out on an expedition before, the ones unknown to Colonel Frémont, the ones least familiar with the arts of survival. Some boiled macaroni cheered us. It was good to get something solid in our bellies. The glazed walls caught the heat, until it seemed we were in a parlor instead of high in the Saguache Mountains, as they seemed to be called by these men. I peered upward uneasily, suddenly aware that the ice-chip stars above had vanished, and I knew that we would soon be inundated once again. The night would not be so pleasant.

"How much food have we?" Ben Kern asked. "Does anyone but the colonel know?"

"I know. I looked in the packs," his brother Richard said. "We have three packs of macaroni, maybe fifty pounds of sugar, salt, and some frozen elk that the colonel is saving."

"Just that, for thirty-three men?" Ned asked.

"That and the mules."

"What good are frozen mules, that's what I want to know," Creutzfeldt asked. "I couldn't hack them up with an axe."

"How far to the Continental Divide?" Ben asked.

No one could answer him. That next ridge west could be days away, with the mules so broken down.

"The mules could be helped with warm water mixed with sugar," I said.

None of them responded at first.

"We'll need the sugar ourselves, I am thinking," Creutzfeldt said.

That's where it ended. Later, it began to snow, thick flakes that soon buried us as we lay in our bedrolls. The snow had become a prison, shackling me. Now there were walls rising in every direction. We could not return from whence we came. We could not go forward. The silent snows ruled us.

CHAPTER NINETEEN

John Charles Frémont

I wondered how Jessie was faring. She probably was still in Saint Louis, readying herself for the Panama trip. She was made of sturdy stuff, and I little doubted that she would negotiate a successful journey to California. A lesser woman could manage it. I felt no qualms about consigning her to the fates of the traveler, knowing she was a Benton. I supposed she was pining for news of me, but I had no means of telling her that I was somewhere close to the Continental Divide, being guided by a lummox who might or might not know the way, and only time would tell.

I had strong men with me during the army expeditions, and some of them were with me this trip, having left the service or taken leave. They were from good stock and had weathered all the adversities of life lived in raw nature. Preuss was a tough little German who knew how to keep himself comfortable. Godey, of course, is the very prototype of his sort, as strong as they come, and a veteran. King is another one, a veteran who was with me in California and who is made of sturdy stuff. Add my California men Taplin, Martin, Stepperfeldt, Ferguson, Wise, Vincenthaler, and Breckenridge, as well as my veteran Creoles, Proue, Tabeau, and Morin, and there is my cadre of hard men, good stock, who never urged on me the counsels of despair. It was the rest who concerned me, but I didn't let them know it. They were soft city men, unused to hardship.

We were being guided by a degenerate, and that caused me some difficulty. It was plain to me that Williams had been a poor choice, though the only one available, so I can scarcely fault myself. He had not lifted a finger the entire trip, reasoning that a guide need not concern himself with food, firewood, saddling and grooming and feeding the mules, breaking a trail, or making and breaking camp. He assumed no responsibility, not even for the mule we provided him, letting my company do every lick of work whilst he meandered about.

That he had led us into a perilous circumstance high in the San Juan Mountains did not escape my attention. He had barely said a word, and I knew he was avoiding me as much as he could. Now we had topped a saddle Old Bill had assumed was the divide, only to discover that many miles distant rose another chain, higher than the one we had topped, and we were far from crossing over to warmer and safer climes. Indeed, I found myself wondering whether this odd degenerate had the slightest idea of where he was leading us, and that morning I decided to find out.

After my morning toilet I sought him out. He was lounging on one of our rubberized sheets watching my company once again prepare to tackle massive drifts and to hack a passage for our weary mules.

My men were busy; the mules had this night eaten saddle blankets, ropes, manes and tails, woolen clothing, belts and shoes and canvas, in the process damaging such tack and equipment as we had at hand. It was almost impossible to keep them out of camp.

I squatted down beside him as he lounged, picking his teeth with twig. I seethed with contempt for the lout but carefully set aside my private thought and smiled.

"Well, Williams, we obviously have a long way to go to cross the divide," I said.

"Goodly way, yes."

"I wonder if you could show me the pass. I see nothing but another wall of white mountains off to the west."

He grinned, his tongue working the gaps in his teeth. "Oh, she's there. I always know it when I see it."

"Is there feed for the mules ahead?"

"Oh, could be, depending on how she blows."

"How steep is it?"

He lifted his cap off and scratched his hair, or maybe it was a cootie he was scratching. "Depends on which way we go," he said. "It don't make a difference."

I found the answer maddening. I espied a knob to the right and saw how it might offer advantage.

"My friend, we'll go up there," I said, pointing. "Then you may enlighten me."

He studied on it. "That's a far piece and full of snow."

"I'm sure it's of no consequence to a man of your abilities."

He offered me no resistance save for some mumbling, and we struck through heavy drifts, sometimes waist high, ascending a rough slope that revealed only the tops of the pines growing on it. In no time he was heaving air in and out of his ill-used body, whilst I ascended easily, the steam of my breath dissipating in the icy air. It was a clear and sunny morning with a cobalt sky, and that would help me accomplish my purpose.

He followed along in my path, daintily avoiding what labor he could, but that was the inferior nature of the man. The last portion was a steep ascent over unknown obstacles underfoot that tripped us, but in time we arrived, blowing, atop the knob, which afforded us a breathtaking view west and north and south. It was at once brilliant and forbidding. The heavens were a bold blue, and before us lay hundreds of square miles of whitened country. In the immediate foreground was a rolling plateau, but beyond was a great range of whited peaks. Overall, the snow lay so thick that it obscured all else, so one could not tell whether forest or plain or rockslide or brush lay underneath.

It was too bright; my eyes leaked tears, which froze in my beard.

"Ah, Mister Williams," said I, "this gives us a view."

He blinked, said nothing. The glare didn't seem to affect his vision at all, and I wondered whether his eyes had dimmed with age.

"Now, sir, we can peer into the future. Where are we going?"

"I don't rightly know from this distance, but I know close at hand, as we pass by," he said.

It was not a response that gave me comfort.

"Now, where is Cochetopa Pass?"

"Oh, yonder there." He waved an arm vaguely north, toward a formidable white range.

"Is that where we're heading?"

"I got my own way."

"Well, then, kindly point it out to me."

He eyed the distant ridges to the west, which probably were the actual divide, and finally shrugged. "I'll know her when we get there," he muttered.

"This was the route you recommended because of its ease and good fodder?"

He smiled cheerfully. "Trust me or not," he said. "It's better than the other."

"What choice have I?"

He laughed, a low muttering that finally broke into an odd giggle. And yet I saw no alternative. He would lead us through, or not. Ahead of us were two or three or four days of passage over a rolling plateau, but it was snow-blanketed open country that afforded little shelter and no fodder unless we could turn the mules into a watercourse somewhere ahead.

We descended in a small avalanche, which in fact bruised my shin, and I proceeded into camp, where my old stalwarts were waiting, having watched our ascent.

"Old Bill assures me that the pass is just ahead," I said. "We have some snowy country to cross, mostly level, and then it's up and over. By Christmas, we'll be down in warm and grassy country, celebrating our deliverance."

"We lost eight mules last night," Godey said.

"And we'll lose more, I'm sure," I replied. "The hardy stock will pull through. The inferior ones will surrender."

I did not see skepticism in their faces, which was good. I've learned over the years that candor is the most excellent means to keep spirits high, and that is what was required at this crucial moment.

"Let's be off," I said.

The men cheerfully finished loading the mules. They had rebalanced the loads, making sure that as our stores diminished the burdens were lighter. Godey took the lead, having fashioned a club of deadwood that would hammer a trail for the mules, and so we proceeded down the canyon where we had harbored ourselves from the icy gale of yesterday. At the van, half a dozen good men hammered the drifts into submission. It swiftly became plain that this day we would work through snows that could well be twenty or thirty feet deep. The V-shaped trench in the soft snow soon blotted out all horizons, save for a narrow strip of blue above. We fell into a world in which the surface of the snow was above our heads, even those of us who were riding the mules.

My men rotated the trail breaking frequently, gangs of four or five slowly making progress through the morning. Scarcely did we see more than the slit of heaven, and at no time did any of us observe the vast, chilling panorama of the San Juan range. I thought it was just as well that no man caught a glimpse of the larger world. This was a mild day, with open skies, and no wind pierced into our trench to chill us. I thought in a way it was rather jolly, though some of my men were fearful of those looming walls of soft snow on either side of us.

A mule gave out, and it turned out to be Ben Kern's. He had urged it forward, only to feel the beast shiver and slowly capsize. Nothing he did could arouse it, and finally he abandoned it. He is an overly tender man but took it stoically. The remaining beasts had to step over the dead one, which they did unhappily, with ears flattened back. But in time we left our troubles behind and completed our descent, heading out on rolling plateau country, with great rounded shoulders of land driving us south and north as we kept as low as we could. The winds had swept some areas fairly clear, and sometimes we could peer over the lip of our trench upon a blank white world, a landscape without landmarks, perfectly submerged by the snows.

We made three and a half miles across that tumultuous tableland, but the plummeting sun compelled us to halt and make a dry camp on a slope. We had scrounged some deadwood and made use of it, for there was none at hand. There would be wood enough to boil some macaroni, but not enough to sustain a fire all night. It would be an unpleasant night for man and beast. I knew the sturdiest would never complain, and I heard not one word of distress. But the silent complaint rising from the mess of the greenhorns was palpable, and I could well imagine what the Kerns were scribbling in their diaries. No matter. I have learned to shrug off the mosquito droning of small men. I would set things straight in my own journals when the time came. My stalwarts soon had their rubberized sheets spread, affording them a dry place to unroll their beds, and I heard no more of trouble. I knew the night would claim more of the inferior mules, and I knew there was no help for it. Let them perish. We did not need them.

I sent Saunders to fetch Godey to me. My deputy commander appeared at once.

"Some stew?" I asked, motioning toward the kettle. Saunders had boiled some jerky and cornmeal from my private stock.

Godey shook his head.

"A few quiet words, eh?"

Godey squatted beside me, mountain style.

"How are the men, Godey?"

"Doing well, sir. I don't hear any complaints."

"What do they think of me?"

"Not a complaint, Colonel."

"Do they know who got them into this difficulty?"

Godey paused. "Old Bill eats by himself, sir. That says all that you wish to know."

"Ah, then they do know where the fault lies. Now, what about the Kerns' mess? That's where trouble will come."

"Quite valiant, Colonel. Doctor Kern was severely frostbitten last night, but he carries on without complaint."

"Yes, but what do they really think?"

Godey eyed me and finally shook his head. I didn't know how to interpret that but let it pass.

"Soft men are a burden to me, Alex."

"I think Doctor Kern would like to save the mules. He headed for the creek and pushed snow aside until he opened up some brush, and pushed a mule into it."

"They're poor stock. We're better off eating them."

"We've lost twenty some and haven't butchered one, sir."

"Choose the weakest," I replied.

I dismissed Godey and watched him hurry into the darkness. He was my most reliable man.

A cruel north wind arose in the night, probing once again into men's bedrolls, ruining hope as well as comfort. My men were already badly frostbitten, with patches of white flesh on their hands and feet, their ears and noses and chins. They had endured these things stoically, as I did, but this night of December 16 seemed to herald a shift in the weather. We awoke to a sullen sky, as dark as the underside of a skillet, with polar air gliding relentlessly past us. Godey lumbered out into the snowfields and came back with the count. Another eight down, but several more so stupid with cold he doubted they could survive another hour.

"Butcher one," I said. It was easy enough to butcher a live and warm animal, and I thought to take advantage of it. He nodded and summoned Sorel, who selected an animal that was barely standing and slit its throat with one sweep of his Green River knife, and we watched the beast sag into the snow with a final spasm as blood gouted from its throat. The butchering was left to the Creoles, who seemed to have a knack for it, and soon they were peeling back hide and slicing skinny loins and rib roasts from the half-starved beast. I wondered whether there would be meat enough to feed thirty-three men one meal.

The rest watched silently. It was so cold that the Creoles had to work swiftly, and soon their hands were covered with frozen red slush. Not even stuffing them under their coats or into their armpits helped much, but in time they did crudely butcher perhaps a hundred pounds of stringy meat and load the freezing red meat into panniers. The head of the mule, now severed from its body, was half buried in snow, its sightless eyes staring at nothing and its sliced-off tongue an open wound between its jaws. It would go hungry no more, and I had done it a favor.

CHAPTER TWENTY

Henry King

I was settling a blanket and a sawbuck on a mule when I spotted Colonel Frémont and Old Bill struggle up to that knob. I thought I knew what that was all about. I grinned and nudged Godey, who was overseeing the loading.

He winked. Pretty soon the rest of the colonel's men were observing the two climbers who were stumbling up that snowy grade. Old Bill could hardly keep up with the colonel. I nodded slightly to Breckenridge, who in turn nudged Scott, Bacon, and Beadle, and that caught the attention of Ferguson, Hubbard, and Carver. Pretty quickly, most of the colonel's veterans were staring up that slope, plainly entertained by the sight.

"Colonel's heading up there to get the Ten Commandments," Ferguson said.

"No he isn't. He's going up there to give God ten or twelve commandments," Hubbard said.

"Saddle those mules," Godey said, but no one paid the slightest heed.

Frémont and Old Bill Williams reached the crown of that knob and began an animated conversation or maybe a dispute, with plenty of arm waving.

"I guess I know what's being said," I announced.

"Maybe you don't," Tom Martin retorted.

"That old coward Williams, he's calling it quits, and he's telling the colonel to turn around and head back the way we came," I said.

"Could be, but I'd suppose they're just looking at the way west. All this snow, it gets hard to see what's what."

"I've been watching that Williams," I said, reaching for the girth that Martin was handing me under the mule's belly. "You know what he is? A loafer. He hasn't done a lick of work, but that's not what's galling me. He don't know the way, and he's pretending he does, and now the colonel's seen right through him and giving him what for."

"I think he wants the colonel to turn around," Joseph Stepperfeldt said from behind the next mule over. "He's half-crazy. He told me once he can see animal spirits. Maybe the mule spirits are telling him to turn around." He laughed. It was a good joke.

I tightened the girth and buckled it. Martin began lifting panniers onto the trembling mule, who stood with locked legs, head low. They were all like that. They had gone three days without a meal, apart from a few twigs.

The wind was howling again, and cirrus clouds ribbed the sky. It would be snowing soon. It entertained me. I'm always wondering how bad it can get.

"I'd bet my last dollar we'll move ahead," I said.

"Of course," Martin said. "The colonel's commanding. There's not one soul over him now that he's out of the army. There is no one to say nay."

I hadn't thought of it that way, but I saw the truth in it. I'd always seen the colonel as a man who let nothing stop him. Our gentlemanly commander would take orders from no one, not even God. And he would succeed in his design, even if he left the entire company behind him. I have the same nature. We were going to go over these mountains no matter what the cost, and that was already decided. We were going to do what no others could do. The Conqueror of California would conquer the San Juan Mountains.

"He's got him a wife waiting out in California," Martin said. "If I had me a wife, maybe I'd be in a hurry, too."

I smiled. "Mine's back East, but you don't see me hightailing it out of here."

"It ain't a wife that's itching old Frémont," said Breckenridge. "He's got some other kind of itch."

No one had a reply to that.

Iron-bellied clouds were scudding in, and we faced another mean day. Breckenridge noticed the clouds, too. "Don't know where we'll be spending Christmas," he said.

"We'll have a feast. Mule-meat pudding, with mule soup," I replied.

He eyed the trembling mules, who stood lock legged with the packs on their backs. "It'd do them a favor," Breckenridge said. "What's the new missus going to do this Christmas, Henry?"

"Pine for me," I replied.

"Like you're pining for her, eh?" Breckenridge retorted.

I laughed. A gust of air wormed through my buckskin coat. I was already frostbit in half a dozen places, two fingers, my earlobes, and there was plenty of dead flesh around my ankles too. "She's not frostbit," I said. "She's with her parents, I imagine."

A burdened mule shivered and slowly buckled, slowly collapsing, resisting its own weakness to the last, but it went down in the snow, half-buried even as it shuddered and died.

"I suppose we ought to butcher him," I said. "I'll ask Godey."

I found the headman loading a trembling mule.

"We just lost one. You think we should butcher before he freezes up?"

"Leave him. We'll butcher another tonight," Godey said.

So Breckenridge and I tugged the packs off the dead one. It was hard work, and I kept feeling I wasn't up to my usual. Sometimes I felt plumb faint. Half the men felt the way I did. Maybe it was altitude, or bad food. We hadn't seen a green in weeks. But some of the company didn't seem affected at all. Preuss, the wiry German, seemed the way he always was, furiously measuring everything, getting the height of every peak in sight, making pencil sketches and notes, and ignoring every hardship. But others, like that Scot, Cathcart, seemed to shrink down every day, and now he was parchment over bones and had great hollow sockets around his eyes. You never knew about those foreigners, whether they could take it.

A fresh gust of bitter air boiled past us, firing pellets of ice into our beards.

"Goddamn the wind," Martin snapped.

I had rarely heard oathing in this company. The colonel's utterances were free of it, and there was an unspoken rule that the rest of us would follow his example. But the colonel was up on that knoll, talking things over with the rotten guide.

I felt the slivers of ice melt in my beard, work down, and then freeze. This would be another day of icicles hanging from our beards and hair.

About then, Frémont and Old Bill skidded and tumbled down that knoll, barely remaining upright. Frémont surveyed the company, the loaded mules, the newly dead one.

"On our way," he said. "We'll walk."

Some of the company seemed irritated by the command and reluctantly slid off their wretched animals. But it was a valuable request. By now the outliers of the approaching storm were overhead, and the wintry sun vanished behind an iron overcast. The trail beaters once again hacked our way westward, this time through windswept country that harbored only two or three feet of snow on the level. The wind jammed so much drift into our faces and eyes we couldn't tell what was descending from the clouds and what was being lifted by the gusts.

It took the heat right out of me, even though I was walking, and I knew ere long I'd be frostbit again and again, and this would be a hard day. I wondered if a man could get frostbit in the privates. What would that do to me? Now that was something to think about. I thought I'd ask Ben Kern about it, not that a greenhorn would know anything. There sure are places a man doesn't want to get himself frostbit, especially me. I've sure got an itch to get to California with all my parts ready and willing.

We rotated the trail breaking, three at a time. When my turn came, I found myself with Stepperfeldt and Ferguson, each of us armed with a deadwood club, which we used to break through the skin of the drifts, hammer down a wide-enough trail to pose no obstacle to the weary mules. Usually I didn't mind the work. It was a way of keeping warm, keeping the blood up, but now a mysterious lassitude gripped me, and it was all I could do to lift the deadwood, smash through snow, and lift it again. And instead of getting warmer, I found myself getting so chilled I thought to find my bedroll and wrap myself. Not that blankets would do much in a wind like that.

So, step by step, we proceeded on. I was glad when Godey sent our relief forward, and I turned over my driftwood snow club and waited for the train to catch up. The rest were a long time coming, and I could see why. The mules were quitting, and even the efforts of several men tugging and shoving couldn't get them to move. So time was flying by and the company was stalled, right in the first foothills on the far side of that plateau. There wasn't a mule that would climb up that trail.

Godey shouted a few things, his voice lost in the wind, and I watched as the company stripped the packs off the mules, tied ropes to the panniers, and began skidding them forward. Even then the mules had to be yanked and shoved, but now the company was struggling up slopes again. I watched Preuss wrestle two panniers up the icy slope, his precious instruments in them. He would not allow anyone to touch the packs and was uncommonly careful whenever he came to a hump or a protruding rock. Well, I didn't blame him one particle. Tough old bird, doing what had to be done. We all protect our jewels.

Godey handed me a rope, but I was so worn from beating a trail I didn't have the strength to drag a pack. But I did. There was no help for it. Drag a pack or give up. Quit. Sit down in the snow and die. And I was damned if I would do that and let them think I didn't have the temper in me. So I learned to drag for twenty yards, pause a while, and go another few yards, and pause, and let my heart settle down.

The snow fell now, driven by the gusts, but these were thick flakes, and in moments they were filling the trench the beaters had pounded up that slope. More mules quit. They would stop, tremble, and slowly collapse into the snow, and we would leave them there. In two minutes they were buried by snow, just a white lump blocking our snow road.

There went more dinner, I thought. Mule meat wasn't much for eating, and the mules were down to bone anyway. But we managed, mostly by cutting the meat up fine and boiling it to a sort of mush. Some of the messes tried slicing it thin and roasting, but it was like eating leather, and pretty soon we were all eating mule stew, mule mush, mule soup, because that was the only way we could get any mule into our innards.

But now we were running through mules in a hurry, and I wondered what we would be eating in a week. I'd heard that Frémont had put aside some frozen elk for Christmas dinner a few days before, and I supposed that would be mighty fine, if we got as far as

Christmas. The way things were going, I didn't know whether we'd make one more day or not.

I'd heard there were some Mexican settlements down the Rio del Norte, but that was some piece away, and that wasn't the direction the colonel was heading. He'd gotten his compass set on west, and west was how he'd go. California or bust. He was stubborn, I'll grant that. That's what I liked about him. There's a type of man who won't quit, and he'd rather die trying. That's what I am.

We didn't make much progress, and by afternoon, with the peril of darkness drawing nigh, the colonel halted us on a slope in a pine forest where deadwood abounded and there would be some shelter from the gale. We had lost mules all day; an animal would simply quit, stand stock-still, and slowly fold into the snow. I surveyed the new camp hopefully and did see some grass on an exposed southerly slope, and I hoped we could put the mules onto it, even though we would have to beat a path through perilous slopes to reach it. Some weary men started at once, while the rest of us collected deadwood and tried to save the mules by rubbing them. The mules either stood inertly, an inch from death, or sought blankets and ropes and leather to eat, making life difficult for us because there was little they would not gnaw on, including what was left of our tents and clothing and tack.

I watched the Creoles slit the throat of the weakest of the living mules, watched it sag into the snow, blood gouting from its neck. They set upon the animal before it was entirely dead. We would have mule stew this night, and mule hide with which to fashion patches for our ruined boots. The prospect offered me no comfort.

Somehow, we made camp and got some fires going in protected snow pits where the wind would not snuff them. The snow had diminished, but the heavens scowled at us, and I had the sense we were trespassers, invaders of a place sacred to others, where no mortal should pass by. I got from gossip that ahead, at the top of a bald hill, one would only find more of the same, no relief in any direction.

The men were all done in. I had thought myself alone in my weakness, but now I saw horror everywhere, men so skeletal and worn they seemed half alive. The sole exception was the colonel, who was calmly erecting his tent, scraping snow away, building a private fire—he always camped apart from the rest of us—and making himself comfortable. I could not fathom it. He had pulled away from us for several days, rarely saying a word to any of us, and never a word of encouragement. It was as if he were indifferent to our fate, or maybe he simply felt helpless to change anything or admit to a mistake or terrible judgment. And if pride stopped him from changing course, his fate was our own, for there was nothing we could do about any of it.

We did get a few of the mules over to that grassy slope, but most could not be budged and stood mutely near our mess fires, waiting to die. I imagined that within a day or so, not a one would be standing. The question that had us all brooding now was whether any of us would soon be standing.

CHAPTER TWENTY-ONE

Benjamin Kern, MD

White on white on white. We called it Camp Dismal, but that understates the case. We huddled on the north slope of a great bald mountain at around eleven thousand feet, in a deluge of snow that lasted for days. There was only misery and foreboding.

We settled in some vast depth of snow, whiteness so deep we could see only the tops of trees, making them seem like needle-bearing shrubs. But below us, buried in snow, were scrub pines, all that grew at this altitude. We could not pitch a tent, for there was no ground under us to take the stakes, so we erected huts of deadwood and canvas, and that was all the shelter we could manage. Each mess managed to build a fire in a pit, which allayed the wind slightly but added smoke to our misery and did little to warm our numb flesh.

Now, at last, we could go no further. We were walled by white, by endless snow falling upon us, a foot or two or three a day. We could neither retreat from the bald mountain nor push forward, so we were trapped there. Preuss led a small party westward, intending to find a way down, but not even that wiry, hardy man, a veteran of Frémont's earlier campaigns, could manage it, and in time he retreated to our camp, where we all sat helplessly, awaiting our fate with each tick of the clock.

Snow engulfed our messes, and we could scarcely find firewood to keep a blaze going in all that stinging white downfall. The misery was compounded by the wetness of our clothing, which permeated every layer of our wool and leather and rendered us so miserable that we wondered how we might endure yet another minute of another hour of another day. We could not dry ourselves or our clothing in that constant blizzard.

We scraped away snow with our tin mess plates, struggled into the treetops to hack at limbs for the fire, retreated into our huts chilled and soaked, our beards dangling icicles, our eyes smarting from the smoke. And lost from us was hope, for the extent of our horizon was a white wall blotting out even the closest scenery, so that all we had before our watering eyes was ten or fifteen feet of whiteness.

But that was only one facet of the horror. Through this whole white nightmare, we heard the piteous whickering of the dying mules, summoning one another for help, telling one another they were departing. I swear, all that first night, the mules we had managed to drive to that windswept dome where a little grass broke through wailed miserably. I swear what I heard was sobbing, the weeping of the mules as they trumpeted their distress to one another, and then the heavy silence that overtook them in the night. I knew they were gone. I knew that the murderous wind had clubbed them senseless, even as they frantically pawed and dug for the thin brown strands of grass that might sustain them in kinder climates.

Thus did the ghastly night pass, and in the gray light of dawn, after we had scraped away new feet of snow with our mess plates, we searched for them and saw none standing on that slope. They had vanished, and we could not find their carcasses even if we had tried with a pole, for merciless nature had mercifully hidden them from our eyes under a white blanket. Yet a few still stood in the woods, protected from the wind, a foot of snow on their backs, icicles dangling from their every hair, rattling under their jaws. Old Bill Williams swore he could see their spirits hovering over them, waiting to fly away, but I could never fathom such a thing. I knew only what my medical training and senses told me: their body temperatures barely sustained life. They had not eaten for days and were surviving on the last of the fat they carried. They were too weak to walk, much less plow through drifts as high as they were. But those few lived, if only for the moment.

At some of the other messes, live mules were being slaughtered. I would hear one last pitiful bleat, and then the thud of an animal capsizing. But it was odd. These messes never dressed out the entire carcass, making the most of it. Those men were as worn as we were, numbed by cold, struggling for breath in the thin air, and soon the slaughtered and mostly intact mule was blanketed by merciful snow. The last mules were simply targets of opportunity and were not systematically butchered to give us as much meat as possible. I had come to love those mules, knew many of them well, and could hardly bear to see them tumble, never to rise again.

I sat mutely as the sun rose and set somewhere above the gray blanket of clouds, too stupefied to write a thing. I'm not sure my numb fingers would have enabled me to write. I didn't have anything to say. Richard managed a few words. I saw him laboriously scribbling some little thing in his bound ledger, probably thinking what I was thinking: those who found us in the distant future would at least have an account of our last hours.

I confess I gave little thought to what transpired elsewhere, in the other messes. We were all wrapped in our misery. But some distance away—it seemed miles away but it was only a few dozen yards, Colonel Frémont was making his own plans. His object, I was soon to learn, was to move our camp from this exposed north shoulder of the bald mountain to the southern side, where we might escape the wind, find forage and a shred of warmth. It was not a bad plan except that without capable mules, we would need to drag our worldly goods to the new locale by brute force, mostly along a snow path of our devising. He sent some of our stronger men to break a trail, and soon we found ourselves slowly dragging panniers and tack over the powdery snow, pausing every little way for breath in the thin air, hoping the ongoing storm would not close in and blind us or strand us. This wretched task consumed two days, and even after that we would need to return to Camp Dismal for the last of the packs. I can't remember a worse time, when I felt so faint and dizzy that I thought I would topple at any time and vanish in a drift.

And yet we succeeded and found ourselves in better circumstances, out of the icy blast and able to collect a goodly supply of deadwood to feed our fires. Such mules as were still standing were scattered behind us, unable to walk the three miles, and we ended up with none at our new refuge. I knew, with heavy heart, that we were now afoot.

In all this I saw Frémont consulting with our guide, Williams, over and over, but the colonel never made me a party to his decisions, preferring to consult only with those veterans of his California expedition. He avoided those of us who were newcomers to his cadre. So I didn't know what was being discussed so ardently, and the others were too weary or breathless at that altitude to inform me. But it was mostly about topography. When we finally settled on the southwesterly slope, we were in a new drainage, which I took to be another tributary of the Rio del Norte, but one more precipitous than what we had traversed to reach this upland of the San Juans.

The brutal cold lessened, and some fragments of a coy sun

caught us up, and we heartened at the better prospect. But I soon learned through the camp grapevine that the divide, which might take us to the waters of the Colorado River, still lay many miles west. It was apparently beginning to sink into the colonel that he was nowhere near Pacific waters and his company was now stranded in high country and had only enough food to last a week or so more. We set out to consolidate the new camp and drag the last of our packs over the ridge, a task so exhausting we could manage only a little at a time. But at last we left the north-slope Camp Dismal behind.

We were more comfortable out of the wind, which lifted our spirits enough so that we could begin talking to one another again. I began to make diary entries. But despite the slight improvement, we were feeling hard used, caught on a mountain top and subject to an ambitious man's whim. Our very lives depended on Colonel Frémont's decisions. Those in my mess knew nothing of his plans.

My artist brother, Richard, wondered aloud one night while the three of us huddled in the cold under a canvas hut, whether there would be any good in escaping the company and making our way to the Mexican settlements down the Rio Grande. He seemed reluctant even to bring it up, lest it seem an act of betrayal and cowardice.

"Maybe we could gather a party and leave," he said. "Take some frozen mule meat and head down this drainage. It will take us to the river, to whatever game is along it, and to firewood and warmth."

"How would the colonel take it?" I asked.

"We don't need to give him any choice."

"We signed on," Ned said. "We gave our word."

That's what was bothering us all. We had bonded ourselves to Frémont and could not simply pull away from the company.

"None of us can hunt," Ned said.

That was one of the most telling arguments.

"We could enlist a few, maybe Micah McGehee," Richard said.

"We lack equipment. This tenting; the axes and mess ware; rifles, shot, and powder—it's all his, not ours," Ned said.

In truth, if we started off on our own, we could take only our personal gear, which didn't come to much and wouldn't help us sustain life for the long trek off the mountain and down the river. We were honorable men; whatever we did had to be done in a proper fashion.

But the speculation came to nothing. We knew we wouldn't. Frémont had some sort of hold on us I could not fathom, a hold on all of his men. It was as if the slightest resistance to his command would be betrayal and leaving the company would be treason. I could not endure it.

"We're at his beck and call," I said. "Our fate is his."

The recognition of our bondage to the colonel did not lift my spirits a bit. Those bitter hours left me feeling trapped and helpless, as if there was not a thing I could do, out of my own free will, to mitigate or avoid the impending disaster. I was yet a greenhorn and ought not to be forming judgments, but I could not help but feel that something in Frémont's nature was leading us straight toward our own doom, and he was not quite right.

"I don't trust him," Richard said.

"I do. I was with him in California, and he was splendid," Edward said.

"All his veterans think so," I said.

Through all this misery I had not heard a word, not a hint, of antagonism or even skepticism about Frémont in the company. It had become a phenomenon that caught my attention. How could a commander, and a civilian one at that, win such total devotion and obedience? I had never seen the like. I had never been in a company so devoid of grumbling. I had never been in a schoolyard or in a town meeting or at a party without some sharp-tongued criticism of some leader or politician or magistrate. The more I studied on it, the more puzzled I became. Something about Frémont was either miraculous or horrifying. The only clue I had was a sense that he was really indifferent to all of us, and if he had no great affection for us, it didn't matter a bit to him what we thought. His perpetual calm was not the mark of a quiet nature, but it reflected his utter indifference to all but himself. Was that the source of his strange power over us?

I knew I wasn't alone in my brooding. But there was little time for it. We were trapped on a mountaintop, Christmas was nigh, we did not know from hour to hour what our fate might be, and our food supply was swiftly diminishing. I heard that we still had some packs of macaroni, some sugar, a little cornmeal, salt, and a few odds and ends. And I had heard rumors that Frémont had put aside some frozen elk meat, which he intended to give us at Christmas.

And there was still mule meat, at least if we were willing to dig through several feet of snow, dig out the carcass, and hack at the frozen animal. During this entire pre-Christmas sojourn on the mountaintop, I had seen no more living mules. Now they were all ghostly remains, white lumps swiftly vanishing in the almost daily snow showers, and it would not be long before we would find no carcasses at all because there would be six or ten or twenty feet of snow over them. If any lived, it would be a miracle.

I found Bill Williams and remembered his peculiar brag that he could see animal spirits.

"Are all the mules gone?" I asked.

"Ever' blessed one," he replied. "I watched them go. I watched them hover above each of them mules, and then slide away."

"How do you know that?"

"Why, Kern, I did sure enough see their spirits fly up into the sky, fly with one sad look back, and vanish up yonder, into the mysterious."

"How can you be sure, Mister Williams?"

"Mister Williams, is it? That's a doctor for you. I'm Old Bill, a renegade preacher that went Indian, and anyone calls me mister's no friend of mine."

I retreated a little, but I did want to know what he saw.

"What do animal spirits look like?"

"How can I tell you that? Like nothing you'd ever see."

"Human spirits, too?"

He clammed up fast. "Ain't saying," he said.

"Are any of our spirits hovering above us?"

"Listen here, you go back to your powders, and I'll just git some firewood, understand?"

Rebuffed, I did. I continued on my way. I also sensed that his occult gifts had somehow given him a foreknowledge of what our fates might be, and his sudden silence about that filled me with unspeakable dread.

CHAPTER TWENTY-TWO

Captain Andrew Cathcart

They called this place Camp Hope because Frémont had announced that he would send a relief party to the Mexican settlements. We had dragged most of the packs over the saddle to the southerly drainage in two days, but even on Christmas Day a few men were trailing the three miles between camps. Ben and Richard Kern were among them and reported seeing two or three surviving mules at Camp Dismal, miserably awaiting their fate.

So much for Williams's claims about seeing spirits, I thought.

Alexis Godey became *chef de cuisine* on Christmas Day, preparing a wondrous feast, given the paucity of our stores. We did enjoy the elk that the colonel had set aside, along with minced mule pies that reminded me of haggis. Godey spread remarkable cheer through the camp, wandering from one mess to another. These were located in snow holes so deep we could not see the neighboring messes or the men at them.

But the good cheer was a damnable fraud. There was not a man among us who did not wonder whether this would be his last Christmas or whether we would ever get off that mountain. The cheer was an artifice, a sweet jam spread over the stark reality of our circumstances. The truth was that this company of scarecrows sat on a mountaintop a hundred miles from the nearest settlement and was running out of food. Its men were weakened by altitude, cold, and poor diet, for none of us could eat enough to replace what was burned away in our labors. We were shod in decrepit boots that shipped snow with every step. Such mules as might still be alive at Camp Dismal were useless.

I kept my thoughts to myself, not wanting to be unseemly. I also didn't want to spoil such miserable pleasures as the men might find on that Christmas Day. What troubled me most was that we were Frémont's prisoners. He held our fates in his hand. And now, having decided to send for relief, he turned to Blackstone's commentaries, once again choosing to impress his eerie calm on us by this means, rather than take an active hand in overcoming the crisis. I was not impressed. I could see that his regulars, those veterans of the previous expeditions, were awed. There Frémont was, reading a law book, while the rest of us wondered whether on the morrow or the next day or the day after that, we might perish.

I both admired and loathed the man, and I itched to make my feelings known but chose instead to honor the birth of the Prince of Peace. I wanted to find the good in the man, but I could not bring myself to it. I wanted to seek peace on earth that Christmas and give Frémont my peace, but it was beyond me. At least I could bury my private thoughts behind a wall of holiday cheer. I had always kept my feelings to myself. I kept to myself in the Queen's hussars, and I would in this place and among these Yankees, no matter how I might seethe inside. Let other men whine; Captain Cathcart would not. By God, I was a Queen's man and I would act like it.

It was a cheery camp, with ample deadwood to feed our fires and good elk steaks to fill our bellies, cut from a frozen haunch the colonel had kept for this moment. It seemed luxurious after the hardships we had endured. But I could only think of those dead mules, whose ghosts would celebrate no Christmas ever. This was an odd sentiment in a born hunter, but it gripped me as I stood there, studying our distant and bland leader who was poring over his law texts in the most theatrical manner he could manage.

He deigned to join us when Godey had the elk roast well seared and sliced for us, and I watched him slowly put the ribbon betwixt the pages and close his leathern volume, smile benevolently at his underlings, and drift toward the nearest mess, Godey's own, where Frémont's manservant, Jackson Saunders, and Godey's young nephew, Theodore McNabb, made their home. With a soft wave of his bare hand, he summoned us. We gradually collected there, around that snow pit where Godey and his nephew were cooking meat.

Frémont stood at the far edge, smiling, scarcely bothering to bundle up. His veins ran ice water, and one rarely saw him smothered in leather and fur and wool.

"We'll take a little detour from the thirty-eighth parallel," he said.

The very idea of it startled me. Was this man still thinking of a rail line over the 38th parallel? And not about his weakened men, his dwindling food, his lost mules, his perilous camp?

"We're not far, actually, from whatever help we may need. Our friend Bill Williams tells me help is available down the Rio Grande, not more than a hundred miles distant, and most of that downslope and over flat river bottoms, which should be full of game. We'll need to reach lower altitudes where we may find game, and tomorrow we'll begin. I'm sending a relief party to the Mexicans at Abiquiu on the Chama River, and the relief party can also continue to Taos on the Rio Grande if more help is needed. I'll appoint Henry King its commander, and he will be accompanied by Frederick Creutzfeldt, Tom Breckenridge, and our guide, Bill Williams. I'm also sending Godey partway, to find a way down the mountain for us. While this takes place, we will begin moving downslope by stages. In short, we'll be moving toward the relief party that will be coming for us."

So the obsessed colonel had finally decided to do something. It seemed sensible enough.

This was indeed a Christmas gift. I looked at the colonel benignly and thought maybe even a testy old Cathcart could endure the man.

They debated how long it would take for the relief party to reach the settlements and return with mules and supplies. It seemed no great trip, and Old Bill Williams supposed it might take four days, and then the relief could be back in a dozen days, sixteen at the outside, given that the company would steadily be descending this drainage and heading into the Rio Grande Valley. It heartened the men, and they plunged into their Christmas repast with relish.

The next morning, after we had scraped away the usual six or eight inches of fresh snow with our mess plates, we prepared to break camp. But before that, we helped ready King's relief party. Frémont gave them four days of rations, enough to see them to the settlements, or so everyone thought. These consisted of a pack of macaroni and some sugar and some mule meat. There was nothing else to offer. Godey supplied himself and made sure his rifle was in good condition. He was a born hunter, and these men would descend to the river bottoms, where game might be found.

Four days, twenty-five miles a day. We watched them slide and skid down this drainage, along a nameless creek that tumbled through a steep and difficult gorge.

"All right, we'll build sledges," the colonel said, and we set about doing that, using axes to shape runners and fashion crossbars, which we lashed in place with rawhide. The progress was slowed by snow. It was no easy task to hack down limbs and shape the runners into anything we could use, but we were inspired by the knowledge that the relief had left, and we would soon follow toward safety.

I was optimistic. We would load the packs and drag them downhill without great difficulty, benefitting from the tug of gravity. Little did I know. But we toiled at that sledge-building project for days, watching our macaroni and mule meat diminish to the point that I wondered where our next meals would be coming from. Then, amazingly, the Creoles managed to drive three live mules over the saddle from Camp Dismal, and we all were heartened. The wretched mules were no good for packing, but we would have meat on the hoof.

On December 27 we set out, dragging the sledges down the creek bottom. The day was mild and we were in high spirits. But the canyon ahead was narrowing and forested right to the banks of the rushing creek. Still we kept on, believing that the relief party ahead of us was making faster time and was now probably out of the mountains and onto the great plain marking the Rio del Norte. What fools we were.

The mild weather held, and we proceeded down the drainage with little difficulty and amazing good cheer. The brooding sensation that we were at the margin left us. We were alive, had food enough, and would soon be in the Rio Grande Valley with its game. I even found myself revising my opinion of Frémont a little; not that I admired his judgment, but at least he had not plunged us over the brink, and it seemed likely that we would soon be enjoying the comforts of the New Mexicans. We made a cheerful camp that evening.

Then we encountered Godey, slogging his way up the drainage. We collected around him, eager for news. But what he imparted was entirely dismaying.

"We can't get through down there," he said. "It's a narrow canyon, choked with downed timber and boulders. You have to cross the creek a dozen times an hour. There's no other way except through this choked-up maze."

"You're saying we can't use the sledges?" Frémont asked.

"No. It's too steep, jammed with boulders, and the only passage is the creek itself in places. Sledges are worthless. And the creek drops so fast, with rapids, there would be no hanging on to packs."

We stared at one another. We were three days down a steep-sided canyon with no way out. What Godey was saying, though no one wanted to put it into words, was that we would have to retrace our steps, drag the sledges back to the top of the mountain, and find another way down—that or leave our equipment behind.

The Creoles responded first. Without a word they turned the sledges and began the weary climb that would take them toward the Christmas camp, and then over the first saddle into the next drainage.

The silence was palpable. I was determined to wrestle my way up that slope, but some of the men just wilted.

"Where are the relief men now?" Frémont asked.

"I'm not even sure they're at the bottom of that canyon. They were crawling over deadfall and rock and wading the rapids."

"They were to reach the settlements today," Frémont said.

"They're hardly on their way," Godey said.

"Did they find game?"

Godey simply smiled and shook his head.

They had a pack of macaroni to hold them. I calculated that they would take two weeks or more to reach the settlements, and food would run out long before, unless they made meat. Still, they had Williams with them. He might make meat. But why had he let them descend that morass? Did he know less about this country than he let on? It was a mystery.

I eyed Ben Kern, who was feeling poor, and wondered if he could make it up that trail. I thought maybe the altitude was weakening him. Whatever the case, he was utterly unable to drag a heavy sledge uphill.

"I'll help ye, Ben," I said.

He simply shook his head and began to drag a sledge mounded with packs up the snowy grade. I watched, worried. His every step was labored. The air was still rarefied, and he had been struggling for breath.

Round and about, the company was turning sledges around and starting the weary hike uphill, through heavy drifts. At least we had broken a trail, but if it snowed, we would be fighting our way up the mountain through massive drifts once again.

No one spoke, but I knew the cheer that had pervaded the company only minutes before had fled it, and now we were all privately pondering the odds and wondering whether fate would visit us after all.

The mild weather held, and that was a blessing. But this climb seemed longer and harder than any I had ever known in my life. Frémont strode ahead cheerfully, oblivious to the suffering behind him. What good was it to haul all this stuff? Most of it was mule tack, though scarcely a mule lived and the last of them would soon be food. He could have cached the tack, but didn't. He plainly was determined to haul it up and down the mountain to save himself the purchase of replacements later. But now we were human mules, and the halters were over our own snouts, and no one objected.

Ben Kern was so weak and gray that now and then I took hold of the cord he used to drag his sledge.

"Take a breath, Ben, and I'll keep us up," I said.

He didn't object but sat in the middle of a snowbank, his lungs rising and falling, his bluish face haggard. Still, the doctor was game, and soon enough he caught up and relieved me of my double burden.

Little by little we ascended that mountain, worn and melancholic and silent. There yet was hope. Down below, somewhere, four experienced men were working steadily toward the settlements. Frémont had entrusted King with some sum of money, the exact amount I did not know, with which to purchase whatever was needed. There would be gold to offer to the New Mexicans, and gold always spoke loudly.

We arrived in Christmas Camp and surveyed the ruin mutely, pausing only to see whether there might be anything to salvage. But such carcasses that existed had vanished under several feet of fresh snow, and we could not cut another mule steak from any.

We needed still to top the saddle to the next drainage, and we did, though I am not sure how any of us managed it. Sheer grit, I would say. Ben Kern was so gray I feared for his life. But we somehow descended to a suitable campsite and quit. We were falling behind the colonel's party, but we could go no further. It was December 30, 1848.

CHAPTER TWENTY-THREE

Benjamin Kern, MD

We were falling behind, and it was my failing. Colonel Frémont and the other messes had worked down the new drainage, finding the way easy. They were even riding their packs on the slopes and enjoying the sledding. I watched them vanish far below, around a bend where the forest projected into the creek bottoms, and then all was quiet.

It was a grand, mild winter day, the sort when the sun warms not just the flesh but the heart and soul. The winds had died away, and only gentle zephyrs played with our coats and hats that last day of 1848. I had never seen a bluer sky. A vast sea of white stretched serenely in all directions, dotted only by what seemed to be scrub forest except that what we were seeing was the needled tips of fifty-foot pines which now lay buried.

I ascribe that benevolent weather to my survival, for surely I would have perished had another storm raked us just then. My brothers, Ned and Richard, and Captain Cathcart had observed my distress. At the worst of it on the thirtieth, when we were struggling upslope and over the saddle, I gave out after a couple hundred yards and could do no more than crawl on hands and knees. They soon gathered around and lifted me up and took my packs, and slowly we worked our way up that awful incline and down. We had to go back once more to collect our rifles, but finally we were settled in a pleasant woods. The next day, the last of the year, was much better. The sun, while making only a brief appearance because of the towering cliffs to either side of us, warmed the air, and we walked and tumbled down the watercourse, enjoying ourselves. And yet Frémont's main party continued to gain ground on us, and all we saw was the swath of disturbed snow marking the colonel's passage.

We were joined by two of the three California Indian boys Frémont was returning to their people, Manuel and Joaquin, whose cheerful countenances added to our levity. Ned and Richard were especially solicitous of me, asking often if I was doing well. In truth, I was feeling a bit better, and the lower altitude was helping me along. My heart was not so labored as it had been during the climb to the saddle.

I am a worrier by nature, and the deepening distance between ourselves and Frémont troubled me. We knew of his passage only by what the snow told us. Still, I am a man of faith, and I assured myself that soon the colonel would send for news of us and make sure we were not in trouble.

"I'm sorry I'm holding us back," I said to Cathcart at one point while we were resting in afternoon sun, which playfully warmed my face.

"We're doing better than they are," he said. "Gaining strength as we go."

We reached the colonel's previous camp that New Year's Eve and found that it offered exactly what we needed: ample firewood, level ground, shelter from the night wind offered by coppery cliffs, and the comfort of sun-warmed rock. Best of all, there were only two feet of snow. So we settled there, knowing the main party would now be several miles down the slope. I looked for messages for us, hoping for instruction from the colonel, but saw none. Perhaps it was a compliment. He was assuming we were fit and able and would find our way as well as we could. But any sort of message stuck in an obvious place would have comforted me.

Ned and Richard were in a gay mood and soon built a warming fire and prepared a comfortable hutch out of limbs and tenting for me. We had rubber ground cloths to keep the wetness from creeping into our bedding at night, and these proved once again to be among the most valuable of Colonel Frémont's provisions. When I examined Cathcart with a medical eye, I was certain he was sicker than I but concealing it. He was down to a skeleton. His face was so drawn that his eyes bulged. It was not just that we didn't eat enough; it was not proper food for good health, and no matter how much mule meat we demolished, it didn't renew us.

We would have mule haunch that night. The colonel had seen to it that all the messes got the last of the meat, and we had received enough to feed us that festive evening and New Year's Day as well. Ned minced the mule meat, which was by far the best way to cope with that stringy stuff, and added macaroni and baked some minced-meat pies for our celebration, which we consumed with gusto. It seemed a grand feast, and for once I was full up, warm, and content as the last light faded and we plunged into the night that would bring us to the new year.

We explained to the Indian boys what all this was about, and they grinned back. I am not certain how much of it they mastered, but it mattered not. They were soon joining us as we sang a few old favorites, and then we crawled into comfortable bedrolls content.

New Year's Day was much like the previous one, mild and quiet. We broke camp after eating the last of the minced-mule pies and dragged our packs down that long slope, which at times became precipitous. But we never lost control, and eventually we reached another of the colonel's camps, this time at the confluence of a creek. This too had little snow. We had passed gulches where snow lay a hundred feet deep or more, burying tall pines. But now, well down the mountain, the snow was thin. We had made steady progress but were uncommonly tired, and I knew I needed rest. There were more worries to trouble me, the worst being that we were now at the very gates of starvation.

"I wish I had a mousetrap. A few mice would look good to me now," I remarked to Captain Cathcart.

"We're not far from the colonel and the rest," he replied.

"They may be worse off than we are."

"They have excellent hunters."

"You're a fine hunter, Captain."

"There would be no game here, not after twenty men passed through. And we're still miles from the San Juan Valley."

That was true. The whole descent from the mountaintop to the valley was eight miles, but in our enfeebled estate it seemed three times farther. This, too, was a pleasant camp, and Richard sketched it. He had somehow sketched through the entire journey, carefully placing each sketch, carefully labeled, in his portfolio.

I was feeling cautiously optimistic in spite of the grave want of food. The relief party would be closing in on the Chama River settlement by now and would soon be back with provisions and pack animals. Still, I began wracking my head, wondering what we might eat from nature if we had to. We had descended to an area of brush, where there might be rose hips, and perhaps we could find trout in the stream or pine nuts, a famous staple of the local tribes. It might be that Manuel and Joaquin could help us with that. We had but a little macaroni, and our trusty rifles if we could shoot most anything that flew. And that was a real possibility. The lower we descended, the more crows and hawks we spotted. But my eyesight was poor now. Bad food and snow blindness had taken their toll, leaving me blurry eyed. I was hoping Cathcart, a fine shot, was in better condition.

"Are your eyes good?" I asked him.

"I can't see a bloody thing," he growled.

Only Richard's eyes were unaffected, and he could barely manage a rifle. It was a fix I had not anticipated.

The second day of January we struggled once again down the drainage, but we were about done in. The packs were too heavy. Sadly, we went through our books and journals, saving only what was absolutely essential and burning the rest. I had ceased writing daily entries in my journal and couldn't say why. Some of those evenings when we were high up the mountain, I lacked the strength even to put a few sentences down, but there was more to it. I had intended from the start to record only those things I would not hesitate to make public someday. Then the day came when every thought in my head was a private one, so I wrote nothing. I had been observing our leader for a long while and realized one day that I did not wish to record the true nature of my thoughts of Colonel Frémont's character. And the worse our condition, the less I felt like writing. But both Edward and Richard pursued their journals, managing to take a moment each day, even now, no matter how exhausted they were. Their journals would be worth something someday; mine, poor dishonest thing, would not. But I didn't discard it, and I included it in the bundle we were putting together to drag over snow to the next camp.

I watched the pages of a botany text darken, curl, and burn.

"There goes my only plant guide," I said.

The weakening of our bodies was insidious. We discovered we lacked the strength to carry all our truck in one trip, so we started down the broad valley, knowing we would have to come back. The day was warm and sunny, but I was dispirited, and so were the rest. We were all diminished by the constant hardship and miserable food. I couldn't remember when last I had some greens. We kept our rifles at the ready, knowing what a folly that was, but the thought of game gave us a thin thread of hope.

At the next campsite we found ample evidence that the colonel's whole party had spent the night. A fire still smouldered. Not all the deadwood had been used up. It was a fine place, a level flat where two streams joined, with abundant wood and plenty of shelter and not enough snow to trouble us. But we were still behind the colonel's party and feeling more and more isolated. We began unburdening ourselves of our packs, and Richard began constructing a shelter, because we had seen mare's tails across the sky and knew another white fury would soon descend on us.

He stayed in the new camp to build us a shelter and collect wood and tend the fire, while Captain Cathcart and I and the Indian lads struggled back to the old camp, which was at a much higher elevation. There were more packs to drag down, packs we could not abandon. But none of them contained food. The others were soon ahead of me, and I found myself giving out. I hadn't gone but a quarter of a mile upslope when I lost the rest of my strength and toppled into the snow. I felt my heart labor, and my muscles quit me, and I lacked the strength to get up. I would have to retreat to the lower camp but didn't know how. I rested until the chill of the snow had worked through my rags, and then began to crawl on hands and knees, a little at a time, grateful that I did not have to cope with a drift. The trail was well worn. I continued in that fashion, resting when I had to, until I reached the lower camp. Richard spotted me, helped me up, and dragged me into the pine-bough hut he was building. I was soon lying on the rubberized canvas, feeling my heart and lungs labor.

"I wore out," I said.

He glanced sharply at me. "We'll stay here," he said.

He was adding boughs, which formed a sort of thatch, and helped make the hut tight against the wind. There would be little snow filtering through all that. The wavering fire threw heat into it, and I lay comfortably, but too worn to go on. I thought maybe the mountains would claim me after all, but I would make a fight of it.

"Richard, take my journal with you tomorrow. It's all that's left of me."

He turned. "Ben, don't talk like that."

"I quit writing in it a few days ago."

"You and your journal are both coming along with us tomorrow," he said.

The next evening we were delighted to welcome Raphael Proue to our humble camp. Proue was the oldest of the Creoles with Frémont and was clearly worn to the bone backtracking from the main party to our camp.

"I bring this," he said, unloading a heavy burlap sack.

We clustered around and found frozen haunches of meat, cornmeal, and coffee.

"Dis here, it's buffalo the Colonel saves and pork and buffalo fat and some meal, eh?"

"His private stores. I didn't know he had any," Richard said.

We were amazed. Where had this provender come from? I stared at the food as if it were gold. The very sight of it sent a wave of strength and energy through me.

"You're worn out, Raphael. Sit with us," Ned said. He knew Proue from the time they both served together.

"I do dat," Proue said. "I got no strength left, not any."

He dropped heavily onto the rubberized tarpaulin before the fire.

"It's gonna snow," he added. "You got some good hiding place here."

We soon were pumping Proue for news. Had the relief party returned? Were food and mules coming, as everyone hoped?"

"They aren't far ahead of us. We can tell, maybe day or two. Dunno what slowed them down, but they aren't doing good."

No relief in sight. That was discouraging.

"The colonel, he's got a place picked out to cache the stuff. Down from here five, six miles. He says we gonna cache everything we can, and then wait. He's gonna take a bunch and head for the settlements himself and leave old Vincenthaler in charge, and after the cache we should maybe keep on going. Good hunting maybe."

I hardly knew Lorenzo Vincenthaler, but I knew he had been with Frémont's California expedition and had served in the army during the Mexican War. He had been so quiet that I scarcely had visited with him, and the only impression I had of him was that he was a stickler for rules and wanted to do everything by the book. Well, I thought, that was an odd choice, but it would be alright.

Proue stayed the night, and we fed him from the fresh provisions he had brought. He looked worn, but so did we all. I was a ghost of the man I had been only weeks before. Captain Cathcart was down to bones, and his clothing flapped on him. My brothers were a little better, but looking gaunt. And the Indian boys were down to ribs. But Proue alarmed me. When he started downriver the next morning, he staggered his way along the trail and staggered his way out of sight.

CHAPTER TWENTY-FOUR

Alexis Godey

When we reached the foothills bordering the San Juan Valley, with the Rio Grande winding through it, Colonel Frémont summoned me.

"We need to cache everything," he said. "There's a cave up La Garita Creek a bit; you probably noticed it. That's where we'll stow our goods."

He smiled amiably.

"Everything, Colonel?"

"Why, yes. My goods are scattered clear up the mountains, and now we'll cache them while we await the relief party."

That was a, how to say it?—formidable—order. There were packs and gear scattered for miles over our downhill route, most of it mule tack and saddles. It made no sense to collect all this useless gear, and I eyed my leader sharply before I surrendered. "Oui, I'll begin at once, Colonel."

"I knew you would," he said. "We'll set up camp under the cliffs there."

He had chosen a sheltered notch on the west edge of the Rio del Norte Valley, a place where there were trees and cliffs to supply some comfort. But to the east, there was nothing but arid plains. Not a tree to stop the wind or supply fuel.

"I'll put the company to it. They're as scattered as the packs."

He smiled, yawned, and walked away.

I corralled various of my best men. "We'll be caching the colonel's equipment in that cave we passed. And that means we'll be heading up the creek, maybe clear to Groundhog Creek, where the Kerns probably are."

They were game but not happy. Every one of them looked worn and ragged. While the colonel and his manservant set about making the new camp, my men and I began the long trek into the mountains again. Fortunately the drainage was wide and the way was easy. But we were trumped by the weather. The warm interlude between Christmas and New Year's Day had passed, and now a bitter wind howled out of the north, weakening and dispiriting all of us. It stung our cheeks, as if our beards weren't even there. Nonetheless, there was a task the colonel wanted done, so we set out to do it. I would do it, as required, but I wondered why. I could not fathom why Frémont had such a grip on me.

We examined the shallow cave in the point of rocks and decided it would do. The colonel had a good eye. But that abandoned gear stretching miles up the trail darkened our mood. I heard no man complain. No one had ever complained about Colonel Frémont, at least in my presence. The question in my mind was whether to obey his command or not. Was the colonel mad? Did he have any grasp of how worn to nothing his men were? I did not give the order I ached to give, by which I would relieve these desperate men of this foolish mission. So we proceeded up the mountain once again.

We hiked up the drainage, step by step. Whenever we found some of the seventy-pound packs, we sent a man or two back with them, while the rest of us continued up the valley. When Preuss and I reached the Kerns' camp we discovered them lying mutely in their blankets, their fire dead. They were in a bad way. Wordlessly, the German and I started their fire going and got some deadwood together and revived their spirits.

"We're collecting the packs," I said. "When you can, work your way down to the colonel's camp. He's on the near edge of the San Juan Valley at the foot of this drainage. Bring what you can."

Ned Kern had revived the most with the fire blazing. "We'll be there. Have you any food?"

I shook my head. What little I had of macaroni and sugar had to go to the men hauling the colonel's instruments and tack and bedding. "You're on your own," I said. "But keep warm. It's the cold that does a man in, not hunger."

Ned nodded. He was the one veteran among them and had been with the colonel in California, but I could see he was the most disheartened.

"Ned, I'm appointing you to keep your brothers and Captain Cathcart warm, and the Indian boys, too. I'll have Micah McGehee keep an eye on you."

The bright fire seemed to pump life into those wretches in Richard Kern's hut, and that was the best I could do. I nodded to my men, and we plodded up again, through deepening snow as we retraced our steps to the mountaintop.

That day we collected fifteen of the packs, but it wore my men to the bone. The north wind was our master, slicing through our frayed defenses and taking the strength straight out of us. We were spread out now, in half a dozen camps up and down the creeks. As January progressed, so did the cold. There was no more cloth or leather to repair boots or make moccasins or fashion into hats or waistcoats or leggins, and we were being frostbitten again—ears, noses, chins, fingers, toes, ankles, lips. Around our miserable fires, which did little to warm any of us because the wind sucked away the heat, we worked thong through our clothing and boots, sewing together what we could, making do with rags and scraps of leather.

Some of my men resented the Kerns because they weren't helping with the hard work of getting the colonel's packs down to the cache. Indeed, they told me that they found Richard playing his flute by the fire one time. Just like some Philadelphians, they said. I was less judgmental, having seen them at death's door. In fact, Ben looked ashen to me, gray of flesh despite weeks of outdoor living, and I knew he wasn't far from his Maker. A man ought to play a flute when he could. A song, a melody, a flute could cleave the living from the dead.

But the men didn't like it, and they didn't like my forbearance. I thought it was best to let well enough alone. On the sixth of January Hubbard shot a prairie goat, or antelope as they are called, and generously divided the precious meat up and down the line. Even the Kerns and Cathcart got a small meal of it, and all were heartened.

We were far enough off the mountain to be among game again, and the very thought inspired every man who was dragging those parfleches and packs through the snow. I lost track of what the colonel was doing down below, but mostly he was simply waiting for relief. It never came. For my part, I camped at the point of rocks and oversaw the cache. The packs had to be dragged into that shallow cave, after we put down some brush and limb bedding to keep the packs dry, and then laid up, one on another, to make use of the small space. And once we finished with it, we would need to seal it and conceal it from the Utes, who roamed these mountains.

The Kerns were boiling up pieces of hide now to make a gluey gruel, but there was some nourishment in it, and I didn't worry much about them. We would soon have relief. By my calculation we were nearly at the end of the sixteen-day period we had allotted for King's party to return with help.

Then Proue died. The old Creole woodsman had shambled

along day by day, getting by until the cold struck, and then he simply began to freeze up. He was dragging packs right to the end, when he tumbled into the snow and said he couldn't go on. His legs were frozen below the knee. Someone wrapped his blanket around his legs, but no one had the strength to help the old man, and so he perished in the snow, the icy wind soon stopping his heart. We had no way to drag him anywhere, so he lay on the trail, frozen to the ice underneath, as man after man passed him by, dragging the colonel's goods down to the cache. That happened on the ninth day of January, and at a time when the cold was the worst I could remember, making us numb and driving us deep into our rags.

I stared at the old man, so cold and still, the snow filtering over his white face, caking his beard.

"Raphael, mon ami, au revoir," I said, watching the crystals collect in his eye sockets. "I'll come for you when I can. I'll let your people know."

If he had any living brothers or sisters, I did not know of them. But I would try to contact relatives in Saint Louis.

Others of us stopped and stared, watching the whirling snow filter through his beard. No one said anything.

That was the fourteenth day since King's party had left the Christmas camp. We were expecting relief within sixteen days at the worst. Proue had missed help by two days. Or was it simply that he had died needlessly dragging the colonel's packs? I refused to think in those terms and set the thought aside. But there was another thought worming through me: Proue's death was the direct result of our effort to drag the useless gear down the mountain. It was a death that Colonel Frémont could have avoided.

I worried about the men, the grunting, laboring men, numb with cold, so cold they could not feel their fingers, skidding the packs past the snow-lost body of Raphael Proue. What were they thinking? Who would be next?

I could not rally them. They were spread out by twos and threes. The company was no longer a single unit but disintegrating before my eyes as men made their own choices and shifted away from their messes. I knew what that foretold and was helpless to stop it. The Frémont company was falling apart.

I paused one last time at the hut the Kern brothers had built and found them huddled within. But the fire was going.

"When you can, make your way down to the colonel's camp," I said. "This wind should quit pretty soon."

"We're out of food," Richard said.

"The relief is due any moment. That's all I can say. Starving won't kill a man. It's cold that kills a man, quick as a knife thrust. Starving men make it through."

"We'll come soon. I'm some better," Ben said.

"Put your packs in the cache at Point of Rocks. You won't miss any of it. Some of the men are camped there. McGehee's there. He's from your mess. You men look after each other."

They nodded but said nothing.

The heat from the fire was welcome. It had warmed my backside. But now I faced my own walk five or six miles down. I was as weary as the rest, but somehow, maybe through sheer willpower, I kept on going. I was dragging two packs, the last we could find. I'd stash them with the rest.

The Kerns stared bleakly at me. They seemed better off than Cathcart, who was a walking scarecrow.

"We'll see you at the colonel's camp," I said. "Help's coming."

I stepped into the murderous wind and felt it burrow through my leather tunic and coat and leggins. But I plucked up the draw-lines and began tugging two parfleches of mess ware behind me, feeling the packs skid, resist, bounce, and sometimes slide ahead of me when I hit a steep grade. I kept my own advice, and when I got too cold, I holed up. There were plenty of refuges from the wind: copses of pinetrees, jagged cliffs, river brush, wind-carved hollows. I set aside my hunger, knowing it would do me no good to cater to it.

I stopped at the cache, where half a dozen men lingered, and stowed the last packs in the cave. These had been concealed with brush as best as my Creoles could manage it. It wouldn't fool an Indian, but we would be back soon enough to recover the goods. The Utes didn't roam far from their lodges in this sort of weather.

Somehow the colonel had gotten us off the mountain. Retreats are chaotic. Retreats are when commands fall apart, and it's every man for himself. But the colonel had held us together, sent for help, gotten most of his goods off the mountain, and so far, except for Raphael, he had kept his men alive. There was something admirable in it.

When I reached the colonel's camp, far below, I reported to Frémont.

"Raphael Proue's dead," I said.

Frémont stared, registering that. "How?" he asked.

"Froze. Lay down and died, dragging a pack."

"What do the men think?"

"He was the oldest of us."

Relief filtered into Frémont's face. "I hoped no one would perish. It reflects badly."

"Sir, it's no one's fault. I'll try to contact his people. I don't know that he had any."

"Yes, do that," he said, absently.

"There's men scattered far upstream; the Kerns are highest up. I've told them to work their way down here as soon as they can."

"Philadelphia people," Frémont said.

I knew what he meant. Yet they were all stouthearted. I thought they would make it.

"Ned is the worst off," I said.

"That's strange," the colonel replied. "He was with us before."

"Ben and Richard seem stronger," I said.

The colonel seemed puzzled. Ben and Richard were the city fellows.

The colonel seemed taut, and as soon as I had reported, he drifted to a place where he had a long view down the Rio del Norte Valley. An observer could see for miles across that barren landscape, where no tree grew and no rise or valley hid a party for long. The vista was so white we soon were squinting and leaking tears.

I joined him. "They're past due. We calculated sixteen days at the absolute worst."

The wind was cutting straight through me in that unprotected valley, and I was more than ready to retreat to the nearest fire.

"They're overdue. Williams misled them again," he said.

"Colonel, it took them four days just to get down that drainage. And they still had eighty miles after that, and they would be hunting, too. I think they're running far behind what we had calculated up on the mountain."

"I never should have trusted him. Kit once told me to watch your back when Williams was around."

"We'll see the relief anyday now."

Frémont shook his head. "Something went wrong. They'd be here."

"It takes time to collect mules or burros and blankets and food and men," I said.

"They failed me."

I changed the subject. "Do you have hunters out?"

"Certainly. There's plenty of tracks, but no game in sight. And everyone's so snow-blind that they can't see much."

That was bad news, actually. "I was hoping to see some meat."

"It's an improvement on shoe leather," he replied. He squinted out on the valley once more, with watering, snow-blind eyes ruined by the merciless white everywhere.

"My men are failing me. They're giving up. They don't have stout hearts," he said.

I hoped he would keep such sentiments to himself. They sounded a little like an accusation, but I believed Frémont was too grand a man to permit himself such thoughts.

"I'll warm up and hunt," I said.

"I'm taking a party out at dawn, if relief doesn't come," Frémont said. "I intend to go to Taos, and on to California, one way or another, with or without this company. Of course, you'll come with me, Alex."

CHAPTER TWENTY-FIVE

Tom Breckenridge

Godey joined our relief party for a while when we started from the Christmas camp, but when it was plain that the main party could not descend the drainage we were following, he returned. The four of us, with King in command, and Old Bill Williams as our guide, fought our way down that narrow canyon, struggling every minute. It was choked with snow, for one thing, and we had little understanding where the creek flowed or where its banks were.

We wrestled our way over or under fallen timber and fought through thickets, and once in a while the way was pinched off and there was no goddamn help for it but to doff our nether garments and wade the snowy creek and then put ourselves together on the far bank, numb and wet. The warm weather quit us, too, and the bitter cold bit our flesh, numbed our limbs, and ruined our hand-grip so we couldn't hold a thing in our fingers.

When nights fell, we carved a cave out of snow and lit deadwood, which failed to warm us, so we shivered in the thin blankets. Because we were carrying everything on our backs, we had but one blanket apiece. We had three Hawken rifles, a fowling piece, and a pound of powder, enough to shoot game if we should be so lucky. As for food, we had very little: some mule meat, a pack of macaroni, and some sugar. And even the sugar was lost to us when the pack tipped and the white powder vanished.

The distance down the slope to the valley was not great, perhaps eight miles, but we consumed four days fighting our way out, and in the process we ate the last of our food. We consoled ourselves that shortly we would reach the Rio Grande, would find plentiful game along its banks, and would soon stave off the hunger that was even then wrenching at our bellies. Fighting our way down a narrow defile choked with logs and rock and snow and brush made us hungry enough to eat bears and elephants. I'd of welcomed skunk stew.

King was a steady man, a veteran of the California expedition, and had a level head on him. He was heading out there to make a home for himself and his bride and had strong reasons to push on and triumph. Old Bill Williams was a different son of a bitch and soon was grumbling.

"This here gulch, it's not right. I didn't say for him to go this way. I know these hills and this isn't a place to go down. He wouldn't listen. He paid his guide no heed," Williams was saying.

"We'll get out of this gulch and be on our way to the settlements, old man," King replied quietly, while the four of us were roasting our bare feet at the fire, sitting around it like spokes on a wheel. "It's downhill, and that counts."

"What'll we eat, tell me that," Williams said.

"You're the hunter," King replied.

I heard so much whining from the old man I wished he would just plain shut his damn trap while we got some blood moving through our frozen feet. Whining doesn't do a lick of good when you're out in the wilds and there's not a thing you can do but keep on going. He was the guide; the veteran of these mountains; the man who could find his way, turn almost anything into food, keep us warm and healthy. He had been silent the whole trip, clear from

Hardscrabble, keeping his own counsel, but now he was belaboring poor King at every opportunity.

Still, Williams was voicing the things that were tormenting us. Up at Christmas Camp, Frémont and Preuss and Williams himself had calculated that the relief party would reach the settlements a hundred miles distant in four or five days, organize help, and be back up the mountains with food and animals in a dozen days, sixteen at the outside. But we were not yet free of the mountains, which were clawing us every foot of the way. There was something dark in it, the horror of it unspoken as we pulled our thin blankets over and under us and shivered the long night away. The truth of it was that the settlements seemed impossibly far.

Frémont had selected us for our strength. He had pulled me aside and said that he had a mission for me, that he was selecting only the strongest of his men, because the task ahead would test us to our utmost. I was the last bastard he approached, apparently, because he said that King, Creutzfeldt, and Old Bill had all accepted. He had come to realize that the company was in trouble and needed relief. That was the first mention of it to escape his lips, as far as I knew. I accepted at once. I wanted to get off that mountain; I was willing to walk barefoot through snow to get off those peaks.

"I'll go," I had told him, which was stupid of me. And so the party prepared that afternoon, and the next dawn, even as day broke, we began our downward trek, with Godey keeping us company.

I wondered whether we would do better in the next drainage, but so forbidding and high were the walls of the valley, and so thick with snow, that it was a foolish fancy. To add to our troubles, occasionally avalanches tumbled down those slopes, some of them beginning with a crack like a rifle shot and roaring their sinister way, raising a great cloud of powdery snow that choked the valley and stung our faces. It was a horror we spoke nothing of, knowing that any moment one of those snowslides could engulf us and end our worldly lives. And yet we escaped these random menaces and finally reached a point where the miserable creek poured into another branch, and the San Juan Valley stretched ahead, a silent white and naked land that looked like a graveyard.

I had yearned to escape the mountains, thinking that things would improve the moment we reached the great plain. But now, as we absorbed the naked valley ahead, each of us knew the mountains had been our friend; that the bleak plain offered no comfort at all. I stared at my colleagues, wondering if the other poor bastards were thinking what I was thinking. That stretch to the river would be tenfold harder than our descent.

That was the last sheltered camp. We found wood enough to warm us that one last night, and we divided the last of our provisions, the tallow candles that Frémont had given us. Never did anything taste so good as that tallow. We each had a half a candle, the white tallow like a king's feast, and then we dug deep into the snowbank, to put ourselves out of the wind if we could, and huddled miserably.

Worse was to come. No sooner had we emerged from the shelter of the mountains than a bitter north wind engulfed us. If it was cold in the canyon, it was murderous here where not a tree, not a shrub, not a cliff stayed the winds. The winds caught us unprepared. Somehow we had expected the valley to be our sanctuary, with shelter and wood and game and quiet air and sunshine warming our frozen beards. Instead it was a blinding white hell that made our eyes hurt from squinting. Had a band of elk marched slowly before us, none of us would have seen them at all, much less shot any for the solace of our ravenous bellies.

How we continued I don't know. I shot a hawk, which we tore to pieces and devoured raw, but it did nothing to allay our misery. We struggled slowly ahead. Far in the distance a thin band of trees marked the river. But the distance from where we saw it to there seemed impossible to negotiate on our frozen feet. We were stumbling now and could walk only a few yards at a time. No man complained, not even our guide.

It had become impossible to walk. Our frozen feet chafed in our boots, and each step tormented us. We would crawl, just to get off our feet, and when we could crawl through the snow no more, we would clamber to our feet and plunge forward another few yards. We were still following the tributary, and after a mile or so that day we stopped where some cottonwoods grew along the bank and dug a shelter for ourselves and our miserable fire. If we stayed upwind of it we got no heat out of it; if we edged downwind we didn't get much more heat, but we got the bitter smoke of cottonwood in our faces.

And for food we did what we had to do. We removed our tormenting boots, cut strips off of our blankets with which to wrap our swollen feet, and tied these makeshift moccasins tight. Then we sliced leather from our boots and set it to boiling. We stared at those slivers of leather, watched the boiling water percolate through them, extracting a thin yellowish paste and softening the leather itself. It took a long time and a lot of dead cottonwood before we had reduced the boot leather enough to eat it. We devoured it swiftly, and it did nothing at all to alleviate the howl of my innards. But we pronounced it tasty. We tied the boots together by their laces and would carry them with us, for that was the only food we had. That night, the temperature plummeted, and there was no way that our thin and diminished blankets could spare us from the brutal cold. Not even the fire was a solace.

I did not know where my feet were or whether they were connected to my body. They were severed from my senses by cold, and only when the fire had warmed them did they start to hurt and prickle. I sat there, shivering, and wondering whether I would live to see any more dawns.

The next day was much the same. We stumbled ahead, ate more of our boots, fought snow blindness, cut more strips off our blankets to wrap around our feet, and in all we made only a mile or two. We had ceased talking: to speak was to waste energy. At one point Bill Williams sat down and wouldn't budge, but we urged him on, and so we reached another place where a little wood might be found, again dug into the snow to get out of the deadly wind, and again boiled up our boots. We had, in all, managed another mile or two; I could no longer reckon distances, and none of us could see a thing, having been so blinded by snow that all the world was a glinting blur.

That night was, if anything, colder than the previous, or maybe our bodies could no longer generate enough heat to keep us alive. Save for the fire, we might have perished. I surveyed the misery around me, and a great darkness filled me. King was gaunt and drawn, the flesh gone from his face, his eyes sunk in pits. Creutzfeldt was no better off but had a little more energy. Williams had crawled inside of himself. There were great icicles hanging from his beard. And the tears from his ruined eyes had frozen on his cheeks. I began to experience a leaden sensation in my muscles, as if they could function only in the slowest and heaviest manner, and I judged that the others were afflicted in the same way. We boiled more of our boots that night. There were still a few miles between us and the Rio del Norte, and I didn't know if we would ever reach those bottoms or see the game we prayed would be awaiting us.

And so we lived, following the ice-topped bed of the tributary, crawling when we could not walk, leaving pink snow behind us from our bleeding feet. Some nights there was not a tree in sight; we dug a hole in the snow, laid a blanket under us and the remains of the rest over us, and shivered through the darkness. The smallest storm would have destroyed us, but we lived. We boiled the last of our boots when we could; started in on our scabbards; and, when those were gone, boiled our belts. After that we had nothing.

One day we found a rotted and frozen otter, half–picked over by carrion birds. We boiled it and somehow gagged down its foul and gamy flesh. It was food. It kept us alive one day more. The only thing in our favor was that the tributary of the Rio Grande had no snow on it. The wind had scoured the ice. In our weakened estate, that meant much to us. Slogging through snow would have been fatal.

We consumed still more of our blankets, wrapping the strips around our ruined feet, but they wore out swiftly, and the cold ate at our ruined toes and heels. At least we were progressing toward the wooded bottoms of the Rio Grande, making a mile or two each day. The promise of the river bottoms, wood and game, was all that kept us alive.

Then, scarcely a quarter of a mile from the bottoms, King sat down.

"I just can't," he muttered.

"We're almost there, it's just one last hike," Creutzfeldt said.

King shook his head. "You go on. I'll rest, and then catch up."

"You must come with us," I replied sharply.

But he slumped inert, barely bothering to refuse me.

"I'll follow along," he said at last.

No amount of urging could change his mind.

"We'll come back for you," Williams said.

With foreboding, we struggled the last quarter of a mile, which took us three hours of our usual crawling and walking. We did at least reach the timbered bottoms and found ample wood, and with our last energies got a good fire going. It would need to burn for an hour before it would throw out any heat, but at least it heartened us.

"I'll go back for him," Cruetzfeldt said, but he was plainly not fit for it.

"He's dead," Williams replied. "I saw the birds circling. I can tell when the birds circle. They circle smaller and smaller, and then come in."

It hardly seemed possible. The youngest and strongest of us might be gone.

"I'll go look," Creutzfeldt said.

We watched him struggle into the dusk. When he returned, out of the dark, he was carrying several pounds of meat.

CHAPTER TWENTY-SIX

Micajah McGehee

The colonel tasked us with caching the packs at the rocky landmark at the edge of the great valley, but we were too far gone to do it. The men were strung up the nameless creek. The Kerns and Cathcart were the farthest behind. With the cruel storms of January upon us, every step was misery, and yet we persisted, sliding the heavy packs downslope or dragging them across flats. All because the colonel required it.

But the food had given out. The Kerns's mess was boiling rawhide and parfleches. Doctor Kern was particularly weak, and I thought for sure he was gone from us. But he lingered on, kept alive by warm fires. The Kerns were reluctant to abandon the hut they had built, but I urged them on. We needed to make our way toward the settlements.

The thing that was gnawing at us more and more was the silence. We saw no relief. We awaited each hour the arrival of burros laden with food, blankets, and needful things, but no one arrived. The sixteen days that Colonel Frémont, Godey, and Preuss had calculated to be the maximum required to get relief to us were almost gone, and I heard that Frémont was anxious, pacing about his camp below us, and sending scouts out every little while to try to locate the relief.

Meanwhile the storms returned, and we were not only starved but also newly frostbitten. Men stumbled on bloodied feet, where frost and thaw and frost again had ruined flesh and set it to bleeding. During all this movement, we passed Proue's body, inert and half-covered with snow, and there was nothing we could do about this horror. Then Elijah Andrews gave out. He and I were trying to get down to the river, but he simply quit, lay down in the snow.

"I'm done," he said.

"Elijah, you've got to come along," I said. "Got to."

He shook his head and slumped into the snow. I knew what lay ahead for him and was determined to prevent it. Just up a shallow slope was a cave, and I somehow dragged him there, where at least he was beyond the curse of the winds and out of the whirl of snow. But he was well nigh inert, and I knew time was fleeing me. I struggled up the slope, needing to reach the timber, but the Arctic blast felled me. Atop the ridge, I found what I needed and tumbled dead piñon down that snowy precipice. I had to work in fits and starts, taking advantage of the slightest cessation of the gale, but in time I tumbled a lot of dry pine down to the cave, and there, in the shelter, with a little powder and flint and steel, I started a fire somehow and watched the wary flame slowly lick at the sticks. It gave no heat at all, but I saw that it cheered Andrews and gave him heart. The warmth was a long time coming, but the cave served my purpose, and soon Andrews was resting comfortably. About then Captain Cathcart and Richard Kern found us and tumbled in, hard-pressed by the storm. And thus we staved off trouble, or so we thought.

We had among us one cup of macaroni and one of sugar, and this we prepared to divide with perfect scruple, there being nothing else. But poor Andrews, still numb, with muscles that did not do his bidding, tumbled the pot over, and the flames soon covered the last miserable bit of provender among us all. No one spoke. No one blamed Elijah. We stared sorrowfully in the fire, locked in our own thoughts. In extremity, I don't think with words, but with images. I saw my mother's bread pudding before me, and a pink rib roast, dripping with juices. I saw eggs frying on a skillet, their yellow yolks mingling with their whites. I smelled my mother's yeasty bread, cooling on her counter. What was I doing here, in this place?

I could never manage my hunger. It had become a dull ache, a throb, and worse, an estate fraught with menace. There was something sinister in it, this conjuring of food, not a thing to eat and a thousand miles from succor, or so it seemed. There was slow death in it. There was weakness; I lurched and wobbled when I walked, as if my protesting muscles were at their limits.

Cathcart clambered to his feet and stepped into the blizzard, and then stumbled back into our shelter.

"I thought I heard the relief," he said. "Could have sworn it."

At least we were warm. Elijah Andrews recovered as the heat of the fire bounced off the walls of our rocky abode. Only two hours earlier, he had stared up at me, surrender in his face. It was cold that murdered; starvation would only weaken us, at least for a few days more.

If only a stray mule would wander by.

The storm never ceased. I discovered a ball of thong in our midst, cut it into strings, and boiled it. I prowled the cliffside and found wolf bones. These we pulverized between stones and added to our thong soup. We knew that others of our company had been caught as well and were harboring in the hollows of that cliff, awaiting whatever fate would bring. There seemed so little we could do; our fates were no longer in our hands.

When the storm lifted two days later we stumbled our way toward the colonel's camp, down in the great valley, seeing no game all the way. If there were animals anywhere near, they had been driven to shelter somewhere. The thing we had hoped for, an abundance of game down in the wide valley of the Rio Grande, was nothing more than a thin dream. I made my body work, one step at a time, step by step on frozen feet, as we staggered toward the colonel's camp. The rest stumbled, too. We helped one another. When someone wanted to quit, we hectored him, made him continue.

By January 9, 1849, we were all out of the mountains, save for old Proue, whose frozen body lay mutely behind us, buried in drifts. A few of us remained at the cache; the rest had collected in Frémont's camp. That day was important. It was the day we should have relief, even if King's company had been greatly slowed. It was sixteen days past the Christmas camp, when the colonel sent King and Williams and Creutzfeldt and Breckenridge off, with our salvation in their hands.

What had happened? No one knew, but the prospects were forbidding. Frémont sent scouts downriver, but they saw only silence and cruel white snow. How we ached for the jingle of harness bells or the crunch of hooves on snow or the shouts or shots that meant our relief was coming. Down there, out of the mountains, the wind was crueler than ever, but we found shelter in the timbered banks along the river, and so endured. The few rations still in the colonel's possession were carefully divided. We got a spoonful of macaroni or a bit of sugar dissolved in warm water. But no one died, and we had ample deadwood and shelter, and since we weren't moving, our tormented feet had a chance to heal. I pulled my boots off and discovered deep cracks between my toes, with raw flesh visible in them. Some leaked blood. Strange white patches pocked my toes and ankles. The terrible truth was that my feet were better off than most.

Then, on the eleventh, the colonel decided that the King party was not going to reach us, and he resolved to form a new relief, consisting of himself; his manservant, Saunders; Alexis Godey; Godey's young nephew, Theodore; and the little scientist, Preuss, who had weathered over several expeditions as a resourceful and tough man.

Frémont gathered us together on his departure. He looked gaunt and hollow eyed and was suffering from snow blindness more than most of us. And his voice had an odd, thin ring to it.

"I'm taking a party with me to get relief. The King party should have been here by now. Take heart; we plan to move fast, make up for lost time. As fast as you can, head for the Rio Grande and follow it toward the Mexican settlements. As fast as you can, bring the baggage to the Rio Grande and meet the relief party at Conejos, Rabbit River, which you can't miss. It's a summer settlement for herders. There will be shelters. Maybe even some stored grains. Look for relief there, eh? You can hunt along the way; we're in game country now. In a day or two, after we collect at Taos, I'll be going to California by the southern route."

I stared at the man, astonished that he was thinking about that leg of the trip, even while we were caught in our extremity far to the north. Had we just heard what we had heard? I saw others staring at Frémont, not believing their ears. But Frémont was oblivious to our disbelief and continued on.

"Now, I'm putting Lorenzo Vincenthaler in command. He's a veteran of my California expedition, and he will see to your safety."

Vincenthaler. I knew so little of him. He was one of the quiet sorts, a part of Frémont's inner circle of veterans, and not one at any of my messes.

I knew he was an Ohio man and a veteran of the war. I saw no difficulty in it and imagined he would be as good as any. And yet one could not help but wonder at the colonel's choice.

The next two days were miserable in the extreme, as we hauled the rest of the colonel's luggage with us and subsisted on boiled parfleche, which produced a repellent, thin gruel. We dragged his barometers and thermometers, spare rifle parts, kettles and spoons, heavy rubberized camp mats, iron rods, canvas, and packsaddles. Then, at last, we set forth along the frozen Rio del Norte, choosing the ice in the middle because it was free of snow and because we could drag the packs more easily. But the farther we pierced into that naked valley, the worse the winds, and soon they were sapping what little energy we possessed. We saw no game and were too snow-blind to kill any.

There was no point in staying. The sooner we headed downriver, the sooner we would meet our relief. Two of the Frenchmen in the company, Vincent Tabeau and Antoine Morin, decided to go ahead. They were veteran voyageurs. They had been with the colonel on all three of his previous expeditions. They were seasoned and familiar with hardship. Now they were going ahead, perhaps to find game, perhaps to meet up with our relief. Whatever their private intent, they left the day after the colonel, with Vincenthaler's blessing.

Our new commander divided the last of the edibles, doling out exactly one cup of sugar to each man, two tallow candles, and a mismatched supply of parfleche leather and thong to boil down to a foul gruel. That was it. There was nothing more to support life.

The rest of us started down the river the next day, January 13, making our slow progress south. We had resolved to stay together and help one another, but the weaker men soon lagged behind. I was among the weaker. I was in the company of the Kerns and Andrews and Cathcart, whose ragged clothes flapped about him. But I didn't suppose I looked much better. And Ben Kern could barely walk, managing only a few paces at a time before he had to rest. Plainly, it would be a slow, hard trip.

Now the dazzling white world rendered our eyes useless. Our heads ached from squinting; we leaked tears that froze to our cheeks and beards. We pulled hats down over our brows, anything that would spare us that glare.

But if the snowblindness was a torment, our frost-ruined feet were worse. Every step was a torment. Our toes and ankles had frozen and thawed and frozen and whitened and blackened and turned to pulp. Then the California Indian lad, Manuel, surrendered. His feet were black. He begged Vincenthaler to shoot him, and when our commander refused, the young man turned back, intending to die in the camp we had left behind us, and no amount of urging on our part could change his mind. The last I saw of him, he was hobbling back, back, back to a sure death. It was a horror I could scarcely swallow. But that was only the beginning.

Later that very day, Henry Wise, a hardy Missourian, simply sat down in the snow and perished. I watched him sit; I watched him slump. I watched him slowly tumble onto his side and await his fate. None of us could help him. There was only that awful silence that comes from witnessing the things our very eyes were seeing, and then we had to leave him there on the river ice and continue on our way, the dark sight we had witnessed crowding our minds and weighing like stones in our bosoms. Joacquin and Gregorio, the other Indian boys, gently covered Wise's body with brush and snow, and I marveled that they had the energy to do it.

That night, as we sheltered as best we could from the bitter wind, a new horror rose among us. Another veteran, Carver, from Wisconsin, went mad. He rambled through our messes, ranting, saying he would go on and find food. He had a plan. All night we listened to his exhortations, and with the following dawn he drifted away, and we could do nothing to oppose it. It is odd, how well I remember my very last glance, remember the exact expression on Carver's face. And the last on Wise's. These were moments when I was staring into the great void.

The horrors had not passed. The Frenchman, Tabeau, who had rejoined us, began to rave. This, he said, was a visitation from God. His suffering was beyond what any mortal can endure, but somehow he survived the night. When we once again started down the icy river, he stumbled along as best he could for an hour or so, utterly blinded by the glare, and then sat down. His old friend Morin sat beside him, the two choosing to depart from this life together, and that was the last we saw of them. They never caught up with the rest of us again.

After we made camp, the rest of us drifted in one by one, each man on his own, all semblance of a company gone. We had gone through the last of our provisions, even the miserable leather.

Vicenthaler had only one thing to say to us as we struck our fires and warmed our tormented feet.

"You're on your own now," he said. " I can do no more."

CHAPTER TWENTY-SEVEN

John Charles Frémont

Ere long, we picked up the trail of King's relief party and followed it. The information it yielded was not good. Preuss noted that the camps were only two or three miles apart and that their progress was so slow that they would not yet have reached the Mexican settlements.

"What do you suppose was the trouble?" I asked him.

He simply shook his head. None of us could know. But it might simply have been the want of food. Now they were somewhere ahead, foraging for food as they went. We had a bit of sugar and macaroni and nothing else to sustain life. But unlike King's company, I had first-rate men with me.

Godey roamed ahead but found no game, and our own position was growing desperate. We examined each of the camps of the relief party, looking for clues, but they yielded nothing. No bones or feathers, no blood, no apparent sickness. Just miserable progress wandering down the middle of the frozen river, camping wherever they could find shelter.

My own party was about to experience the same fate. We ate the last of the macaroni, boiled up the sugar, and prepared to feast on our boots and scabbards, when one of those fateful turns of fortune caught us up. Our own progress was slowed. Theodore, Godey's nephew, could scarcely walk, and I feared for Preuss. There, ahead, was an Indian. I was so snow-blind I could scarcely make him out and thought he might be one of King's party, but as we approached Godey told me this was an old Ute. He was all alone, or so we thought.

I made the peace sign, palm up.

He stood somberly, wrapped in a leather cape, his gray hair falling in two braids. He carried a bow and quiver of arrows, one of which was nocked. His face was seamed copper, and his cheekbones ridged his face. He surveyed us one by one, reading our hunger.

I knew little of the hand language and feared we might have trouble.

He said something in a tongue I could not fathom. I remembered that this people had generations of contact with the Mexicans and tried Spanish.

"Buenos dias," I said.

"Hablo un poco de espanol," he replied.

After that, with much hesitation, we conducted what surely was one of the most critical negotiations in my life. He seemed slow, almost ponderous, all the while weighing us in ways I could not fathom.

I learned that he was with a small Ute hunting party camped nearby. Yes, they had seen the other party and had seen their smokes but had not visited them. The other relief party had spilled much blood in the snow.

"Are they alive?" I asked.

He hesitated, and finally nodded.

"How far ahead?"

It was not a question he could answer, so he remained stone silent.

"Have you food we could trade for?" I asked.

He eyed us, seeing our rifles and powder horns and the bedrolls we carried on our backs.

I told him we needed horses or mules, food, and I wanted a guide who would take us to the closest Mexican settlements on the Chama River. He studied us, uncertain whether we were true friends or somehow dangerous.

"I have blankets, a rifle and powder and shot to trade," I said.

I could not make out his reply, but then he beckoned, and we followed him up a drainage to the south and came suddenly on a small encampment of brush huts with skins thrown over them, with perhaps a dozen men in it, all of them warmly dressed in skins. I did not see a woman. They circled around us, wary but not hostile, and I once again made my wishes known to them. I feared ambush; their numbers were large enough to put arrows into us. But it didn't happen. Instead, they invited us to sit at their council fires.

We received a thin, hot meat broth. As I downed this blessed soup, drinking directly from a pottery bowl that was being passed around, I noticed several bony horses gnawing at bark and sticks in the brush nearby. A sorrier lot of horses I never did see, and how they had survived in this white world I could not imagine, and I thought maybe the horses couldn't imagine it either. But I knew one thing: I wanted those horses. I wanted them so badly I would trade anything and promise anything to get them. They would carry us to safety.

I needed to give them some sort of gift and settled on my camp hatchet, which I laid before the coppery old man. He nodded and examined it with pleasure. Anything of metal was a treasure to a Ute.

That broth was so savory we could have emptied their kettle, and I know every man of us stared hungrily at that soup, but it was time to negotiate our salvation.

I told him my name was Frémont and waited to see whether it brought a response. He said he was known as San Juan, a chieftain of the Utah people. That was a good start.

I told him, fumbling for simple words, that we needed food and horses and a guide to the settlements. We had things to trade. What would he want in return?

He arose, came to me, touched my Hawken rifle, shot pouch, powder horn, and bedroll, which held two blankets in a canvas groundsheet. He pointed to the horses and held up five fingers, and then to a parfleche, which he opened. It was brimming with jerked meat, probably venison. There were twenty or thirty pounds of it as far as I could tell.

"More food?"

He shook his head. That was all he could give us, and it wouldn't sustain us long.

"If you guide us to Abiquiu, I will reward you when we get there," I said.

"How?" he asked.

"I will see to it," I replied, for I had no idea what I might discover there.

He arose, sharply commanded a youth to follow, and then headed into the brush. In the space of a few minutes he and the boy returned with four scrawny nags, so poor I wondered if they would carry us far. He laid the heavy parfleche before me. I slipped my rifle off of my shoulder and handed it to him, along with the powder and balls and patches, and then pulled my bedroll from my back.

He smiled broadly, baring gaps in his browned teeth. It was our moment of triumph, and I felt my burdens slip away. It was my destiny.

But it was not quite as I had thought. The horses would carry us or our baggage but would remain his. We would borrow them.

He would come with us to the Mexican settlements, and then he would reclaim his horses. He was being abundantly paid for this service and a little food, but I ignored his extravagant demands. These tribesmen put a larger value on things than they're worth.

I explained my negotiations to Godey and Preuss, who congratulated me.

We started at once, the four bony nags hauling our truck, and San Juan leading the way. We cut across an oxbow of the river and soon picked up the trail of the relief party. Both Godey and Preuss, who had become a keen mountaineer, noted that the camps seemed fresher. We were gaining on King's party. I had become so snowblind that I could barely see and gladly left the navigation to the old Indian. For the moment, we walked, but there was not a man among us who didn't wish to throw himself over a bony horse and be carried to safety. Either that or eat the horse.

We made good time. The guide was able to bivouac us in drainages where thick brush supplied a little fodder for the starved horses, as well as some shelter from the relentless wind. We boiled up a thin soup of jerky and a few roots the old man dug up from the frozen earth, and so mollified the demands of our stomachs, though we were just as hungry after as we were before.

We rejoined the Rio Grande and were quickly comforted by firewood and the prospect of game. I left it to Godey to hunt, since I no longer had a rifle, and I noticed the old chieftain was walking wide of us, hoping to scare up game. Then, not far from the frozen river, we came upon a disturbance in the snow, some blood frozen to the earth, giving it a pink pallor. But there was no sign of life here or habitation or a camp. Maybe they had killed an animal and dragged it to the river.

"Something live, or newly dead, was butchered here," Godey said. "If there's blood, it was not a frozen animal."

It was a good observation. There were skid marks, so we pursued them the quarter or third of a mile to the frozen river, and there we found another campsite, fresher than the others, and with some sign that it had been used for several days. There had been two fires, and not all the wood they had collected had been consumed by them. But there was no sign of the animal they had consumed, which led me to believe that they had devoured every scrap of it.

But the German was restless and began a slow circle of the camp, poking and probing the dense river brush. What he was hunting for was quite beyond my imagination until he stopped suddenly.

"Ach!" he exclaimed.

We headed at once through dense willow brush to Preuss, who stood sourly, his lips curled down.

There, at his feet, was King. Without trousers. And without legs. King's open eyes stared upward. The carrion birds had not yet plucked them out. In fact, there was no sign that any animal at all had discovered this frozen corpse caught deep in the tan brush. The man's legs had been crudely severed, perhaps with an axe, and there was no nether part of him in sight.

"So," Preuss said. "They should have put an apple in his mouth and baked him whole."

I knew at once whose work this was.

"Williams! I'd been warned about him. That man's a degenerate. He'd eat the whole party if he had to."

Godey knelt beside what was left of King and attempted to roll him over, but his shirt was frozen to the ground. With some effort, Godey pulled King loose and turned him over. There was no evidence of violence, other than the lost legs.

"Froze to death," Godey said.

"It was Williams. No man of my company would do it." I said.

Preuss grinned at me. He was an oddly cynical man and could annoy me at times.

"I want that body removed from here, far away, buried in brush. I don't want this known," I said. "I want this kept entirely between us and of course request your silence."

I waited. Godey nodded. Preuss grinned and nodded. Young Theodore frowned. The boy was the most likely to talk.

"Theodore, I want your word of honor. Some things must never be mentioned, not ever."

"Yes, sir," he said.

The Indian stood quietly. I knew the more I urged silence from him, the more he would whisper, so I ignored him. No one would believe him anyway. He stared at the body, then at us, a deep curiosity in his seamed face. Then he looked away, into the white skies.

Godey found a canvas and rolled King onto it, and he and Preuss slowly dragged the corpse through brush, into timber, and finally to a frozen swampy spot. They put King out among the cattails, where he would sink as soon as the thaw came. Then they heaped brush over King's body.

I thought it was a good choice.

I did not want Senator Benton to know, nor Jessie. Or my sponsors. I didn't want the army to know, nor the public or the press. I didn't want the rest of the company to know. I did not want it said that there was cannibalism on my expedition or in my command. But if word did leak out, I knew exactly what I would say. Old Bill Williams was the responsible party; men of mine would not do such a thing but would choose to perish before eating the flesh of any other mortal.

It was a good and valid riposte. It was well known that the beaver trappers and mountaineers had sometimes resorted to desperate measures in starving times, and many a man now living in Saint Louis owed his life to the flesh of his companions. So, if whispering began, it would not be about Frémont but about the guide, who had deliberately slowed the party, let it starve, and finally had partaken of the forbidden.

"Are we going to say a word over this man?" Godey asked.

"A word? I've asked you not—oh, you mean a prayer. We'll have a moment of silence," I said, and doffed my fur hat and felt the icy fingers of the north wind filter through my ragged hair.

Later, I wondered how his widow would receive the news.

CHAPTER TWENTY-EIGHT

Tom Breckenridge

I hated Creutzfeldt. I despised Williams. I peered at them through snow-ruined eyes, the tears freezing on my lashes. I had partaken of the meat; I was helpless to stop myself. I swallowed it as soon as it was half-cooked over the wind-blown fire. King ham. Precious little of it, too. What good were two skinny thighs of a half-starved man? There were hardly ten pounds of flesh for the three of us. I have no recollection of the taste; it didn't matter. It could have been chicken or elk or beefsteak. It was poor food, and it went down with my stomach clawing at it, and my revulsion vomiting into my soul.

I could never again walk through the doors of my church. I could never receive the bread and wine of communion into my mouth.

I looked at Creutzfeldt and loathed him. He was the devil. He had tempted me. He had turned into something grotesque, some gargoyle or griffin guarding a dark building. His cheeks had sunk, his eyes bulged, his matted hair flapped out from his grimy hat. Williams was quieter, and I loathed the man. It was he who had built up the fire, sliced meat from King's hambone, and set it sizzling in the miserable snow pit we occupied. I stared at myself, at fingers that had held the dreadful meat, the devil's fingers. And yet my belly stopped gnawing at me, at least for the moment.

By unspoken agreement, we set the rest aside. We could go two days on it, a pound of King a day for each of us. It would get us a few miles farther toward the northern settlements. Or Taos on the Rio Grande. I didn't care which. If we made it, we would walk into the village and they would know. The mark of Cain would be on our foreheads. We could not hide ourselves.

I looked into the sorry sky, knowing nothing had been hidden. Later, I imagined our conduct might be hidden; life would go on. But there are no secrets; every foul deed is made known, sooner or later. By agreement, the three of us dragged King into some brush, hoping wild animals would obscure our sin, then fled the abattoir and stumbled southward once again, carrying six or eight pounds of King. The snow wounded my eyes; I could see nothing through the frozen tears but followed mutely along. Williams led the way; we stumbled behind, Creutzfeldt and I. And so we passed a day, camped in some sheltering brush that night, hid under the cutbank against the wind, and ate another parcel of King. We had made only a few miles before we had all given out. And then we tackled the next day, crueler than the previous, and made a few more miles. Who knows how many? That eve, Old Bill settled us in a riverside woods, where shelter and firewood were plentiful. And there we demolished the last of King. Our friend had given us only a reprieve. We were still forty miles from the Chama River villages. What had King's flesh bought us but a stone in the bosom for the rest of our days?

The next day, with wind lifting and whipping snow, we set off again, this time aware that no meal would await us at the end of the day. We resolved to hunt; I checked my load. I fantasized. I would find a few deer; I would steady myself, aim, and drop one, and we would be saved. There would be venison enough to see us through.

But in my feverish imagination, I saw myself shooting an antlered King and slicing him up. Still, we had put King behind us; we were three days along the river road from that horror. If I could have run, I would have run and run, day and night, run away from that place. And we were seeing signs of game in the snow; hoofprints, tracks, marks of passage everywhere. Surely, surely, I would find a deer, and that would somehow wipe away our shame. We would eat clean, well-cooked venison, and be freed of the stain. I even pushed ahead, weary as I was, so that I might have first crack at any game we found. But the afternoon stretched away in silence, and the winter sun plummeted, and we made camp in a good place where we would be warm—and starving once again.

None of us could see much anymore, and that was why we scarcely knew what was coming upon us until men and horses plunged into our camp. I arose, startled, to see the hazy shapes of horses, some bearing men. Other men were walking. They collected silently around us, peering down.

"Breckenridge? Is that you?"

The voice was Colonel Frémont's.

"Yes, sir," I croaked.

"And Williams? And who is this?"

He was pointing to Creutzfeldt, and indeed, the scarecrow in rags bore no resemblance to the man the colonel knew.

"I'm Creutzfeldt, sir."

"I see now," Frémont said.

He dismounted and peered about, and I suddenly was glad there was no meat in camp and no sign of any cooking.

"I have men with me; we thought you were lost. I'm the relief this time," Frémont said.

I could not tell what men were with him, so terrible were my eyes. There was an Indian among them.

"Have you food?" Williams asked.

Frémont ignored him. "Twenty-two days ago you started out. What happened?"

"We had food only for four," I said. "It took that just to get out of the mountains."

"Rough country, like I say," Williams added. "I been saying it."

"Two or three miles a day?" Frémont asked.

This was accusation, and I didn't care for it. "No one could have done better," I replied.

"Have you chow?" Williams persisted.

"Not up to your tastes?" that was Preuss talking. I still hadn't figured out who all was with Frémont.

"We got a little jerky from the Ute," Godey said. I knew the voice.

I managed to focus long enough to see the whole party. Frémont had the German with him, Preuss, tough little devil. And his manservant, Saunders, and Godey's nephew, Theodore. And an ancient Ute.

"His horses, not ours," Frémont said, to allay any instinct of mine to slice the throat of one of the miserable animals. What those starved beasts fed on, I could not imagine. "He's taking us to the settlements. We'll get help there."

Now I could see that these scarecrow horses were the poorest I had ever seen. They carried packs, except that the strongest carried Frémont. There were four. The rest of the company, along with the Ute, walked. Or maybe they exchanged rides.

Preuss studied our camp, poked around its periphery, as if looking for something, but we had nothing to show him. We had bedrolls, a few tools, and a rifle or two. I thought they would stay, but Frémont had other ideas.

"We're going to put in another hour,' he said. "I've got hungry men upriver waiting for relief. We can't dally."

He let the word hang in the air. We had dallied. On the other hand, we had not met any Utes with horses and food to trade, either.

"We have no food," I said.

"I can imagine," Frémont replied. He studied us a moment. "Alex, how much jerky is there?"

Godey dug into a pack on the back of a scrawny horse. "Maybe thirty pounds," he said.

"Give them a third," Frémont ordered.

Godey parceled out a third of the jerky and handed it to Williams. Old Bill instantly handed a piece of jerky to Creutzfeldt and me, and I jammed it between my teeth.

"Follow along. I'll send relief out as soon as I can."

"How do we get to the settlements?"

Frémont stared at Old Bill Williams and me. "Charts show some hills west of the river below here a mile or two. Leave the river there. Circle around the hills and bear southeast across open country. There won't be any running water, and not much wood."

"Our feet have given out," I said, wanting leather or blanket or anything I could get. We were walking on strips of blanket.

"We could use some canvas for our feet," Williams said.

"So could we," Frémont replied.

"You'll send the Mexicans?" I asked.

"I'll send relief as fast as possible. And I'll be outfitting for the California leg while you others come in."

"California?"

"The next leg. We'll head south and then west to the Gila River and across. I'll be buying livestock and stores. I'm going to reorganize, recruit a company, head down the Rio Grande. The place where we head west is near Socorro. That will take us to the Gila drainage. It should be a warm and pleasant trip, that far south."

"California?" I whispered.

"Don't lose heart," Frémont replied. "You'll make it."

With that, he reined his pony and the whole party drifted away, leaving us behind. I watched, hating Frémont and Godey. I hoped the Ute would steal away with his ponies in the middle of the night. I loathed the man. They could have taken us along. Abandoning us was probably a death sentence.

Preuss had looked through me, as if I were transparent. The others were cold. Godey, usually the most affable of men, had stared quietly. Surely we had been found out. But I was beyond caring. I stuffed another stick of jerky in my mouth and tried to make a meal of it, but there is nothing less satisfying. It is nothing but an emergency ration, and not a good one at that. Still, if we resisted the temptation to devour it all, right then and there, we might make it.

"Bill, maybe we should divide up that jerky," I said.

He grinned wolfishly, but then he did arrange the sticks of meat into three piles and beckoned. I grabbed one, the others caught up theirs. It would suffice us or we would die. I ate mine in small crumbs, letting my saliva release the flavor. If I could not really eat, at least I could pretend to and let the juices linger in my mouth.

We stumbled back to our campfire and collapsed in the small circle of heat it threw out. We ate more jerky than we intended, since none of us could slow down.

There was something gnawing at me: "He didn't ask," I said.

"No, I reckon he didn't," Old Bill said. "Like maybe he had that part of it all figured out."

"They know," I said.

"Anyone coming by, they'd sure enough know," Williams said. "So what? It don't matter none. Happens all the time, and a man can be glad of it."

The unasked question haunted me. They knew. It was in all their faces. It was in the ginger way they talked. It was in their politeness. It was in their silence when I asked for food.

I should have just accepted it, but instead I was enraged.

"They'd have done the same," I snapped.

"Maybe more," Williams said. "There's a lot more to King than a pair of hams."

I stared into the twilight. Not far south the second relief party was cheerfully marching into the dusk, accusations in the minds of them all. Still, maybe none of them would say a word. If I knew Frémont, I knew he would bury it deep.

We started the next morning in a whip of snow. The restless wind would not leave it alone but drove it into drifts and carved hollows in it. Still, we made our way slowly along the route that angled away from the river. It would save us miles by cutting across the oxbow, but we would lack shelter.

In many ways, those legs of our trip were hardest of all. There was no wood for fires, no shelter from the wind, no comforts at night. We could only huddle in our thin blankets, one beneath the three of us, the other rags heaped over us, and endure until the next cruel sun would blind us but offer no heat. We sucked our jerky, gathered our strength, and marched out on another blinding day.

But our feet were failing us. They were frostbitten, bleeding, numb, and painful all at once. We left pink trails behind us. We took to crawling for a hundred yards at a time, just to relieve the pain that was lancing our every step. We exhausted ourselves on our hands and knees; that consumes more energy than walking, but our feet rebelled at every step we took, and we had no leather or cloth to ease our torment.

I raged because Frémont didn't take us with him. They could have carried us. They saw our feet, the ragged bits of blanket, and yet they paused only for an hour and then hurried on.

But we didn't die, and I credit the jerky for it. By the third day we had consumed the last of it and were more starved than ever, but we pushed on. The settlements were nigh, and the reality that we were close to help and comfort was the only food we possessed.

I gazed ahead, with snow-blind eyes, aching to see our rescuers coming toward us, bearing food and blankets, mules and warmth. But we saw nothing at all, nothing but the great, hollow snow-swept valley, and we stumbled on.

CHAPTER TWENTY-NINE

Benjamin Kern, MD

It was only later that I grasped the horror of Frémont's intent. With men starving to death and frozen and weakened, his thought was of his equipment. We spent days ferrying the truck that had been scattered up that creek down to the cache, days spent consuming the last of our energy.

I was too numb to see it, and so were the rest. If the colonel wanted his equipment collected and cached, then it was up to us to do it. I heard in that awful span of time no complaint at all. The colonel had a mesmerizing effect on all of us, and we would have followed his instruction unto death. I do not know where or how he acquired that grip over other mortals, but he had it and used it, his soft polite voice sealing our doom.

His choice of Vincenthaler is instructive to me now. The man was a dutiful sergeant, incapable of doing anything but following the colonel's command no matter what new circumstances arose. I think Frémont intuitively understood that; in Lorenzo Vincenthaler he had the man whose will was a slavish copy of the colonel's own. So without question or cavil, our new commander set us to the task, no matter that his own eyes told him we were all on the brink of collapse and our sole chance lay in leaving the mountains at once, reaching the bottoms of the Rio Grande, and finding game. But he did not abandon the mountains. He didn't send his best hunters ahead to scout for game. He didn't send the strongest of his men to prepare a warm camp that might sustain us for one more night. As the perfect surrogate of the colonel, he required us to drag the last of the colonel's stuff over the snow and stow it in the cache. Then we set out across the valley, in a gale out of the north that began murdering men before we were a mile or two out of the mountains.

Then, with several men down, he chose to abdicate.

He collected those of us who had survived a day of stumbling along with our rifles and blankets and nothing more and announced his decision:

"You're on your own," he said. "Some of us are stronger, some weaker, and I can't let the weaker delay the stronger. So, I'll take the stronger men with me and try to get relief. I can do no more."

It made sense in a way, if you wish to excuse the days we had spent sliding the colonel's stuff down the mountain. We devoured the last bits of tallow candles that night. The next morning Vincenthaler's chosen party sneaked away before the rest of us were even aware. He took with him the two California Indians, Joaquin and Gregorio, as well as Scott, Martin, Bacon, Hubbard, Ducatel, and Rohrer. There was hardly a man among those of us left behind who could lift a rifle to shoot a passing raven. There was Andrew Cathcart, skin and bones but doughty and alive; Micajah McGehee; Captain Charles Taplin; Joseph Stepperfeldt; Elijah Andrews; my brothers, and I. We were on our own, we who were so worn we could scarcely walk thirty paces to collect firewood. We vowed we would not leave one another, so long as there was breath in us, and so strengthened ourselves in our solidarity.

Still, we were not yet defeated. If we had no flesh on us, we still had heart. I surveyed the creek where ice did not cover it, looking for anything, water bugs, fish, aquatic plants, that might sustain us, but it was a feckless search. I did find some wild rose shrubs and collected some rose hips and shared these with the rest. They are known to allopathic medicine as being therapeutic. It behooved us to be off. The farther ahead the stronger party got, the worse would be our chances. If they might shoot a deer, they would send a fair portion of it back to us if we didn't lag too far, or so I believed. I should have known better.

All that day we proceeded along the river, sometimes a few steps at a time, but never failing to make headway. By dark we were spread out again, but some of us went back for the stragglers whilst the rest got a fire going and made some warmth. I was one of those stragglers and had fallen insensate only to have the rest get me to my feet, and by that means I staggered into the camp and the welcome warmth. There remained only Andrews not accounted for, and soon we heard one hoarse cry and nothing more. We found him a hundred yards back and got him in, but he lay inert, in a stupor that awakened a dread in me. I have seen that sort of stupor all too often in my practice.

Then Rohrer came in, rising out of the dusk, much to our surprise.

"Couldn't keep up," he muttered.

We welcomed him to our campfire, where he collapsed in a heap. Soon he was warming himself, but I eyed him sharply and didn't like what I saw.

We were much too famished to break camp the next morning and resolved to hunt whilst we had strength enough to shoulder a rifle. The whole lot of us were so snow-blind I couldn't imagine we would have much luck, but my friends persisted, and in time, they brought in two prairie hens. Oh, that was a fine moment, even if it meant only one bite apiece for the nine of us. We divided everything, including the entrails, and felt that single morsel slide into our gullets.

One of us, Taplin if memory serves me, found a dead wolf and dragged it in. It was mostly gone, gnawed away by raptors and other hungry creatures, but we got some well-boiled flesh out of it, boiled the hide for more, and ground up the bones and gulped them down, too. That barely sustained life, but in truth we could travel no more. We were worn out.

Elijah Andrews lingered in a stupor, and nothing I could do induced him to live, and so he perished quietly in the night. He was a Saint Louis man and had served long years in the navy, only to meet his Maker out in the middle of the continent. He had struggled to live but had weakened steadily. McGehee had saved him earlier in the mountains, but the span of his life was only a few days more. I wondered what little family in the city would soon be sorrowing.

We found a small gilded bible in his pocket and resolved that if any of us should live, we would deliver it to Andrews's relatives in Saint Louis. It was a most sacred vow: that bible would be carried from one end of the continent to the other, if need be, but it would come home in Saint Louis. We laid Andrews out flat; the cold wasted no time permeating his flesh, and we covered him with brush, for that was all we could do.

My eye was on Henry Rohrer, who was mumbling and ranting and drifting to and from the fire. He was a millwright, making his way to California, where his skills would be greatly valued. I knew the madness as a prelude to what would come next, but I was helpless. I had no remedy but hot water, which I attempted to put into the man and thus warm his innards, but he would not drink it. I could not fathom what he was saying, but the flow of words told me he was off in his own memories, or his own world, and already lost to us. So our camp began another deathwatch, as we waited for the maddened man to quit life. It did not happen at once. By unspoken agreement, we planned to head downriver as soon as Rohrer left us. I don't suppose anyone wanted to remain in camp with two of the dead.

But ere long, his breath stopped. And so we had lost another. We stared at the bodies. That's when my brother Ned, one of Frémont's trusted lieutenants in the conquest, offered the proposition:

"It's a hard thing to say, but that meat's as good as any other," he said.

I wasn't surprised. Or rather, I thought it might be Richard, the weakest among us, who would raise the prospect. Ned had his ways in the wilds and managed to pull bits of food from everything he passed. I once watched him dig up cattail root and mash and eat it. But now he had come to his Rubicon and was proposing that we all cross that river, even as Rohrer's body began its long and fateful cooling.

I had no objections. Men do what they have to do in extremis. My own empty stomach groaned with need. Captain Taplin, who was the strongest among us and had stayed with us to hunt if he could, simply stared. The awful prospect hung among us.

"Do what you must, but out of my sight," Taplin said roughly. "I will not see it."

But McGehee, courageous lad from the Deep South, offered his own plea. "Let us wait. Relief is coming. It might be here tomorrow. We can endure. Give it three days, and then we shall do whatever we must do."

That was a sensible and courageous suggestion. We nodded, feeling the hollowness of our bellies, our tongues and teeth and throats and stomachs rebelling against this great moral act Micajah had proposed. But for the moment, we subsided. I pulled a bit of canvas over Rohrer, the millwright who wanted to live out his life in a sunny, warm land. The canvas cast a veil over him and made a small, redoubtable barrier.

"Who's going to write them?" I asked, thinking of all the newly made widows and orphans, mothers and fathers, brothers and sisters scattered across the country, but most commonly in Saint Louis and Missouri.

"Someone must," McGehee said.

"The colonel, of course," Taplin said. "It's his duty."

It's odd how that thought dispirited me.

Hunger doesn't abate. It's there, down in the gut or under the ribs every waking moment and during sleep as well. It is not only a physical pain but an incompleteness. It feeds a gnawing worry; life isn't right. Now this hunger afflicted us all. The faces in these men, as I watched them in the flickering light, were almost unrecognizable. Something had scooped and shrunk their faces, like a lingering disease. I wondered how well I might read the sign of my own failure, and thought I could well enough.

I forced my mind to other things. Tomorrow, if I had any strength, I'd chop through the river ice and see about fishing. A morsel of fish would go a long way among us. I had nothing to fish with, but the dream of catching one fevered me.

Captain Taplin was a saint. He was hardier than the rest of us but chose to shepherd us and hunt for us instead of joining Vincenthaler's party ahead. If we survived, he would be the rock of our salvation. It was he who collected wood and fed the fire and drove away the misery of the icy night. It was he who helped me up when I fainted away and got me to this place.

My thoughts returned, as I knew they would, to those two departed men and the meat of their shoulders and arms and thighs that might support us for a few days more. Would it be so terrible? It's odd that I debated the moral ground for it, when all I wanted was flesh, any flesh, to eat. And yet my mind persisted in examining the issue, perhaps with a clarity that only a starving man can experience. I thought it would not be so bad; the dead might even have wanted it. And yet, somehow, I was grateful when McGehee suggested we wait for our rescuers. It came to me as a vast relief, a release from my own temptation.

That was a long night, filled with strange phantasms. I thought the Utes had fallen upon us, but that was not the case. By the cold light of dawn I surveyed our number and saw that the living lived; the dead lay just apart. It was plain that we were going no farther. We would either be rescued here or perish here. Most of the men did not bother to sit up but lay in their miserable blankets, staring at the white sky.

I urged upon them the last medical advice I had, which was to drink hot water, as scalding as they could endure, for in the heat was life, and it was cold that would steal in and murder them. Some did. We had a single kettle among us, and Taplin kept it filled and close to the flames. I was worried about Cathcart, who didn't stir, and I managed to get some hot water to him. It was all I could do to get him to sit up and swallow it, but he seemed better for it after he had downed a good hot cup.

That day was the beginning of helplessness. There we were, sensate, aware of our world, and utterly helpless. Our bodies failed us. Taplin, the strongest, tried to hunt, and he managed to walk to a copse a hundred yards distant and sit on a log, awaiting whatever game might wander. Nothing came, and he made his way back to lie down beside the fire.

Helplessness is a strange sensation. I wanted to live, to walk, to eat, to sit up, and all I could manage was to lie close to the flickering fire, turn myself occasionally to warm the front or rear parts of me, and peer half-blindly off to the south, from whence our help must come, if it were to come at all.

The others were in the same case. I was too weak to attempt my plan to fish or find anything aquatic to eat. I could not wield our camp axe enough to breach the ice. And so the helpless day passed, followed by an even more helpless day, and then another, while we slowly wasted the last of our strength.

I had reached the point where I could barely raise my head to look after my brothers. I had tried to doctor them all along, but now I stared into the whiteness until my eyes blurred and smarted, and I waited for whatever fate would bring.

Of the two dead I knew nothing. Whether any among us chose to slice aside the men's shirts and britches and find some meat, I could not say. If it was done, it was done so furtively in the deeps of the night that I had no inkling of it. I supposed it would be some-one's deep secret and unknown to me.

Then on the third day, or perhaps it was some other day, for I had lost count in my perpetual twilight, we heard a shout. I could no longer lift my head and don't know what it was about. But I managed to rise a little, by dint of determination, and saw men and horses approaching. Whether our relief party or Utes I did not know.

CHAPTER THIRTY

John Charles Frémont

We reached the Red River settlement late of a winter's day, and no place looked more like heaven. Here, in an arid brown valley off the Rio del Norte, lay a northern outpost of the Mexicans, a scatter of low adobe homes surrounded by snow-ribbed grain fields and pumpkin patches. The usual adobe defense tower guarded these farming people from the sallies of the Utes and other tribes. White smoke drifted from their chimneys, but we saw no other sign of life.

We five stumbled in, guided by our Ute chief. His horses were so poor they barely moved, so it had taken us four more days from the time we encountered Williams and Breckenridge and Creutzfeldt to reach the settlement.

The Mexicans soon herded about us, warm and sympathetic, and swiftly brought us into a heated, if austere, one-room jacal, where they hastened to feed us with a corn gruel and bread. Never did anything taste so elegant. The walls were festooned with strings of dried red peppers, a local delicacy. There, before the hearth fire that cast its thin heat into the adobe room, we found warmth and comfort. Bronzed, jet-haired neighbors wrapped in serapes crowded in, watching us silently as we wolfed our food. The children were shooed away, and perhaps for good reason. We were a shocking sight. I am adequate in their tongue, and Godey spoke it passably, and we made our needs known: we had starving men upriver. We needed men, mules, bread, blankets, and livestock feed, and fast.

The villagers simply shook their heads. There were not food stores and blankets and mules and burros enough in the whole settlement to meet our needs. A man who introduced himself as the alcalde, Juan Solis, said he could spare but three burros, five mules, and a little cornmeal, but maybe more food might be found. A goat or two might be slaughtered. He and his villagers would do all they could. They would also prepare for the next arrivals. A little goat milk would help them.

At Taos, one long day's ride south, they told us, there would be everything a relief party would need, as well as a detachment of American soldiers who had been there since the conquest. The next dawn, well fed and greatly strengthened, I set off for Taos, along with Alexis Godey, my man Saunders, and Godey's nephew, Theodore. The Ute chief, having delivered us, retreated after receiving what remaining gifts we could manage, which were Saunders's and Theodore's rifles and powder flasks and shot. The Mexicans treated the old man kindly, offering him a bowl of the cornmeal, which he ate swiftly before he left. I watched the old chief wander off with his weary nags, two powder horns dangling about his neck and his new rifles slung from his saddles. Preuss, who was unwell, stayed on at the Red River settlement, to gather strength and deal with the survivors as they straggled in.

It was an itch in me to send relief at once, but these things take time, and I could only hope that my men could endure a few days more. The horror of it had descended on me, and I could scarcely look northward without feeling the lances of tragedy stab at me. We four, mounted bareback on borrowed mules now, made our way to Taos in a long day and reached town as an azure twilight, the heavens transparent as stained glass, settled over the village.

Snow topped the tawny adobe homes, while the incense of piñon smoke hung over the place, delighting my senses. Off to the east the forbidding Sangre de Cristos caught the red light of the dying sun and threw it back on the settlement like some last benediction from the Creator. It was a hushed moment, all sound blotted up by the lavender heaps of snow.

But at last we rode into the old town, past low adobes with tight-closed shutters, toward the small plaza and merchant buildings hemming it. Taos stood on a plain at a great altitude, and the winter had not treated it kindly. There were dimpled drifts about and footpaths through them. Still, this was the place of our succor.

We were a sorry lot, wild and savage looking, and starved down to nothing, and we wrought a great malaise among the staring villagers who saw us make our way to the heart of town. A black-clad older woman could not bear the sight of us and turned away. I wanted to find Carson at once and sought a certain cantina where he might be at an early evening hour.

"Godey," I said, "begin the relief, and make haste. Take whatever you can find. You and Theodore. I'll be at La Tristeza, if not Carson's house."

He nodded, smiling. Thus commanded, he set off at once, looking for the soldiers stationed there. I had done all I could and now looked forward to a needed rest. I wandered into the cantina just off the plaza, adjusted my snow-ruined eyes to the flickering firelight, and spotted Carson, along with Dick Owens and Lucien Maxwell, old stalwarts and friends, gathered at a hewn trestle table beside a beehive fireplace, enjoying the crackle of piñon logs and some aguardiente. So far was I removed from the man I had been that they didn't recognize me at first.

As I approached, they surveyed me, noting my unkempt manner and hollow cheeks. Then they turned away.

"Kit," I said, tentatively.

He stared a long moment. "Is that you, Captain? You?"

"It is."

Lucien Maxwell sprang up. "My God, man."

"I took bad counsel," I said. "And now I have starving men scattered clear to the San Juans."

"They want relief?"

"Yes. Godey's with me. He'll do it."

"How much time is there?"

"We've lost the first. Frostbite, starvation. There's no time. My topographer, Preuss, is at the Red River settlement organizing them."

"Are you going back with relief?" Owens asked.

"I'll leave that to Alexis."

"Then you'll stay with me," Carson said.

"Major Beall can help. He's commanding here," Owens said.

"Godey's looking for him."

"They've got some men and rations and mules," Maxwell said.

"What needs doing now?" Owens asked.

"It's up to Godey. He plans to leave in the morning with relief."

"Who else is here?" Maxwell asked.

"My man Saunders and Alex's nephew."

"Are they all right?"

"A little sleep and a feast or two will make them new. They're with Godey."

"What happened, Captain?" Carson asked.

"I listened to Old Bill Williams, that's the whole of it. He got lost, bumbled into the wrong drainages, and led us into snowy traps. I kept asking him about his course, but he just ignored me. I think the man's addled. He had no idea where he was."

"What about your mules?" Carson asked.

"Lost every one."

"Didn't you eat them?"

"Buried under drifts almost before we knew they were gone."

"Who's lost?" Owens asked.

"Raphael Proue, for one. Henry King. You know him from the conquest."

"Not King! Proue! I knew him, too."

"These men—some of them weren't made of the same stuff as my battalion. It was a mistake, you know. Men without heart. With more heart, we'd now be over those mountains and on our way to California."

"What is their condition now?" Carson asked.

"I don't know. I put Vincenthaler in charge. Remember him? From California? He's charged with caching my equipment and getting the men down to Rabbit River. He'll do his duty. Wait for the relief there. That's what I directed. But I've men in that company who don't heed me, so there's no telling where they are. I imagine Godey will deal with them."

"The San Juans, Colonel, can be tough. Especially with a winter like this," Owens said.

"If I had better men, they would not have yielded," I retorted. I was feeling testy. The company had thwarted my design, mostly from the lack of manhood, and now I had been forced to retreat. I knew one thing: I'd be off to California in a day or two, and I would take none of the malingerers with me. The Kern brothers would remain here, and so would Old Bill Williams, and maybe some more.

I told them my story, even as the stout proprietress plied me with sugar cakes. But ere long the pleasant heat from those piñon logs wore away my resolve. I knew that in moments, I would tumble to the earthen floor. The warmth and comfort were engulfing me.

"You come with me, Captain. It's not a hundred yards, you know. Josefa will help get you settled."

I knew that. Carson's rambling home, built around a courtyard, lay just to the east.

"You'd better plan on a couple of days in bed," Carson said.

"I'm not going to dawdle here—off to California in a day or two."

Carson remained uncommonly quiet. We pushed through the gated wall into his yard, and soon he and Josefa steered me into a tiny bedroom and laid a bright fire in the adobe fireplace. In my weariness I scarcely had a look at Josefa, Carson's young bride. She seemed more a servant-girl to me, though I did notice she was heavy with child.

I fell into a luxurious sleep, well deserved after my ordeal, confined in a warm room with ample blankets above me and a corn-shuck mattress beneath. I was confident that Saunders and Theodore and Alexis Godey all found a suitable loft.

Well into the morning I was finally awakened by a stirring and realized Josefa was peeking in. She was a pretty young thing. When she saw me stir, she smiled, and brought me a tray bearing a pottery mug of hot chocolate. I had not expected such a delicacy in Taos, but there it was, warming my body with its medicinal powers and making me whole again. I thanked her and sipped while she watched anxiously.

"Bueno," I said.

She fled at once.

I was not yet up when I received a caller, who proved to be Major Beall, commandant of the detachment there. I received him whilst I sipped. He wore his blue winter issue and eyed me with some curiosity.

"Colonel, I'm pleasured to meet you," he said.

"And likewise, Major. Do have a seat."

"I'll get right to it, sir. Your man Godey reached me at supper last eve with news of your distress, and I hastened to supply from my stores whatever is needed. He left at dawn with several mules and muleteers, and my men will follow with more supplies. I've sent along rations and blankets. He's taking several dozen good round loaves of bread, some blankets, and some maize to feed his mules and horses. I'm sending a squad behind him with more food, salt pork and hardtack; some horses we can dispose of; and some manpower to assist."

"Most gracious of you, Major. I will make a point of repaying the army as soon as I reorganize."

"It's a pleasure to meet you, Colonel Frémont. Your reputation as an explorer precedes you, and I take a delight in placing myself at your service, sir."

I nodded, taking the measure of the man. "Even a man in my circumstance?"

He nodded, amiably. "By all accounts, you were caught by conflicting orders, sir."

I was satisfied. "Major, this railroad exploration has come to grief because I didn't have well-trained regular army men with me. Even at that, this guide I was forced to hire against my better judgment turned out to be worthless. Keep it in mind."

"I've heard similar about him."

"I don't mean to be unkind, but I do wish to warn away the army. Use Carson if you need anyone."

"So I've heard, sir. But what's happening up there?"

I told him that my men were giving out and that I had directed them to reach Rabbit River, where they could find shelter and expect relief. But I suspected some were still higher up. Hadn't the first relief party dawdled its way south for twenty-two days now, and had not yet reached the Red River settlements?

Beall nodded, as I briefly apprised him of the ruinous decisions of our guide and the lethargic response of some of our summer soldiers, as I thought to call any who had not hardened themselves, and thought the trip to California would be a lark.

"But of this, say nothing, sir. I wish to deal with the matter privately," I added. "I'll be in touch with Senator Benton, with a full report, and I want it to be the true and accurate account of my travails, so he can deal with the repercussions. I'm afraid that some of those men, who were plainly chafing at my direction, might say things of no substance and thus cast aspersions on the honor of my good veterans and my company."

I ended the interview there, having already grown weary of politics, and begged leave of the major.

Carson saw him out and a moment later joined me.

"What's the word, Kit?" I asked, still abed.

"Godey left at dawn with four muleteers and about ten mules. He said to tell you he'll hurry on ahead, getting bread and blankets to all who are still alive, and he hopes that will include most everyone."

"I could not ask for a better man than Godey," I replied.

"He'll pick up more provisions and mules and blankets at the Red River colony and should be intercepting your men within a day or two," Carson said. "Beall's men will be a day behind with some slaughter colts and will do some camp tending, getting the survivors up to a trip here."

"Tell me candidly, Kit; what do you think of Old Bill Williams?"

Carson pondered it a while. "Well, I've heard it said that in starving times, you'd best not let Old Bill walk behind you," Carson said.

"I think I'll tell that to Jessie," I said. "Have you a pen and ink and paper?"

"Never had much use for those," he replied. "But Lucien Maxwell ought to."

"I want to set down the facts," I replied. "Before anyone else attempts to."

CHAPTER THIRTY-ONE

Alexis Godey

I labored ceaselessly to put a relief mission on the trail. The great-hearted Mexicans were ready and willing to help. I found muleteers willing to travel through the perilous winter. They offered their services with a shrug and a smile. For payment they would soon have gaudy stories to tell their families. Families donated blankets woven from unbleached wool. Others volunteered their mules and horses and saddles. I loaded golden cornmeal into sacks, collected the coarse round loaves of bread that would sustain lives, found some multicolored maize with which to feed our livestock in those snowy wastes, and soon had enough collected for temporary relief.

Major Beall's soldiers would follow with some rank condemned horses, hardtack and other rations, and the manpower to tend fires and feed the desperate until they could be recruited to travel again.

"But are you going back, sir, after your own ordeal?" he asked me.

"I am. My friends are in great peril. I will not stop."

"But look at you. You're worn."

"I've had bowls of cornmeal mush. They call it *tole* here, and it revives me. If I can eat, I will be alright."

"It's a solid meal, that's for sure," he said.

I would do what I had to do. At dawn, my Mexican muleteers

and I hastened upriver, through a frosty gloom I can barely describe because it seemed hostile and dark. But my men, mostly wearing heavy wool serapes, hurried the sluggish animals with switches. Their burros and mules were all half-starved. But on their backs was life itself. The day of our departure was January 22. A disastrous four weeks had elapsed since Colonel Frémont had sent the first relief party from the Christmas camp, and we began making our way out of the white mountains.

We reached the Red River settlements late that day. Preuss, who remained weakened and unable to travel, told us that none of our company had come in, which alarmed me, so we didn't tarry except to collect more bread and blankets and shoe leather from worried villagers and hurried north once again. Surely our men could not be far ahead. But they were. It took us four days to cover the first forty miles, and finally we raised the original relief, Breckenridge, Williams, and Creutzfeldt, huddled miserably around a flame, unable to move because their feet were ruined. They had staggered along on strips of blanket until at last they could go no farther and were waiting for help or death in a sheltered arroyo where there was some wood.

I scarcely recognized any of them, but one thing will remain with me. Breckenridge clasped the loaf I gave him and began sobbing, and soon the others wept also, as they tore at the bread.

Creutzfeldt was the weakest, and I wondered whether he could even eat the bread, but he nibbled, gained a little strength, and began tearing at chunks of it, tears leaking from his eyes the whole time.

This was clean and honorable food. They were eating something that evoked no shame. I thought the tears had something to do with that as well as the joy of their salvation.

"The army's on the way with rations. They'll tend camp here until you can be moved," I said. "Eat sparingly."

"What will they think of us?" Breckenridge asked.

"Whatever you think of yourself," I replied. They would have to live with themselves, and if they couldn't, they faced sad days and years.

I left those hand-woven, hand-carded Mexican blankets with them and a little cornmeal to boil up. The muleteers gathered firewood for them and wrapped them in thick blankets and made them comfortable, and that was all we could do for the moment.

"Look for help tomorrow," I said, eyeing those tear-stained, smoke-blackened faces.

"You have saved us," Breckenridge said. "We would be dead."

"Are the others alive?" I asked.

None could answer.

It was snowing again. Never had anyone seen such a winter. But these three, with bread and meal and blankets, could endure. Reluctantly, we parted. I was shaken by the encounter. These men were but hours from crossing that bourne from which no mortal returns. If Colonel Frémont had not sent me swiftly back with aid, surely these three would have perished.

We hurried upriver, the snow biting at our faces and driving the heat from us. I marveled that these good-hearted muleteers braved the hardship with such cheer. They had a way of coiling their serapes around them that protected them from the stinging snow. We reached Vincenthaler's camp suddenly, out of the white whirl, men slowly rising out of their snow-covered rags beside an almost-extinguished fire.

"Relief! It's the Colonel!" Vincenthaler cried.

They were so snow-blinded and deaf and devoid of their senses they scarcely knew who had come.

"It's Godey," I said. "The Colonel sent me."

Now these ruined men stirred. I wasted neither time nor words but dug into the sacks and began handing out those brown loaves.

"Bread!" someone cried. I could not make out one man from another, so ruined were their faces, blackened by wood smoke, their dull eyes peering out from the parchment over their skulls.

Two of my muleteers, Carlos and Esquivel, swiftly handed each trembling man a round yeasty loaf. One lacked the strength to pull it apart, and Carlos attempted to help, but the man would not let go. The man finally bit into the side of the loaf and tore bread loose. For the life of me, I could not tell who was who.

"Don't eat fast," I cautioned. But it landed on unheeding ears. They would wolf it down just as fast as they could.

I waited for Vincenthaler to demolish a few pieces before seeking to know how they stood and who was where. I dug into a sack of blankets and wrapped Martin in one, and found another for Bacon and another for Ducatel, who stared numbly at me, looking demented.

"Bread," Ducatel said. "I live. The bread of life, thanks be to God."

It was some sort of communion, and I found myself the priest distributing this sacrament.

I squatted beside Vincenthaler. "Who's here? I scarcely recognize these men."

He took a long time, as if he weren't sure himself. Somehow, most of these men were confused, including their leader. "Hubbard quit us a while ago. He couldn't go another step and sat down."

"We'll go for him. Where's Scott?"

Vincenthaler shrugged. "Left us."

"That's two. Where's Rohrer?"

Vincenthaler didn't seem to know.

"You've got Joaquin and Gregorio. Where's Manuel?"

Vincenthaler shrugged. "They thought they'd be eaten so they came with us."

"Eaten?"

Vincenthaler nodded.

"The Indian boys came to your camp because—they feared for their lives?"

Vincenthaler shrugged.

I saw that my men had fed everyone and had covered the most desperate with blankets.

"The army's coming. Be here tomorrow. They'll tend camp and feed you and then help you out of here."

"Leave a mule."

"No, but some colts are coming, and you can have them. We've some cornmeal we'll give you. Boil it up. It's a sturdy food. It'll satisfy until you get some army rations and meat. You should have horse meat and hardtack in a day or two."

We could do no more except collect ample deadwood and build up their fires and make sure these man had blankets. We also built up their shelters a little. The longer I stayed at each camp, the itchier I got. Maybe, just ahead, would be a man I could save.

The snow lessened, but we had miles to go, and if need be I would wrestle up the river in the dark. If the sky was clear snowy nights could be quite bright. My muleteers had given the wretched beasts a few ears of maize, but that was all there was for the animals, and I marveled that they moved at all.

But then we plunged into the wintry dusk, a wild hunger to move ahead impelling me.

We stumbled on John Scott, scarcely a hundred yards ahead. It was incredible. He was within shouting distance of the camp. He sat stupidly in the snow, unmoving, and I thought he had perished. But his eyes tracked me. Life flickered.

Swiftly, Esquivel wrapped him in a blanket.

"Scott! We're here. Hang on!"

Scott, a veteran of the California battalion, simply stared. He was bone cold to my touch.

"The Colonel sent me! I've bread for you."

This time Scott's eyes focused a little. Whether he comprehended any of it I could not say.

Esquivel drew a bladder canteen from his bosom, pried open Scott's mouth, and squirted. Scott coughed and sputtered.

"Aguardiente!" the muleteer explained. Taos Lightning, the fiery brandy made locally.

"What?" said Scott.

"Frémont sent relief."

I tore some bread from a heavy loaf; his hands could barely lift even the small piece I gave him, but in a moment he was masticating, swallowing it. I rubbed his shoulders and back, willed life into him. He ate another bite. And another. My muleteers lifted him onto canvas, and we dragged him back to Vincenthaler's fire.

"I'm cold," Scott said.

The sight of Scott alive energized some of the party, and they drew him close, built the fire, and began feeding him.

"Look after him," I said. "This is his loaf."

They would.

My muleteers started out once again in the whirling snow and soon stumbled across Hubbard, sitting upright, like Scott, staring at us as we descended on him. He was a Wisconsin man, used to cold.

"Hubbard! We're relief!"

Hubbard stared stupidly.

I shook him, a deepening dread in me. His body flopped about, but I saw no life in it.

"Hubbard!" I rattled him hard, and he simply sagged over.

Esquivel shot aguardiente into his mouth, and it dribbled away. Hubbard was dead. And he had died so recently warmth lingered in his body.

We stared at one another.

"Ah, Madre," he cried.

These Mexicans had come to share my passion to save lives. Hubbard toppled the rest of the way, lying on his side. I knelt, straightening his limbs, folding his hands over his chest, until he stared sightlessly into the falling snow, which still melted on his face. We had come so close. A half hour, maybe fifteen minutes was all that separated this man from our relief. So close. A terrible melancholy swept through me. If only we had hurried a little more, driven a little harder.

How many had died? I could not say.

We pushed ahead another hour, until a snow-choked dusk caught us and we were in peril of losing our way, and then we huddled through an overcast night. We could go no farther. My own body was rebelling. My sainted muleteers boiled a pail of *tole*, the hot cornmeal mush that did so much for me, and I recovered my own strength as I lay buried under blankets. They fed the bony mules a few ears of maize, but it was not enough, and the plaintive bray of a hungry beast we were abusing sometimes lifted me out of my doze. It was an especially black night, without stars or moon, and I felt almost strangulated by it. I wanted to be up and off. There were men ahead whose lives hung by a thread, if indeed they still lived.

Restlessly, even before dawn, I arose, built up the fire, and boiled up the mush. When first light permitted us to leave, we burdened our mules and horses with packs and set out in dull gray light. A thick ice fog lay over the land, and I knew it could cloak the survivors, making them invisible and muffling our shouts. I would shout every little way, because it was possible we could pass them by. And so we proceeded in a cold and lonely morning, making such noise as we could all the while.

It turned out that we did pass the camp of the Kerns, Cathcart, Taplin, McGehee, and Stepperfeldt, striking a camp of Josiah

Ferguson, who had a fire blooming, though the thick fog caught the choking smoke. He was another of Frémont's veterans, an able man in the wilderness, and somehow he had survived.

He smiled broadly. "Thought maybe that was no elk drifting through the fog," he said.

"The Colonel sent me. You alright?"

Ferguson shook his head and gestured toward a dark bulk lying in the snow a few yards distant.

"Ben Beadle," he said. "I thought maybe a pair of Show-Me Missourians could beat the game. He's dead."

I felt something give way in me. Esquivel handed Ferguson a loaf, which he tore apart and began steadily chewing. I pulled out a blanket and wrapped it around the man's shoulders.

"Colonel got through and sent us with relief. The army's coming along behind, with rations."

"You mind if I eat one of them mules?"

"There'll be some horse flesh tomorrow. We've got the bread and some *tole*, good cornmeal mush, that'll put some warmth in you." I nodded toward Beadle. "How long ago?"

"Yesterday. We couldn't keep up, me and Ben, so we made camp. The Kerns, that bunch, are below us."

"Below? We passed them by?"

He nodded. It had been a thick, cloistering fog that muffled sound.

Ferguson quit eating and buried his face in his arms, the blanket wrapped over him to hide himself from us. I knew he was crying. We quietly built up his fire. I looked at Beadle's body. It was intact, though snow had drifted over it. He lay sprawled on his belly. Another of Frémont's hardy veterans from the third expedition gone from this world.

In time, Ferguson recovered some and resumed his meal, while we heated up some cornmeal for him. "Is there anyone above here?" I asked.

"Manuel, but he's dead. He quit first day out of the mountains, froze up, his feet black, that was some days ago, and he headed back to the cache. He said he'd be there. Stay warm there, if he could. All the rest, they're down in the camps below."

Ferguson seemed to rebound a little more than the others with some food in him, and we helped him onto a mule, which shuddered under the weight, and headed downriver through the morning fog, which was composed of tiny, mean ice crystals that bit at us.

Even at that, we almost missed the Kerns' camp.

"Halloo?" someone yelled.

"Relief," I yelled back.

"Who is it? We're all snow-blind."

"It's Godey," I replied.

We rode in and found a few men huddled in misery, too worn to greet us. I stared at Cathcart, wondering who he was. And Taplin. And young McGehee and Stepperfeldt. And the Kerns, all unrecognizable. But soon we would have their story, too. All alive.

CHAPTER THIRTY-TWO

Benjamin Kern, MD

That shout rising from the mists was the most welcome I ever heard. In short order, Godey burst into our midst, along with some Mexican men and mules. They wasted no time. One dug out round loaves and handed one to each of us; another man tugged blankets out of packs and wrapped one over the shoulders of each of us.

"Who's here?" Godey said, as soon as he and his men made us comfortable.

We were too busy tearing at our bread to reply. I could not answer; my belly cried for this bread, and I was jamming it into my aching mouth faster than I could swallow it. All the cautions of my medical training were trumped by the wild taste of something in my mouth.

"I can't tell one from another," Godey added. "But I need an account."

I paused long enough to warn the others to eat slowly, but the words would not form on my lips. Cathcart was the weakest. He hadn't the strength to tear that big loaf open, and I pointed at him. Godey caught my gesture, knelt beside the Scots captain, and gently broke the loaf into small pieces, a great tenderness in this act.

Cathcart nodded. I saw tears swimming in his blue eyes. I felt like weeping myself.

Godey built up the fire, which was almost out, found our camp kettle, and poured a golden meal and water into it and set it to boiling.

"Cornmeal mush, what they call *tole*," he said. "It's the best we've got to build a man up. I've lived on it the whole way."

I was ready for the cornmeal. I was ready for anything. I lacked the strength even to sit up, so close had I come to perishing. But I knew I would soon gain some command over my helpless body. I felt that bread in my belly. It was amazing. Something real down there, something being transformed into life. My stomach was ready for ten more loaves. I didn't feel stronger, but I knew I soon would.

After helping us all he could, he turned at last to me. "You Kern brothers are here. Captain Cathcart. Stepperfeldt over there. McGehee yonder. We brought Ferguson with us. And Captain Taplin, who seems to be doing alright, over there. Am I missing anyone?"

I did not want him to visit the places just outside our camp where others lay.

I nodded, miserably, the gesture pointing Godey toward the ones who had fallen. I knew what he would see. Some of those bodies were not whole. I had not partaken of any of that flesh, but some had, each furtively cutting his own piece in the deeps of the night. I thought Godey would find us all guilty, and there was naught I could do about it.

Godey left camp and soon enough found Andrews and Rohrer, or what was left of them, and returned wordlessly. I somehow expected recrimination but instead found only silence and the same gentle affection he had given us as he set about feeding the starved. To this day I know not what he really thought. He found legless and armless bodies there and let it pass.

He hunkered beside me, waiting for the mush to heat. "The Indian boy, Manuel. Ferguson says he went back to the cache?"

"He did. He could walk no more on frozen feet. His calves were black from frostbite. Dead flesh. We had gone only a mile or so when he turned back. He'd be gone. There wasn't a scrap of food."

"But warm, at least."

I nodded. That was a good camp, sheltered in a cave, with abundant deadwood. But he had been there a long time.

"I'm going to go. I need to account for every man. And maybe I can bring some of the colonel's equipment."

"Equipment!" I glowered at him. We had died shuttling the colonel's equipment instead of escaping to safety.

The bitterness welled up in me. "You say the Colonel sent you?"

"He did."

"What is he doing?"

"He's outfitting for the next leg."

"He did not come with you."

Godey rebuked me. "He sent me, and it was my honor to come, and his honor to do his best for us all."

"He summoned the army?"

"He asked me to."

"His friends there, Kit Carson and Owens. Did they help?"

"Every way they could. The colonel is Carson's guest. They made him welcome. The colonel needs to reoutfit, you know. He needs credit and contacts, and that's what Owens and Maxwell and Carson have been doing for him."

"What did he tell them about us?"

"He had men stranded on the Rio del Norte and was sending help."

"What happened to the first rescue party?"

"They starved and froze and made no progress, and finally King died."

"Young King? The strongest?"

Godey suddenly drew into himself. "You would not have liked to see them, Ben. I saw the survivors, if you can call them that. The colonel gave them some jerky and headed for the settlements. We had the whole company to relieve and couldn't spare the time to help them much. The colonel did the right thing exactly. I would have done the same."

I nodded, not liking that story and all that was missing from it. "Would you?" I asked.

"An army detail will come here with rations and a few slaughter colts in a day or so. They're dropping men off at each camp."

"Who's below? Who lives, who died?"

Godey tolled the names of the dead.

"With Manuel I count eleven," I said. "A third of us. You spared the rest of us."

"The Colonel did. He sent me."

I wondered why I hated that statement so much.

Godey saw to our comfort, left a muleteer to tend camp along with more *tole*, and headed across open country, going clear to the edge of the San Juan Mountains, another day's travel. I watched him and his remaining Mexican men vanish into the fog and was overwhelmed with an odd sadness I could not explain. That was January 25, a month after our Christmas camp, when we all still lived and enjoyed health.

Alexis Godey was everything a man should be; more man than I could ever be. He was carrying the world on his shoulders.

The army failed to come that day. I was beginning to see the scope of this rescue. It would be several days before any of us could gather the strength to leave. We were the living dead, and nothing anyone could do for us would spring us back to life in one or two days. There we were: hairy, gaunt and ragged, our faces so sunk down and fire blackened that Godey could not recognize us. Cathcart was the worst off, I thought. He was so reduced that he could barely swallow his cornmeal, and we had to break his bread into small pieces he would nibble and drop. Relief had come, but I wondered if Cathcart would yet perish.

I collected Edward and Richard to me. They looked better. Ned was stronger, and Richard had some color in his face at last.

"Colonel Frémont's busy outfitting. Are we going?"

"Not with him," Richard said. "I will not travel with that man. I will not be a part of any company he assembles. I bear him no ill will; I just don't trust his judgment. None of this needed to happen, and that is the hard rock lying in my bosom."

My younger brother spoke for the three of us.

A pair of soldiers hallooed the camp that evening, driving four bony horses. They looked colder than we were, in thin army coats that plainly didn't provide much warmth.

"Corporal Hochshuth here, and this is Private Grubb," one said.

Captain Taplin managed to get to his feet. "You sure are a welcome sight," he said. He introduced himself, leaving his rank unspoken, and then the rest of us.

"We're going to slaughter a colt and use the others to carry you out when you're fit for it," the corporal said. He eyed Cathcart dubiously. "Mister Godey, he's gone ahead?"

"Yes," I replied. "That's the last, up there."

"Alright then," the corporal said. The pair saw to their camp, got firewood, saw to our comfort, and settled in.

"You have any news about the men below? And the colonel? Frémont?" I asked.

Grubb replied. "Played out, sah. We got there in the nick. The explorer, he's in Taos looking after his affairs."

I wondered what those might be.

"Has the colonel said anything about this?"

"I wouldn't know, sah. Well, yes, I know a bit. He's saying it's the guide, Williams, that let him down. I don't suppose I should be repeating it."

"I'm glad for any news I can get, Mister Grubb."

"Most things, they're nobody's fault, sah."

"Sometimes, the wrong man takes the blame," I replied.

The men doled out army rations, hardtack and salt pork. My teeth were loose in their sockets, but I didn't let that stop me from gnawing that food. I got it all down and was ready for more, and so were the rest. I wondered whether this would stop my bowels, but I did not suffer trouble.

I ached for simple comfort: a room, a roof, a fire, but that was still a long ways off. In truth, I didn't see how the army could get us down to the settlements. We were all too weak to walk, and most of us too weak to ride a horse. But somehow, we were going to get there.

Alexis Godey and two muleteers returned the next day, and with them was the California Indian boy, Manuel, clinging to a mule.

"Alive, alive?" I cried. "Let me look at him."

They gently pulled Manuel off his mule, laid him on a tarpaulin, and covered him with blankets. Gingerly I drew back the blankets and stared at those ruined feet and ankles. At least they weren't bleeding. There was dead flesh peppered over those feet, flesh that would slough off in time. I could do nothing at all, lacking my powders and kit, but the several days spent in the warmth of his cave had wrought some improvement.

"I'm glad to see you, boy," I said.

He nodded. He understood enough English to get along with us. Frémont had brought him east with the California Battalion.

"You're going to get well," I said, and I felt sure of it, so long as Godey and the army could get him to the settlements.

"We fed him some," Godey said. "He came right along, with some of that cornmeal and bread in his belly."

"This makes me very glad," I said. "We'd given him up for lost when he turned back."

"He had a regular nest, doctor. He got him into an open-sided cave and got warm, lots of wood, and stayed warm, and waited."

The arrival of Manuel lifted the spirits of the whole camp, and for the first time in many days, I saw men smile.

"There's not much I can do with him. I don't think binding that frostbitten flesh would be a good idea." I turned to Manuel. "You eat up, and stay warm, and keep those feet clean if you can."

"Si," he said.

I stood slowly. It made me dizzy. "What's the count, Alex?"

"Of the lost? Ten. Until I found Manuel, I was counting eleven."

"It would have been all of us, but for you, sir."

Godey turned away, hiding his face from me.

He and the muleteers and soldiers spent the next day burying our dead. They hacked the two bodies free from the blood-caked snow and ice while we watched in utter silence. The soldiers moved those two lost men to a bushy area, heaped brush over the bodies, and added deadwood to weigh it down and protect the remains from animals.

Which animals? I thought. I suppose the rest of us were thinking the same thing. We had not seen so much as a coyote track. We broke camp the next day, working toward the settlements in easy stages. For most of us it was a grim trip, as desperate and painful as any of the rest of it. There weren't enough horses and mules to carry us all, so the stronger rotated, but some, like Captain Cathcart, clung desperately to manes and saddles all the way and barely lived to reach the settlements, even on horseback.

It took days, and we were well into February when we reached Red River and were greeted by Preuss, who rejoiced to see us and accompanied us the rest of the way. It took more days for us to stumble south to Taos, but eventually we collected in that earthen outpost, the sorriest lot of men imaginable. Godey shepherded us the whole way, gentle and yet insistent that we come along, keeping us fed and warm and comfortable.

Taos, rude and humble, billeted us. Godey saw to it. There we were, bedded under roofs by smiling Mexican people, fed and warmed, in comfort. We did not see Frémont at first but heard he was busy assembling the gear and livestock for the California trip. I wondered about it, why he did not show his face, but in time he did collect us together. I marveled because he looked quite the same as always, his lithe body no worse for wear, his beard trimmed, his gaze benign and secret. I detected in him no great interest in us or our condition and heard no words of comfort.

"We'll be leaving in two days," he said. "Those of you who wish to join me, please make your wishes known to me, and I will take them under advisement. Those who are unable will find good company in Mister Carson and other of our friends. I'll be taking us over the Gila River route, first to Santa Fe and Albuquerque, and thence to the point where we will abandon the Rio del Norte and strike west to the Gila drainage, which will take us to the Gulf of California and across. It ought to be a mild trip. I'm provisioned, we have stock, and nothing impedes us."

He paused.

"Perhaps you've heard. Gold has been found in California. In great quantities. Even now, people are rushing there. I have heard that some has been found near my own Las Mariposas, which I acquired during the last expedition."

Gold. I had heard something of it while we were being settled in Taos, but now the colonel confirmed it.

I consulted with my brothers and Captain Cathcart. "Are we going with him?" I asked.

"Not for all the gold in the world," Captain Cathcart replied, and my brothers seconded the sentiment.

CHAPTER THIRTY-THREE

John Charles Frémont

It was imperative that I set the record straight. I contemplated what I would put into a letter to Jessie about the troubles I had encountered in the San Juan Mountains and knew what I wanted to say. Only by prompt communication might I head off public criticism drawn from sensational accounts. Jessie had probably departed for California via the isthmus, but I intended to write her at Saint Louis anyway. Maybe I could still catch her. The mail in that direction was fairly prompt, and communication was assured by both army and civil post. I would soon see her in California and could tell her privately the things that I thought should not be put in a letter.

So while I waited for news of Godey's relief operations, I penned a letter to Jessie.

"I have an almost invincible repugnance to going back among scenes where I have endured much suffering," I wrote to introduce her to the worst, "and for all the incidents and circumstances of which I feel a strong aversion. But as clear information is absolutely necessary to you, and to your father more particularly still, I will give you the story now instead of waiting to tell it to you in California."

There was but one thing to convey, and that was the utter incompetence and stupidity of the guide, Old Bill Williams, who took us into country he obviously didn't know, got lost, and gravely endangered my party. He took us into snow-packed defiles, cost us our mules, and cost the life of Raphael Proue, who froze in his tracks. All this I conveyed to Jessie at length, along with my plans to depart for California at the beginning of February. I also planned to write my father-in-law, Senator Benton, a briefer letter that might set the public straight. There was no need to impart any details, but I wished to make it known that the army detachments posted hereabouts had been most cordial to me and had helped with the relief. I thought it might gain me some ground for us in the Senate. But I deferred writing that one until such time as I heard from the relief.

There was ample to occupy me in Taos. The stark reality was that I had lost nearly everything save for some instruments and lacked funds to outfit myself. Thanks to Carson and Maxwell, I discovered an old Saint Louis friend, F. X. Aubry, was in town. He had business interests in New Mexico. I welcomed him heartily, and soon we were recollecting good times at the Benton household. I borrowed funds from him against the surety of my cached saddles and tack and other equipment up in the San Juan Mountains and used the thousand dollars of credit to purchase fresh livestock. It was my hope that Godey might return with the materiel, and if so that would spare me much grief.

I obtained further aid from my old friend and California companion Major Beall, who opened army stores to me, offering livestock and rations. I had the distinct pleasure of working with officers who possessed none of the jealousy or animosity that had been poured out on me by those higher in command. For these able men, I was simply one of their own.

I spent a most amiable time in Taos among old friends and new acquaintances but was never far from uneasiness about the relief. Day after day slipped by with no word from Godey or those upriver. I wanted only to put the whole business behind me; it was something to bury and get past, but the delay gnawed at me, until I thought I should saddle up and discover what had become of my party. I was certain that the hardened veterans of my California Battalion would fare better than the easterners who had joined up, thinking the trip would be a lark. I could trust my old soldiers to endure through the worst.

Early on, I had discovered that the Kerns and their friends were slackers, a drag on the whole expedition. What was Richard Kern doing while my veterans sweated? Playing his flute. If they had pulled their weight, we would have topped the San Juans and continued on our way, despite Bill Williams's bungling. The men of my old command were able to deal with the snow, while the newcomers slowed us day by day. More and more, as I waited for news from upriver, I determined to settle the blame for the calamity on the Kerns. I had imagined that an artist like Richard would provide valuable sketches that would augment the railroad survey, and a doctor like Benjamin would serve the injured, but little did I know these pampered Pennsylvanians would slow the entire company to such a degree that precious days were lost high up in the mountains, when haste was our salvation.

In time, the survivors did drift in, by twos and threes, assisted by muleteers and the army. They were a horror to see, still snow-blind, starved to nothing, weakened by their ordeal. I wished they had stayed in the Red River settlements longer, cleansing themselves, trimming beards, repairing their attire, so they would not be a spectacle to the citizens of Taos. Indeed, some did linger there, unable to travel the last lap. From Vincenthaler I finally received the bad news. Ten had perished: Proue, King, Wise, Carver, Hubbard, Beadle, Tabeau, Morin, Rohrer, and Andrews. Godey was bringing the last and weakest along and would report to me in a few days.

I was impatient to be off and waited restlessly for the remaining men to drift in. I thought of leaving without them, knowing they would be weakest, but I stayed on out of a sense of duty.

It was clear that in my absence there had been no effective leadership. I had held them together, and on my departure, their discipline had vanished and they had fallen into small fragments, no one of these wandering groups helping any other. Yet I could not regret leaving them. But for the relief I sent to them, all would have perished. I saved their lives. One thing puzzled me: of the dead, all but two were veterans of my California Battalion. Only Rohrer and Andrews were not with me in California. It made little sense to me that softer men, like the Kerns and Cathcart, had survived while my resourceful veterans had died. I had intended to make a point of it with Jessie and Senator Benton and thought better of it.

We gathered at last on the sunny plaza in Taos, on a particularly pleasant February afternoon, with little sign of the grave winter we had endured. Banks of rotting snow persisted, but the earthen town was shaking loose from the worst. I looked them over, not liking what I saw. Some of them were too diminished to stand while I addressed them. Curious villagers, including heavy-boned women in black shawls, and urchins had collected and watched me quietly in the amiable sunlight. I doubted that any could understand English, for which I was grateful.

"Gentlemen," I began, "tomorrow at dawn we leave for California. It's clear to me that some of you are not able to travel and will stay here to heal. I'm adding several new people to my company. Now, I regret not being able to take all of you with me, but my first choice rests with those seasoned men who were with me during the third expedition and others, old friends and veterans of past campaigns. Those who I've decided should, for their own sake, remain here until they are better able to travel include the Kern brothers, all three; Captain Taplin, Captain Cathcart, and Mister Stepperfeldt.

As for Mister Williams, I no longer require his services. I wish to thank all members of this company for engaging in this enterprise and offer my heartiest best wishes to those I will be leaving behind here."

That wrought silence, at first, and then smiles. These doughty veterans would actually gather strength with regular meals, warm weather, and horseback travel. We would enjoy a mild climate the rest of the trip. Altogether, it seemed a good choice. I saw no one objecting. Those whom I had excluded gazed silently from within a little knot.

But Doctor Kern did speak up.

"Colonel, have you notified the families of the departed?"

The question caught me utterly off guard. This wasn't an army command, and it really wasn't my duty to do anything of the sort. But I understood his sentiment.

"Why, Doctor, I shall attempt to do so when we reach California," I said. "This is neither the time nor place, and I have no information about them."

"I'm sure you will look after it," Ben Kern said.

Was there something in his tone that offended me?

That was an oddly disturbing moment, as if Kern wanted to revive memories of what we had all just been through, instead of burying them and getting on with life.

"I will," Taplin said.

"That would be most appreciated, Captain," I replied.

Everyone seemed well satisfied with that.

I caught Ben Kern and Charles Taplin afterward, and privately offered them a mission. "I've a great deal of equipment cached up in the mountains. It's worth several thousands. If you gentlemen could quietly retrieve it when the weather is more favorable and turn it over to my creditor here, Mister Aubry, you would do me a great service and one I would reward. I fear the cache will be plundered by the Utes if no one gets to it soon. You'll need to employ some men with mules here to haul it all to Taos."

"I'll make the effort when I am able," Kern said.

"I know I can count on you."

I spent the evening at Carson's house, absorbing what I could of the southern route from charts and from his recollections. He had been over it several times. At an hour before dawn, February 13, I collected my men on the south edge of town, in gloomy moonlight near a big adobe church, and by first light we were off. I had with me Kit's brother Lindsay Carson, who would serve as guide, as well as Tom Boggs, the former Missouri governor's son. I even had Charles Preuss with me. My topographer had recovered his health in the Red River settlement and arrived just in time to join us— tough little fellow, and I had forgiven him his derelictions. We were in fine fettle and glad to put our trials behind us. Just as I had hoped, the trip down the Rio Grande was easy, and the weather remained perfect for traveling. The nightmare of the mountains swiftly vanished from all our minds.

At Albuquerque, another little mud town without the grace of Santa Fe, I did more outfitting, and soon we were en route through the arid river valley, an empty stretch not fit for human occupation. A man could only wonder why the United States wasted its energies on such country. It was infested with hostile Indians, was worthless for crops other than what might be produced in a melon patch, and added nothing to the United States.

That first sunny afternoon south of Albuquerque, I invited Preuss to ride with me. We were, actually, at the rear, where we could talk peacefully. The reliable Godey was at the van.

"Ah, Charles, it's good to be on our way again," I began. "I should like to talk about California. You have a position with me, if you want it."

"Doing what, Colonel?"

"The Las Mariposas, which Larkin bought for me. It will need some topographic mapping. It lies in the gold country, and if there's gold on my property, I'll need metes and bounds. The boundaries were rather vague. I'll need to lay out wagon roads and locate villages and camps."

He simply grunted.

"The gold stretches along the western flanks of the Sierra. My grant's right there. Taos is buzzing with stories about the gold. With your geology and topographic skills, you could be a most valuable employee, and a well-paid one."

"I have my own plans, sir. I'm sorry."

That was a disappointment to me. I did not inquire into his plans but ventured some other business. "Alright. I have other business to transact. I plan to complete the railroad survey and intend that your topographic data should be completed as well. As soon as I'm settled out there, I'll plan the rest of it. We'll approach from the west, and connect where we left off."

Again, he said nothing.

"We were so close," I said, showing him two fingers a fraction of an inch apart. "If Williams had followed my instructions and taken us north, up the Saguache River, we would have topped the San Juan Mountains, descended into the drainage of the Grand, and continued west. That close," I said.

"I'm very sure of it," he replied.

"Well, I intend to finish it up."

"In winter?"

"No, I've proved whatever needed proving. We'll complete the link, and I'll report to Senator Benton and his business friends."

"I don't think so, sir."

I wasn't sure whether he was turning down my employment or was simply skeptical about the route. "There might be a better route still farther north," I said. "We can survey it."

"No, sir. In California, I will be pursuing other matters. It is a territory that remains unmapped and little known."

"I see. Well, I still plan to engage your services once we arrive."

"I am honored by your attention, sir."

The German seemed as amiable as ever, and yet something had changed. We had been colleagues all this while, in previous expeditions and this, but now he was clearly separating himself from me.

"I suppose you'll be making your journal public," I said.

"I keep an account for my own reference, Colonel Frémont."

"I plan to write about this expedition at length. What especially pleases me is the strength and courage of my veterans, the ones like yourself who were with me in the conquest."

He didn't respond, and we rode some while through the mild day before we arrived at Socorro. Plainly, this Preuss was not the Preuss who had measured every mountain and valley we had crossed together and shared his every measurement with me.

At Socorro, the southernmost town in the area, I enjoyed the hospitality of Captain Buford, who commanded a detachment there and helped me complete my outfitting. While at his quarters I penned a brief letter to Senator Benton, wanting my father-in-law to be well apprised of all events. I made reference to the calamity of January but did not dwell on it beyond a bare account. There was no reason to dwell on it.

CHAPTER THIRTY-FOUR

Jessie Benton Frémont

Mr. Frémont's letter reached me while I was the guest of Senora Arcé y Zimena, in Panama City. It was dated January 27, 1849, and was mailed from Taos, where my husband was a guest of our friend Kit Carson.

I read it and trembled. Before my eyes was an account of deprivation, cold, starvation, and death. And yet Mr. Frémont had escaped except for frostbite, and at this writing was recovering among friends. How close he had come, and he was only a third of the way to California. The letter had found its way to Saint Louis and had been forwarded downriver, ultimately arriving in Panama, where postal authorities diligently tracked me down. Mr. Frémont and I had known Senora Arcé's nephew when he was his country's ambassador to Washington.

I was most grateful for her hospitality. Panama City bulged with Americans and others from all over the world, waiting for transportation to the goldfields of California. They were camped throughout the old town, and many were sickened or dying from mysterious tropical ailments. I was fortunate to have the connection. The flies and biting bugs were terrible, but at least Lily and I had our own room, with a blue couch, hempen hammocks to sleep in, and a bit of privacy. It was a paradise compared with the steaming cauldron of the rest of the city.

We were all waiting for the mail steamer to California, which didn't come week after week, while we hung on desperately, most of us without funds and no way to go forward or return to our homes. Somehow Lily and I had eluded the awful diseases that caught and killed the flood of immigrants. We had been transported across the isthmus, first by river canoe, and then on foot over the mountains, following a path overarched by jungle. Through the courtesy of so many of our countrymen, we made the trip unscathed, though I was certain I would never attempt such a venture again.

It was gold that changed everything. Mr. Frémont and I had planned all this before its discovery; we had no inkling of what was about to happen. I read and reread the letter, concealing it from Lily for the time being, looking for signs that he was past the worst of it. He seemed eager to put it behind him, and it was clear to me that he bore no guilt or responsibility in it; the fault lay in the incompetent guide he had been compelled to employ. It was Mr. Williams who had almost felled my husband and wrought the deaths of a third of his company. It was this Old Bill at whose doorstep this tragedy must be laid.

But that did not allay the tremor that shook me when I considered how close my beloved husband had come. I was stricken with anxiety, because he had yet to travel the main part of the trip and was gravely weakened. In time, once I could choose my words carefully, I did summon Lily and explained to her that the Frémont family had narrowly escaped disaster.

"Your father is safe and on his way overland, but on a different route, milder in wintertime," I told her.

"He likes trouble," she replied.

I almost reprimanded her for expressing such sentiment, but for some reason didn't.

I ached to travel north, but all I could do was wait helplessly, like the teeming thousands living on the grubby old streets and filling the cemeteries. Street vendors sold monkey meat and fly-specked chickens and filthy fruit, and on these things my countrymen survived or sickened.

I was among them. A newspaper account of Mr. Frémont's disaster in the mountains reached Panama City and greatly disturbed me. I fear the shock of Mr. Frémont's catastrophe unhinged me, for next I knew I was gravely sick with brain fever, which also afflicted my lungs, and both a Panamanian and an American doctor attended me. I ceased to think or care, and scarcely knew where I was. There were no leeches to bleed me, but some croton oil from a ship at anchor blistered my chest and wrought a healing. I remained greatly enfeebled, and my condition worried Senora Arcé and others who knew me.

But one May day the Pacific mail steamboat did appear, with great fanfare, and a welcoming shot from the shore battery. A virtual brawl ensued as to who would occupy its few berths. The ship could accommodate eighty in its cabins and finally embarked with hundreds more deck passengers, so jammed on board that each man's bedding ground was a chalked-off rectangle. I was given a narrow cabin, but in that small, dank chamber my lung fever returned, and I arranged to live in a tent hung over a mast on the quarterdeck, which I shared with Lily and another proper woman. I felt better in the fresh sea air. I even came to enjoy the company of all those men as we sailed north, filled with hope and adventure. Actually, they all treated me with respect.

Still, those days were wrought with anxiety as well as hardship. There was not food enough on board to feed that mob, and the steward was lining his pockets by selling the ship's tinned food at exorbitant prices, so many on board sickened just as they had been in Panama. It was rumored, too, that the steamer hadn't enough coal to make San Francisco and might be set adrift or forced to use its spindly masts and pull out its canvas. Indeed, it was true. The ship reached San Francisco only by burning its deck planking.

Our first California stop was at the Pueblo de San Diego, and I so dreaded it and the news I might receive of Mr. Frémont that I reclaimed my old room and barricaded myself within, unable to face what I dreaded. But in time a knocking summoned me to the door, and with dread I received the news from the ship's purser, who had been asked to convey it from someone on shore. Mr. Frémont had arrived in California safely, though his frostbitten leg troubled him, and was even then making his way north to rendezvous with me in Yerba Buena on the bay of San Francisco. I accepted the news with a flood of relief that left me unable to stay upright for a while.

We reached San Francisco, as it was being called, June 4, 1849, steaming through the strait my husband had named Golden Gate, into a vast inland sea. A cold fog swirled over the scabrous little village on our right. Before me stretched a graveyard of bobbing sailing ships, their rocking masts a forest beside the shore. Their crews had decamped for the goldfields. There was no pier, and our sole recourse was the lighters that took us to the shore. Scores of little boats swarmed us, and I peered anxiously into the cold mist, hoping to discover Mr. Frémont among them. But I was soon disheartened. Men everywhere, scarcely a woman in sight, but the colonel was not there.

The city climbed into hills just beyond, but all its vitality seemed to collect close to the water's edge, where mountains of supplies, wagons, tents of all descriptions, and hundreds of males were congregated. If Mr. Frémont should not be present, I scarcely knew what I might do; Lily and I would be at the mercy of a lawless and savage lot of people. The mail steamer suddenly seemed a safer and better place than this cold, wretched camp along the inner shore.

Then a stranger, in one of those bobbing lighters below, hailed me, pointed directly at me until I was sure he was addressing me.

"I'm here to get you settled, Mrs. Frémont. Your husband saw to it. William Howard's my name, and I've a room for you at Leidesdorff House. It's up that hill, and it's all there is for you."

He helped us into his boat and took us to shore, where his hesitant and embarrassed sailors lifted us over the surf and settled us on the strand because there was no pier.

Mr. Howard did settle us in a single, well-furnished room in the private home. There was no wood for its parlor stove, and it was as cold and dank as any place I have ever been. I drew my shawl tight about me. But it had walls and a roof and was some distance from that fierce crowd below, and I accepted gratefully, thinking that Mr. Frémont had looked after his wife and daughter, even while some distance away. I was curious about the delay, how he could be elsewhere. Mr. Howard soon enlightened me.

"He went directly to Las Mariposas, madam. He needed to have a look at once, assess its value, and determine what to do if gold should be upon it. He'll be along soon."

I thanked the man, who immediately hurried off. The mail steamer was unloading cargo, and he needed to claim his own.

I learned that food was scarce, services impossible to find, firewood and lamp oil nonexistent, and I would have to fend for myself. Still, we were fortunate: in a canvas city, we had an adobe room and a roof over us, and I would see what I could see about food.

So Mr. Frémont was nearby. I did not yet understood the size of California and didn't know that the grant he had purchased through the consul, Thomas Larkin, was far distant and not easily reached. He had told me it was seventy square miles, a size beyond my fathoming. How could one person hold so much of the earth?

"Well, Lily, we're here; our trunks are here; we'll look for food if you wish."

"All those men," she said.

"All those men," I said. We had scarcely seen a woman.

Fearfully, we ventured out into a maelstrom of life, knowing there was no law to protect us from whatever savagery might exist. We would depend entirely on the civility of those around us. Plainly, gold fever had created the frenzy we walked through. Men stared but never paused as we passed by. We found canvas gambling halls, and I hurried Lily past them, and there were drinking stalls and hardware stalls, all open-air or canvas, where things might be purchased at outlandish prices. There were thousands of males arriving and nothing to sustain them. We found at last a vendor who had a little rice, which he was parceling out to eager buyers at a breathtaking five dollars a pound. Reluctantly, I bought some and tumbled it in my reticule for want of a sack. It looked like we would be eating rice, if we could find enough wood to boil it. On our way home I salvaged some wood from packing crates to cook our dinner.

Thus did we occupy our first day with the sheer necessities. I had only a small sum and dreaded that I might run out. Later, gentlemen callers arrived in great numbers, to my relief. The colonel had not been forgotten here, and many of them brought precious gifts of food, hoarded or garnered from somewhere. I swiftly learned that there was scarcely a young man in California tending herds, butchering meat, hoeing gardens, hauling produce to market, gathering eggs, feeding poultry, milling wheat, baking bread, cutting firewood, or milking cows. They had fled to the goldfields, leaving these tasks to old men and women, who were somehow carrying on and getting amazing prices for whatever foodstuffs they were able to deliver.

I learned to accept gratefully whatever was presented to us. We were soon entertaining army officers, diplomats, businessmen acquainted with Colonel Frémont, politicians, and strangers, some of them brandishing heavy leather sacks burdened with nuggets.

We endured day by day, in what surely was the coldest place I had ever lived, its fogs and skimpy sun laying an icy chill over the whole place, which was rapidly affecting my lungs, until I feared I would contract the lung fever once again unless I could escape.

Then one blessed day he appeared. I saw him walk quietly up the slope, survey the Leidesdorff House, and approach the door. My heart leapt. I wrapped a shawl about me and hastened to the door, admitting him into the house, into my arms, and into the quiet circle of my embrace.

Lily found us embraced, and I hastily retreated, my instincts always decorous. He paused, smiled at Lily, and clasped her hands in his own.

"You're a young woman now," he said.

She stared uncertainly at this father she had not seen for almost a year.

As I examined this husband of mine, I discovered the marks of his suffering. He was gaunt; his cheekbones seemed to protrude under parchment flesh. There were great pits below his eyes. His gray-shot brown beard, without a shred of gray before, now bore the streaks of hardship. He walked with a visible limp.

"I've heard you suffered greatly in Panama," he said, his glance taking in the darkness that lingered under my eyes.

"She almost died," Lily volunteered. "They blistered her chest. She's still sick, and this cold air isn't doing her any good."

"Then we'll move at once to Monterey," the colonel replied. "This is not a proper place for my family."

We three trailed into our icy room, and my cough told me that this place was a menace to me.

There was so much catching up to do. "You went to Las Mariposas?" I asked.

"I did. I know this much. There's gold there. I hired some experienced men, Mexicans who know about these things, to prospect. And even while I was looking over this holding, they found gold everywhere."

"Gold, gold?"

"Mrs. Frémont, I am going to be very rich." He dug into his old coat and pulled out a small sack, and poured nuggets into my hand. Heavy, glimmering rounded bits of gold, cold to my touch. "This is from my land," he said.

And that is how the news came to me.

I ached to hear his story, everything he could tell me about his harrowing journey across the continent. I ached to tell him my story, that odd, sinister trip from Chagres to Panama City, surrounded by parrots and monkeys and buzzing insects and serpents and a world I could scarcely fathom, in which we traveled in canoes propelled by near-naked men.

But within the hour, he was out the door. He said he needed to see people, make arrangements, hire miners, talk to lawyers.

I buried my yearnings in my heart and let myself bask in the joy of our reunion. But somehow I grasped that things were different. That this man, my husband, was not the man I had left in Missouri, but I didn't know how or why.

Over the next days, I felt more than the chill of San Francisco Bay. I felt a growing chill that had settled around my heart. Mr. Frémont would gaze at me, smile as he often did, and yet he was not seeing me, not hearing me. His own gaze had turned inward, and I no longer knew what his thoughts might be, and he no longer shared his deepest yearnings.

We would sit at table, just the three of us, and he would say all the right things, thank me for the rice pudding, comment on the fog and cold, and yet nothing was the same. There were only two of us at the table, Lily and I. I did not know where he had gone. Was this the man I had eloped with? Was this the man who once lay beside me, talking through half the night? Was this the man whose journals I had transcribed day by day, sharing every moment? Was this my beloved?

I wondered if I would ever know this other Mr. Frémont, or whether he would ever love me as he once did. And I wondered what had happened in the San Juan Mountains that had taken him away from me.

An Afterword

The character of John Charles Frémont has fascinated me for years. Although I have read a great deal about him, he remains a mystery to me. He was a man of considerable courage and ability who nonetheless was constantly getting into grave trouble, often from lack of judgment.

His early biographer, Allan Nevins, did not look deeply into the causes of the Pathfinder's checkered career. But later biographers took a harder look at the man. Andrew Rolle, in his study of Frémont, concludes that Frémont was a narcissist. David Roberts describes a ruinous recklessness in the man. Pamela Herr, Jessie Benton Frémont's biographer, notes Frémont's inability to live within ordinary social boundaries, including those of marriage.

Frémont seemed indifferent to the needs and hopes of others, and yet his soldiers greatly admired him. He ultimately treated his wife badly, and yet she adored him. He could not bring himself to obey the commands of his superior officer in California and was court-martialed and convicted for it, and yet he became a national hero. He was involved in the shadiest sort of business dealings, and yet he was a reformist presidential candidate. He led his fourth expedition into desperate circumstances for no good reason, and yet most of those who went with him supported his leadership unconditionally.

In this novelization of Frémont's disastrous fourth expedition, I have attempted to draw Frémont as a man with all these conflicting traits at work in him. He remains, however, an enigma. Since he had failed to locate a suitable railroad passage over the Wet and the Sangre de Cristo Mountains of central Colorado in the vicinity of the 38th parallel, why did he plunge into the far more formidable San Juan Mountains in the dead of winter? One thing is certain: he was not pursuing a railroad right of way, no matter that he continued to talk about it and use that as his rationale for crossing the mountains in winter.

But his fourth expedition makes no sense. I was tempted to look for other motives, such as his wish to acquire a reputation as someone who could do most anything or to show the army, which had disgraced him, what he was made of or even to enter politics. But at bottom all these rationales for his conduct fall short, and I remain as mystified by his reckless assault on the San Juans as I was when I first looked into the strange fourth expedition. He led ten members of his company to their doom, yet we find in him little sympathy for them or their families, virtually no regret, in any of his writings or utterances. He was somehow disconnected from everyone else, including Jessie.

For some reason, he could not fathom boundaries, no matter whether they were imposed by society or nature. These were impediments to his will, things to be surmounted. When the Bentons resisted his courtship of a very young Jessie, he eloped with her. When he commanded early topographic expeditions, he grossly exceeded or ignored his orders. When General Kearny arrived in California late in the conquest period and required the subordination of Lieutenant Colonel Frémont to his command, Frémont resisted. When Frémont was warned not to cross the Sierra Nevada in winter, he ignored the warnings and imperiled his entire command. And even though he had lost ten men and a hundred and thirty mules in the calamitous fourth expedition, he attempted the same perilous winter trek over much the same territory in the fifth expedition, losing another man and escaping disaster only because some Mormon villagers rescued him. He was made wealthy by the gold on his huge California estate and yet managed to squander his fortune through mismanagement.

One trait that ran through his life was his remoteness. He always seemed distant, and to be surrounded by invisible walls, which deepened as he aged. He was private and even secretive, largely keeping his feelings to himself. His real hurts, angers, bitterness, delights, and satisfactions were hoarded—kept on the private shelves of his mind—and were not in public view.

His remoteness was ironclad. The exception was Jessie, the only person he admitted to the privacy of his heart, but as the years went by, he distanced himself even from her. At times he seemed to be scarcely aware of the needs or the suffering or the joys of others, and he did not share his own. During his campaign for the presidency he was ineffectual, remote, and formal, so surrogates did his campaigning for him. The paradox is that many loved him and devoted themselves to him. People reached out to him, even if he did not return their affections, or maybe because he didn't.

I cannot explain this man. But neither can I explain Jessie, who knew about his failings, his philandering, and his dubious ethics and yet devoted her life to making him into a national hero. She was his enabler, to use modern parlance.

Virtually all the primary source material written in English that deals with the disastrous fourth expedition has been collected, annotated, organized, and introduced in a single volume by Leroy and Ann Hafen. *Frémont's Fourth Expedition: A Documentary Account of the Disaster of 1848–1849 with Diaries, Letters, and Reports by*

Participants in the Tragedy is the bedrock source for most of what happened during the expedition. Patricia Joy Richmond's *Trail to Disaster* is a valuable resource. She located all but one of Frémont's camps in the San Juan mountains, and provides a powerful narrative of the unfolding tragedy, along with maps and illustrations. Dale L. Walker's *Bear Flag Rising* is a superb history of the conquest of California and offers a shrewd and balanced evaluation of Frémont's character.

The sources are so contradictory and self-serving that it is impossible to sort everything out, and my novel is based on educated guesses instead of well-anchored facts. Some scholarship noting the contradictions, evasions, and self-serving interpretations of events by those in the Hafen collection would be welcome, but this is not the place for it. Suffice it to say that another novelist could portray these events in quite a different light and be just as grounded by primary source material as I believe I am.

—Richard S. Wheeler